Heal Me

Jennifer Lanzilotti

Published by Mirror Publishing
Fort Payne, AL 35967
www.pagesofwonder.com

Printed in the USA

Chapter 1

Lily knew someone was in the room with her.

She woke at the creak of the floorboard, before catching the outdoors scent, like a child who'd played in the grass all day. She listened to the shallow breathing as she slowly reached for the weapon under her pillow. She'd always been a stomach sleeper. With her face half-buried in the pillow, she was able to maintain the pretense of sleeping, while she wrapped her hand around the metal baton.

With her heart hammering in her chest, she waited for him to stand by the side of her bed. Her eyes rapidly adjusted to the dark as she rolled back and her arm went into swinging motion. She whacked him hard with the baton, hitting the side of his head. He stumbled back into the dresser as she sprang from her bed and out the door.

She had just enough time to sprint down the stairs to the front door. She'd jumped the last two steps, unlatched the door and glanced up just as the man reached the balcony. She didn't hesitate, and ran for the forest.

Fear was nothing new, but she'd panicked focusing entirely on flight mode. It wasn't until she scraped the bottom of her bare foot that she realized she needed her shoes. She also should've kept the baton. Not only because she might need it again, but because her brother, Alex, gave it to her. He'd wanted to give her a gun, but she was too afraid to hold one, let alone keep it under her pillow.

The air felt damp, as a warm mist hovered above the pine needles and brush that surrounded her. The sun was just beginning to rise, offering only the faint light early dawn brings. Being in the forest barefoot was a problem. A deer jumped through the woods, making her heart race again. She wished she could move through the woods that quickly. The forest would hide her. She could probably climb a tree or bury herself under a thicket, but not barefoot and not in her boxer shorts and t-shirt. Though August was a warm month, it was cool in the Appalachians and Lily needed her supplies. She tried to calm herself while contemplating returning to the house.

"Where are you, Lily?" the man shouted from the doorway. He was holding his head and blood was smeared across his cheek. She was careful to hide her body behind the tree, crouching low so the tall brush concealed her. He wasn't as tall as she thought. He seemed bigger standing over her bed. Still, he was much taller than her 5 foot 5 inches.

His arms looked muscular, but the broad shoulders could merely be fat. She hoped he was hefty and out of shape.

The man half stumbled out of the cabin, gripping the railing on the wide deck. He stared into the forest. "There's nowhere to go!"

Lily brushed a bug off her foot and wiped sweat from her brow. She needed her pack with her supplies and she really wanted her shoes.

"You know we will find you!" the stranger yelled into the woods. "You can't keep running away. No one will hurt you, Lily!" He stepped off the porch, looking contemplatively at the forest trying to decide which way she may have gone.

It was decision time. She had to either escape by running barefoot through the woods, or somehow make her way back into the house. If she could reach the bedroom, she could easily slip her shoes on and grab her emergency backpack. It was vital to her survival to have her supplies.

Glancing around the forest, she found what she needed. There were enough thick trees and shrubs to keep her hidden while she diverted him. She picked the stick up slowly, waiting for him to turn away. The moment he angled his body toward the right, she threw the stick as far as she could along the left side of the wrap-around porch. His back was turned, so he didn't see the stick flying through the air, but he obviously heard it. He immediately ran in that direction, disappearing to the back of the cabin.

As soon as he was out of sight, Lily darted to the house and back up the stairs. She'd only been in the cabin one week, but she knew which floor boards squeaked and what part of the railing rattled.

The emergency backpack was under her bed, so she pulled it out before quickly slipping her shoes on. She crept toward the window which offered a decent view of the thick forest beyond the grassy lot. No sign of the stranger.

She whipped around, reaching for the baton when she heard the squeak on the stairs and the rattle of the banister. The man stood in the door, breathing heavily and smiling. "You won't be using that thing again."

Lily grabbed the lamp and threw it at him, but he simply batted it away. Fear overwhelmed her as she realized she had again misjudged his size and now felt trapped. The window was behind her, but there was no way she could open it in time.

"Please don't do this," she pleaded. "I have a right to my freedom. I have a right to say no to them." Her grip on the baton tightened.

"Normally, I might agree with you, but..." he lunged at her. His arm came up blocking her swing, and next he was on top of her, securing her hands above her head. "I don't want to hurt you." He clipped metal handcuffs to her wrists. "Stop struggling, so you don't hurt yourself."

He sat on her legs, keeping her from kicking out, and pulled her up by her cuffed wrists. "Now listen, damn it!" He pushed her long coppery red hair out of her face so she could see. "The whole world is depending on you, and no one wants to see you hurt."

She pushed at him as hard as she could, but he didn't budge.

This was no soft, out of shape man. "Let me go!"

"Look at me." He pulled on her wrists. "I'm not going to hurt you, but you have to cooperate." There was something in his tone that made her stop struggling. "I'm sorry I've scared you. I didn't want to." Their eyes locked, and he searched her face. He always wondered what it would be like to finally meet the most famous, sought-after woman on earth. She was more petite than he'd expected. There was fear in her eyes, but strength in her struggle. "I'm not going to hurt you," he promised again.

"Then just let me go," she pleaded. She stared at him a moment. Then her eyes widened with alarm. "You have cancer." She looked him straight in the eyes and squeezed his arm with her hand. "I can feel it."

His eyes narrowed. "You're lying. You're desperate, and they warned me you might try this."

"I am desperate, but I'm telling you the truth." She felt the heat radiating from his arm, and sucked in a slow, deep breath. "It's possibly a tumor. There's cell damage from radiation. Have you been exposed?"

"Damn it." He stared at the unusual color of her irises. He knew Lily McCallister and her deceased twin sister, Kate, shared the rarest form of eye color; a red copper, like the color of her hair, with flecks of gold. He sighed, and then stood up. Lily quickly got to her feet and stepped back. The only chance she had was to convince him, and make a deal.

"You know I can heal you," she said tightly.

He crossed his arms. "If I let you go right?"

"Yes."

"I don't believe I have cancer. I had a physical this year."

"Are you having headaches?"

"I work for the government. Of course I get headaches."

She needed to convince him. "I can feel the energy flow of your illness. I sense you've got out of control cells destroying your body, perhaps even a little radiation poisoning." She knew throwing that in was a good idea, since so many people suffered from small amounts of radiation exposure. He'd be foolish not to worry about that. "You'll die like everyone else, if I don't heal you."

He thought about his family. His parents back in Michigan, his brother who struggled financially and needed help. He knew she could be right.

"This is what I do. You know I'm telling the truth," she stated quickly. She could see he was considering her offer.

"I could make you heal me, then still take you in."

"You just promised you wouldn't hurt me." She was feeling calmer. He hadn't secured the handcuffs too tightly, and he appeared to believe her.

He ran his hand through his hair and winced at the cut she'd given him with the baton. "I'll give you a head start. You can run, but I'll be right behind you. Next time I catch you, you come willingly. It's the best I can offer."

She thought about this. Was he really going to let her go? She stared into the brown eyes she hoped were sincere. "Okay. I'm taking your SUV though, and I want the keys." She held up her hands.

He unlocked her cuffs and slipped them back in his pocket. "You can't drive my Nav. It's my favorite vehicle, and you probably don't even know how to drive."

She rubbed her wrists. "I'll manage. What's your name?" Hope for escape made the churning inside her stomach subside.

A wry grin stretched across his face. "You'd probably like my brother's nickname for me better than my real name."

"What's that?"

"Prick. It's my brother's version of Patrick. He took the 'at' out."

"It's a bit fitting." She wouldn't smile along with him, but part of her appreciated his attempt to humor her.

"Look," he handed her the backpack. "Where will you go? If I don't take you in, someone else will. They won't stop hunting you, Lily. Your power is too valuable. You're not safe anywhere."

"I know." She felt that familiar ache in her chest.

"Do I really have cancer?"

"Yes." No way was she giving up the only card she could play.

Patrick handed her the car key. "This is an odd turn of events. You will cure me?"

"I will." She followed him down the stairs. His hair was sandy brown and thick. She wondered if he'd once had it cut military style before deciding to let it grow out. "Are you married?" She wasn't sure what made her ask, but he somehow seemed more human now. He had a name, and kind eyes.

"I'm a widower."

"I'm sorry." She hesitated at the bottom of the stairs. "How did she die?"

"Cancer."

Chapter 2

Lily drove carefully down the narrow dirt road that led off the mountain. The cabin was a perfect place to hide, until Patrick found her. Apparently, the department decided to split their men up to cover more territory. She'd caught a break with only one man sent to bring her in rather than the typical three or four.

The road was gravel, full of potholes, and almost as narrow as a bike trail. The Navigator was bigger than anything she'd ever driven before, and she felt swallowed up in it. Her brother told her the road was private. She hoped there wouldn't be oncoming cars, especially since she was driving faster than she should. The wheels of the white Navigator were dangerously close to the edge. There was nothing to stop her from going over the long drop filled with trees and rolling hills. She clutched the steering wheel with both hands.

Once she turned onto the main road, she reached in her backpack for the cell phone. It was a throwaway per-minute phone, meant to be used only in an emergency. This was an emergency.

With no idea where to go or what to do, she called her only contact. "Danny, it's me."

"Are you okay?"

"They found me." She glanced around for a sign indicating where she was. "I'm in a government vehicle alone, near Purple River." She could hear Danny pressing keys on a keyboard. He could locate her position from the phone. It was another reason she chose to go back in the house for it.

"Go left at the next intersection. I'm sending someone to pick you up. Are you hurt?" Concern etched his deep voice.

"No, I got lucky. It was only one man, and he didn't hurt me." It was her good fortune that Patrick was actually a nice guy.

"Good. How did you get his car?"

"He let me take it."

Danny chuckled. "You had to heal him first, I take it."

"Of course."

"I don't trust it though. I want you out of that car immediately. I'm sure it's got a tracking device."

Lily glanced at the dashboard feeling a twinge of panic. Of course there would be a tracking device built into the GPS. She shouldn't have taken the car, but it was that or run, and Patrick seemed to be in excellent shape.

"I'm glad you're okay, Lil."

"Yeah, me too."

Danny was her best friend. She'd grown up with him as her neighbor. He'd been madly in love with her twin sister, Kate. Unfortunately, all Danny's computer skills and inside connections couldn't save Kate in time. Now he'd do whatever he could to protect Lily.

"Can you drive the car into the woods? It would be best to hide it."

She slowed, letting a small Honda Civic pass her. Since gas was a rationed, expensive commodity, the majority of cars were smaller and most people only drove when necessary. "It will be hard to hide. I think the best I can do is…" She saw an unmarked dirt road. "Wait, I think I can turn down a hidden road."

"There shouldn't be too many people. Most civilians have already evacuated."

"A car just passed me." She noticed a folded, queen sized mattress over by a large tree. She could imagine a family rushing to evacuate, loading it on top of their car and simply leaving it when it fell off. Parents were anxious to protect their children from potential radiation. The Virginia nuclear power plant was bombed, but not all detonators had gone off, leaving only partial damage. It gave workers time to prepare for a meltdown, buying time for people to evacuate.

"I've contacted, Alex. He knows not to go to the cabin." Danny knew she'd worry about her brother.

"Where will I go, Dan? I'm running out of places to hide. How do you think he found me?"

"We shouldn't have let you stay there so long. I won't make that mistake again. I've got a plan."

She sighed. "No, it's not your fault. I should've heard him coming. He drove a darn SUV up the mountain. I should've been more alert." She was exhausted last night, but for the first time in a while she'd felt safe. She was foolish to let her guard down.

Pulling off the side of the road caused a cloud of dust to block her view. She slowly got out of the car, and slipped her backpack on. "Where to now? Do I walk back to the main road?"

"No. I want you to follow that dirt road. It should lead to a house, but stay clear of it. A car will soon be coming for you."

The sun rose just above the trees, and Lily felt the warmth on her skin. She glanced down at her watch. Eight AM. Only two hours ago she struggled with Prick. That name should seem fitting for a man who tried to abduct her, but somehow she couldn't call him by that name.

She pretended to heal him, and he'd allowed her to change into a pair of beige hiking pants and a white t-shirt. She'd even brushed her teeth and used the bathroom.

They weren't on friendly terms, yet he'd been kind in answering her questions. He told her how he'd worked for years as a police detective. There was something about his voice and eyes that softened her fear when she learned his investigations helped convict rapists. Patrick was just a man, fortunate enough to have a position that paid well and didn't require working for the CCC. Many people who'd lost their jobs and were struggling to survive were forced to go to work for the Contamination Cleanup Corporation. The CCC was created by the government to help employ people while cleaning

13

up the destruction caused by the terrorists' bombing.

The country had been attacked on July 4th, 2063. On the day Americans celebrated their freedom, Radical Jihadists had succeeded in bombing three of the nation's nuclear power plants. Days later, radioactive "dirty bombs" were detonated in several major cities and factories. The plan was to destroy large sections of the U. S. and eliminate electrical power in more than half the country. The terrorists' plan worked. It was the most devastating act of terror in history, crippling the nation.

"You're quiet. Are you still there?" Danny asked.

"I'm still here. Just thinking."

"Yeah, well don't hurt yourself."

She laughed. "I miss you."

"I miss you too."

A picture of Danny popped into her mind. No doubt he was hidden away in some garage somewhere, pushing his long blond hair out of his eyes, while multitasking on at least three different computers. When Danny was eleven, he'd knocked on Lily's front door smiling that wide, crooked smile of his. "I need two more players for touch football. My parents are going to confiscate my phone if I don't start doing some outdoor activities," he'd told Lily and Kate as they'd stared at him from their doorway. Kate was the first to step out on the porch and reply.

"So the 'back of the bus' boy finally wants to talk to us," Kate said. Lily knew her sister had been crushing on Danny all year. He'd lived next door to them, but rarely was outside. He always sat in the back of the bus, barely speaking two words in the three years they'd known him. But that day, playing touch football in his backyard with three other neighbor kids had been the start of a close friendship and the beginning of true love for Kate.

"The car is coming now," Danny said, bringing Lily's thoughts to the present. "Her name is Sage. You cured her baby brother and she joined the 'Save Lily Foundation'."

"You're just full of jokes today." A compact shiny red car approached her. "It's a red car, right?"

"That's her. Turn the phone off and then call me when you're at the safe house."

She knew the routine. "Okay."

"Be careful, Lil."

Danny would get her someplace safe and then her brother, Alex, could join her. She relaxed her shoulders in relief. All that really mattered was keeping Alex safe, and as long as she was out of danger then her brother would be also.

A familiar, attractive blond with white sunglasses smiled and waved from the red car. Lily vividly recalled the day she'd first met Sage. It was the year before the terrorist attacks, when Lily decided to stop holding healing conventions. There were too many people in need of help and when she had to turn away the sick and dying, it made her feel horrible. People would travel for days to meet her at a designated time and place, but she had limited time and energy and the demand was simply too great. She cried when she saw the lines of people still waiting, praying for the opportunity to be healed. She wanted to cure them all, but couldn't. Healing conventions were her way of using her gift to help others, but she soon realized it wouldn't work.

Sage, however, had managed to draw Lily's attention. She was young at the time, only twenty-one, small in stature, yet she held her four year old brother in her arms for hours. Her brother, Joey, had developed a rare bone cancer when he was three. All medical treatments failed, but Sage refused to give up hope, even when their parents began to plan his funeral. Lily admired Sage's strength and devotion and selected the siblings from the other sick and dying people who waited in line that day.

Immediately after healing Joey, he could walk slowly on his own, no longer needing to be held. There's a bond between siblings Lily knew was sometimes even stronger than that between parent and child. Joey was the last person Lily healed that day, and Sage pledged her lifelong devotion to Lily with gratitude.

15

Sage raised her hand in greeting. With a wide smile, she stepped out of the car and wrapped her arms around Lily. "I'm so happy to see you!" She kissed the side of her cheek. "We need to hurry, but I had to hug you."

"It's good to see you." Lily stepped back to look at her. She'd filled out and her hair was longer, sweeping just below her hips. "How is Joey?"

"He's wonderful. He—"

Sage fell forward into Lily, just as Lily felt a pain in her right leg. She caught Sage in her arms and carefully lowered her to the ground. She turned in time to see Patrick aiming his gun at her. She reached down, pulling the sharp dart from her calf. Although her body had the ability to heal itself, she knew the dart's poison would absorb long enough to stop her from escaping.

"We had a deal, Lily." Patrick approached her quickly. "You have to come willingly."

"No!" She tried to get in the car, but her vision blurred as she felt her knees give way. Her hands hit the dirt first, next to Sage who had a red dart protruding from her neck. The dart was the last thing she saw before darkness took over.

Chapter 3

Slowly waking, she smelled his scent again. "You need a shower," she whispered.

"I'll keep that in mind, Lily."

As she slowly opened her eyes, she felt her stomach turn.

"Here, take this. It will help with the nausea."

She pushed his hand away. "I don't trust you, Prick." This time the name fit perfectly. "You were supposed to give me a head start."

"I did. You took my damn Nav."

"Yeah, knowing you could track me in it. Very convenient." She glanced around the motel room, a standard model with two full-size beds stripped to white sheets. The walls were beige with the usual trite ocean paintings hanging over the wooden headboards.

"I told you I'd be right behind you." He helped her sit up. "You gave me one hell of a workout. I normally prefer a shower after a long run."

Her mouth felt dry, so she took the water he offered and drank it slowly. "Go ahead and take one. I'll wait here."

He smiled at her, placing a pillow behind her head.

She pushed his hand away. "Where are we?"

"Purple Valley Motel." He rose and walked to the corner table where a tray of food waited. "Are you hungry? I figured you must be, since you didn't eat this morning."

"Please let me go, Patrick." She'd beg now, given that she had no other options.

"Sorry." He handed her the tray.

She lifted the lid and found an appealing turkey croissant sandwich, applesauce and coleslaw. "Are you waiting for more men to come, or a helicopter?" She wondered how much time she had alone with him, and what his plan was.

"I haven't called it in yet." He rolled his shoulders uncomfortably. He wasn't sure why he brought her here, or hadn't requested a chopper. His superior would fire him instantly if he knew he'd found her and not reported it.

The air conditioner rattled just before shutting off. Lily studied him as he turned the TV on and stretched out on the bed beside her. He didn't seem too worried about her trying to escape. He hadn't handcuffed her, probably because of her promise to go with him willingly if he caught her again. "Why haven't you called your superiors yet?"

"Would you like for me to call them right now?" He pulled out a thin glass phone.

"No!" She set her hand over his. "Please don't." She read humor on his face, and almost smiled herself. She wasn't sure what to make of him, but she certainly wasn't going to encourage him to call more government agents.

He glanced from her to the TV. "That nuclear plant nearby is like a bomb waiting to explode. They're trying to cool the reactors, but there's not enough water. It could go into full meltdown any moment."

This was nothing she didn't already know. It was why Danny had chosen that particular cabin to hide her in. Many had already fled the state months ago. Virginia's plant was the only one the terrorists' bombs had failed to completely destroy. Although the reactor was still intact, the explosion caused structural damage, leaving it extremely unstable. Most people in the area had chosen to evacuate, joining thousands of other evacuees living in government safe zones.

It was odd the motel wasn't closed. "Do we still have housekeeping?" she wondered. Not that it mattered to her what order the room was in. It was simply more comforting knowing there were people around.

"The owners are living here, running the place. Their teenage daughter is handling housekeeping. Why, do you need more towels?"

She ignored his sarcastic grin, and the dimples at the corners of his mouth. She watched the TV and took a bite of her sandwich.

The TV was showing the ubiquitous infomercial for air purifiers "guaranteed to remove airborne radiation." It was followed by a bleached-blond reporter with the latest news. Suddenly, Lily's name was being spoken. Was there ever more than five minutes on television when her name didn't come up? She hated seeing herself on TV, and even worse was the appearance of Kate's photo. "Turn it off."

Patrick hit mute and turned to study her. He'd seen that sad look in her eyes before. It was just after she'd healed him, and they'd spoken briefly. "I'm sorry about your sister."

"I doubt that." She forced herself to chew, knowing she needed the food. "You plan to take me to the same people who killed her."

"That was an accident. No one killed her."

She tried to dismiss his words. There was a heavy pain associated with her sister, and she didn't want to cry. She didn't want to explain to Prick just how very wrong he was.

Patrick didn't need audio to know what the news was saying. The pictures of the protesters, the images of desolate damaged areas of the United States, the interviews with angry survivors… it was all the same. Always the same. "Half the world wants you in government hands, and the other half wants you safely hidden away."

"I know which half you belong to." She finished her last bite of sandwich.

"I'm feeling better, you know."

She glanced at him. "No you don't. You only think you do."

He narrowed his eyes. "What the hell does that mean?" He sat up straight. "Did you lie to me? Did you not actually heal me?"

19

"You were never really sick."

"What?" he said incredulously.

"It was all I could think of to get away."

He ran a hand through his hair. "Damn. You really had me going." He gave an apprehensive sigh. "Does your power really even work?"

"It's not a power, Prick."

"I shouldn't have told you my nick-name. You're enjoying it too much. Call me Patrick."

"No."

Impatiently he moved closer. "Well, does it?"

"Does it what?" She stared at the side of his face where she'd seen blood, and wondered if she'd given him a concussion with the baton.

He handed her the applesauce before setting the tray aside. "How does your healing ability work?"

She shrugged her shoulders. "Haven't you heard all the theories?"

"Some." He'd heard scientists comparing her to light. They believed she somehow had the ability to send invisible electromagnetic waves into another person. Those natural energy waves could alter abnormal cells, breaking down their malignancy. One doctor said her body was able to emit a current that manipulates white blood cells to work faster, accelerates clotting, and allows proteins to heal the body in a matter of seconds rather than the typical weeks. The Christian faction believed her power was divine, perhaps even messianic, with the power to heal the devastation in the world. "I'd like to hear your opinion."

"I don't think I'm alien offspring, though it's a common theory." Many people thought she was the product of an alien abduction. Conspiracy theorists believed an alien raped and impregnated her mother. It was true her mother had been raped, and afterward retreated into a general denial of reality. But she'd been functional enough to raise her children until that terrible day of her psychotic

20

break.

Lily was never able to block the painful memory. She could still hear her mother's voice: "You're not human, you're not human." How could that eerie, sing-song voice evoke both fear and love at the same time? "You're not human, you're not human."

She closed her eyes and tried to force the image away. But she could still feel the grip of her sister's hand. She could still smell the scent of kerosene. Her psychiatrist had told her years ago it was healthy to remember... that if she relived it enough, her mind would come to terms with it.

At age ten, she'd shared a bed with her twin sister, Kate. Kate always preferred to sleep on her back, while Lily slept on her tummy. Lily had been half-asleep, thinking the voice was part of a dream. There was the chanting of a calm, whimsical song by a voice she recognized as comforting, except that the words didn't make any sense. "You're not human, you're not human." It hadn't been until Kate squeezed her hand so tightly she felt the bones crack that she opened her eyes and turned to her side. There stood their mother holding a lit match over Kate. Lily didn't understand, and her mind had been still foggy as she listened to the gentle song, "You're not human, you're not human." Suddenly Kate had been a glow of raging fire. Lily had felt the intense pain the moment her sister screamed. An ear-piercing scream that threatened to burst her eardrum. Pain had radiated from the side of her face all the way down to her toes.

Engulfed in flames, her mother had been singing still, because her lips were moving, but there was no sound. Only the sound of Kate's long, bloodcurdling scream. Lily wanted to protect her, to shelter her, to put the flames out. She rolled on top of her sister. Her body went numb, except for a strange stabbing pain in her stomach. Lily ignored it, because her only thoughts were of shielding Kate. She managed to raise her head up, and stare into her sister's eyes. They were glazed over, and fixed on the ceiling. "Kate?" she felt the words on her lips, and swallowed against the smell of burnt flesh.

21

She heard her brother, Alex, yelling at their mother, "What have you done?" It became a new chant that seemed far away. Lily set her cheek on top of Kate's. The heat was beyond painful, and she closed her eyes, feeling consumed by it. Kate's soft whimper made Lily realize she was still holding her sister's soft, still hand.

"I'll heal you," Lily whispered into her ear. She didn't know what made her say that, other than she had a powerful overwhelming urge to take her sister's pain away. She wanted to absorb Kate's body into her own, and take that intense heat out of her. It felt like tiny needles stabbing her skin everywhere, and all she could think was, "I'll heal you. I'll heal you, I'll heal you."

After setting fire to her children, Lily's mother was committed to a psychiatric hospital. She hadn't stopped chanting, "You're not human," until four months passed. She'd been given intravenous drugs, because she'd lost the ability to eat, to move, to live. Her mind had entered a new landscape, and this time it didn't allow her to function. It was Lily's twenty year old brother who had taken over raising his younger sisters.

"Hey." Patrick's voice brought Lily's mind back to the present. He laid his hand over hers. "I don't buy the alien theory either. Will you explain it?"

She glanced down at his hand, and didn't find it uncomfortable when his thumb softly grazed her fingers. There was compassion in his touch, and understanding in his eyes.

"I'm human," she whispered.

"I told you, I don't buy the theory that you're not."

She struggled to hold back tears.

"Damn." He rose and walked to the window. He didn't like to see women cry, especially not Lily, who was somehow able to display every emotion she was feeling on her beautiful face. "Look, I don't think you're an alien. I just wanted to know if you could explain to me how you're able to heal people. It's a completely mind-blowing ability that you have."

Taking a deep breath, Lily tried to block out her mother's face.

She ran her fingers along her midriff. She had not one scar on her body to remind her of that horrible day, and neither did Kate. When Kate was alive, they'd had only the memory, and now she needed to push it aside. She glanced over at Patrick, who was clearly uncomfortable with her emotions.

Something about that made her smile. "I can feel when people are sick. I can't explain it." She'd tried putting it into words thousands of times when doctors and scientists pressed her for answers. "It's like I can just feel energy. You feel the wind, but you can't see it. You know it's there, because it blows trees or you feel it on your skin. My ability is like that. I just feel it."

Patrick slowly walked back to the bed, and sat beside her.

"I first discovered my ability to heal when I was ten." She knew she couldn't share the actual experience without crying, so she skipped that part. "I can touch you," she set her hand on top of his knee, "and I feel heat. I feel normal wave pulses. If you had abnormal cells in your body, I'd feel ripples." She moved her hand slowly up his leg and lifted it to the side of his head, just above his ear. "I feel the waves where your skin is damaged. I cut you with the baton. Your body is trying to repair itself, and if I wanted to, I could heal it in a matter of minutes."

"I wondered why when you claimed to have healed me, my cut was still there, but I didn't want to press my luck." He smiled and took her hand, moving it from his wound. "So I really don't have cancer?" He stood up, feeling the need to step away again. His muscles were tense; his legs were beginning to ache from the long morning run. His jeans were filthy; his blue t-shirt had dried sweat spots down the front. He'd love to take a cold shower.

"You don't have cancer." Her slender legs were stretched out in front of her, and she leaned back against the headboard. "But you have a different form of malignancy. It's called trusting your government."

"I don't trust the government, Lily."

Chapter 4

She smiled halfheartedly, and gave him a look that said she begged to differ.

"You have a gift, Lily. If scientists can determine how your body works, and how you cure people, then lives can be saved. We can change the future." He remembered what his wife had gone through, how the treatments destroyed her immune system and made her sick. There were long waits now just for medication. He'd spent many hours in agency meetings, being taught that Lily McCallister was the answer to the world's sickness. She possessed some new DNA strand that could prevent and cure cancer. They needed her body and stem cells to make the technological advancements.

Lily hated that speech. The same lecture the doctors gave her and Kate. It worked at first, because Lily wanted to help save lives. She wanted to change the world and give people hope.

"The answer to salvation isn't in me. It's in our choices. What good does it do, if I can cure your body of cancer, but tomorrow you walk around in a nuclear wasteland of chemicals that just cause more free radicals and cancer down the road? Mankind needs to rid the earth of pollutants, and stop building things that destroy our planet."

Patrick looked at her as if he was actually contemplating what she was saying. "We're trying. What do you think all those people are doing working for the Contamination Cleanup Corporation? They are cleaning up the earth."

"You're a fool." She pulled her legs to her chest. "Those workers have no choice. They need food and supplies for their families. The government is providing that on one condition: that they risk their lives for it." The nation had become almost completely dependent on the government.

"Hey, the government is trying to save the lives of everyone in this nation. Look how they generated electricity by building thousands of windmills. That created jobs, and gave the economy a boost."

Lily shook her head. It was hard to argue with someone who so strongly supported the government. It did little good. They didn't see that the authorities should have built the windmills to begin with. "I'll admit they've done some good, but only because people were desperate to survive. The windmills were developed because Americans rose to the occasion and demanded it."

"You mean because Americans can't live without Wi-Fi!" He paced the room. He didn't know why Lily's dislike of the government bothered him so much. Sure, the people worked together to rebuild, to reestablish electricity, and to rise above the destruction and chaos, but wasn't the President also helping? A tremendous amount of good came from the government. He'd been told Lily was uncooperative. She wouldn't share her ability with the scientists who swore they could learn valuable information from her.

"The government is feeding starving and misplaced people. The military is keeping people safe, and the rest of the power plants are under heavy guard now. Many of the terrorists are dead. Parts of the nation have been destroyed, but the government is fixing what it can." He said tensely, and then sighed realizing he defended the government more than he'd meant to.

"Please!" she stood and put her hands on her hips. "I can't listen to your nonsense anymore. This administration is no better than the last. It's their fault the world is suffering today. They have no choice but to try and fix it. There is barely any world left now. Everyone's going to die from cancer or radiation poisoning!"

"Except you." He blocked her path to the door, as she tried to push past him. "Where do you think you're going?"

"The bathroom."

He stepped aside, knowing she couldn't escape in the windowless room. "Fine."

After she slammed the door shut, he walked over to the bed. He slipped the silver phone from his pocket and stared down at it. Jeffrey, his agency superior, was expecting all operatives to report in. Patrick flipped open the phone and pressed the power button, turning it off. "What the hell am I doing?" he whispered to himself.

He knew the moment he made the call a helicopter would arrive within an hour. He might have longer if agents were sent by car. It took longer to drive anywhere thanks to road closures. Many main highways were no longer accessible. Large sections of the country were now uninhabitable. Nuclear plants were destroyed, resulting in widespread contamination. The only states not affected were the western coastal states and a few of the northern ones. But Patrick and Lily were in West Virginia, which was mostly evacuated, and it was only a matter of time before a fourth nuclear disaster would occur.

Lily stepped out of the bathroom. "I need to find a store." For a moment she considered bolting for the door. Would she be fast enough to make it outside?

"Don't even think about it." Patrick turned to face her, his arms folded across his chest. "What do you need?"

"A female product."

He raised an eyebrow. Did she want deodorant or what? He'd looked through her backpack, and hadn't seen any. "Look, you can take a shower. You'll feel better."

"I plan to shower, but I still need a feminine product from the store."

"What exactly do you need?"

She rolled her eyes. "It's that time …"

"Oh."

"Yeah." She held her breath in the hopes he'd believe her. Then she slowly released it, trying to appear uncomfortable.

He wasn't sure if she was telling the truth, but he'd been married, and knew from past experience that when a woman needed something, she needed something. "Crap." He wasn't prepared for this. If he left her chained, he could inquire at the front desk. If he took her with him, she would only try to escape. Hell, she was going to attempt escape either way. "I don't suppose I need to remind you, you made me a promise."

"You can stick that promise—"

"Look," he walked to the nightstand phone. "I'll call the front desk. There's a girl working here, and I'm sure she can bring you something."

"I need more than one, Prick, and this isn't a five-star hotel. I doubt feminine products are included in their complimentary supplies."

He ignored the use of his nickname, and the irritation on her face. "Let's find out." He'd call the motel's front desk and offer to pay the girl, or anyone, to get him what she needed. Damn her, for making him have to use those words.

Suddenly a loud siren sounded outside. They quickly looked out the window. Patrick pressed TV volume, so he could hear the emergency broadcast message.

Lily laughed. "What are the odds?" She didn't actually find the situation funny. A reactor thirty miles away just exploded. The core of the West Virginia Power Plant was in full meltdown. Citizens not already evacuated were being told to stay indoors. The loud sirens were installed months ago to warn people when to seek shelter.

The news showed various clips of the ways people tried to make their homes radiation proof. Protective canopies over windows and roofs, electric filters, and dug out basements with lead paneled walls. With so many displaced Americans coping with the loss of land, many people chose to stay in their homes, preparing for the worst. Patrick was sure the hotel owners had a fallout shelter, and were probably already in it. Perhaps they'd be willing to share it, but he had no intentions of being stuck inside a bunker with a bunch of strangers. "Let's go." He slipped a handcuff to her wrist and cuffed the other to his own.

"Seriously?" She watched as he slung her backpack over his shoulder. "Is this really necessary?"

"Move."

He had her enter the car first, told her to slide over, and then got in.

"Where are we headed?"

"Back up the mountain to your cabin." He'd seen a storm shelter behind the house, along with a well. At least there was plenty of forest surrounding it, and large trees to hopefully protect the home from nuclear debris. He also knew the cabin was stocked with plenty of food.

Cars were flying along the two-lane road, and Patrick laid on the horn as a frantic driver cut him off. "Damn, people are panicking." He was going 95 mph just to keep pace with traffic. He almost missed the turn to the cabin. A black pickup was traveling directly in front of them.

"This is a private road, he shouldn't be here," Lily said nervously, pressing her hands to the headliner to keep from bouncing as they drove over potholes.

"I'll take care of it." He was going to have to deal with a frightened driver who was only trying to get up the mountain to safety. How many others would follow? He glanced in the rearview mirror, but could only see dust.

"Watch out!" She threw her hands out in front of her. "My God, slow down! You're going to go right off the mountain." Her stomach clenched at how fast he was driving.

He handed her the handcuff key. "Un-cuff yourself before you pull us off the damn road." She was yanking his hand with all her movements.

She was more than ready to free herself, and desperate to get away. She was worried about her brother. Where was he? Was he safe from the radiation? She hoped Sage made it to safety. She handed the key back to him, studying his relaxed face. He didn't appear stressed or tense, the way she was. "If I were to run, would you risk your life to come after me?" The sirens were still going off, which meant radiation was already in the air, carried on the wind, probably for a radius of many miles. It wasn't safe to be outdoors.

"Yes."

"Yes?" She couldn't believe it. "Why?"

"Because you're too valuable."

She knew this was going to be an ongoing battle. The government had thoroughly brainwashed him.

The radio played mostly static, but Patrick found a news station. Reports of explosions were happening at the plant. He turned the volume down. "This isn't good."

"We were stupid to build so many nuclear plants." She remembered how nine years ago, when she was fourteen, her brother, Alex, dragged her and Kate to a protest. Danny laughed at what a waste of time protests were. The world was already full of nuclear plants, and some were built on seismic fault lines. Danny was wise for his age, and seemed to know things most teens didn't even care about. He'd discussed how the EPA was pushing for more green energy instead of nuclear plants, but to no avail.

Patrick braked as the truck in front slowed abruptly. "Damn it," he slapped the steering wheel. The driver in front was stopping. "Put your head down!" He reached over and pushed her head into her lap. "He's seen you."

"So what?"

"He could be a fundamentalist." Patrick was aware of the dangers involved with the fundamentalism movement sweeping the nation. Many Christians were on the hunt for Lily as well.

Lily wasn't sure what to think of the more radical people who believed she was the messiah. Her brother thought perhaps they could be trusted to keep her safe. However, Danny believed they could be harmful and it'd be no better to end up in the hands of a fundamentalist any more than the government. "How do you know?" she asked Patrick, as she pushed his hand away from her.

"His bumper sticker: 'Christians stand as one nation under God; Government stands for one nation under itself.'"

"That's hardly proof he belongs to the radical faction. Maybe he's just a Christian who, like me, isn't a fan of the government."

"Do you really think it's safe for you to be with anyone right now? Every person on this planet probably has someone they love that is sick or dying. You don't think they'd try and use you to heal their loved one?" Patrick checked the rear view mirror. There was no way to back up, and nowhere to go but up. He pulled his gun out, and checked the chamber.

"You're not going to shoot him, are you?" Lily placed her hand over her chest as if she could calm her racing heart. "Please don't kill him."

"Don't say a word." He rolled down the window and peered at the man who carefully stepped from his truck. The stranger appeared harmless, an older man with silver hair that framed his face. He wore a blue plaid short-sleeved shirt and jeans.

"I wanted to ask you how far this road goes and if you know what it leads to?" the man asked Patrick. He didn't even glance at Lily. He was pressed against the side of the truck, as there was no shoulder on the narrow road.

"This is a private road to my cabin," Patrick informed him, leaning his head out the window. "Just a quarter mile up and it ends."

The man shook his head. "I panicked." He glanced over his shoulder at the vast wilderness. "I have my gear, but don't have much water."

Patrick relaxed his grip on his gun. The man was obviously a drifter. He'd probably been traveling with his camping gear, looking for food and odd jobs. Many people chose that way over government shelters.

"I've got a well. You can get some water, then be on your way." He couldn't exactly turn around, and Patrick felt sorry for him.

"I appreciate it," the man said. Just then he set his eyes on Lily for the first time.

Patrick immediately knew the man recognized her. He raised his gun, quickly opening his door. "Don't move!" he shouted. He glanced at Lily. "Get out of the car, and get into his."

"It's you! It's really *you*?" The man stared at Lily as if she were God himself. "Will you see if I have anything? Will you heal me?"

It was always the same. Every person she met immediately wanted her to check for cancer or radiation poisoning. If necessary, they wanted to be healed. It's what she was famous for. She had the one gift of supreme value to every human being on earth.

"Please... I know I've been exposed."

Patrick moved to the front of the car. "We all have, buddy." He kept his gun carefully trained on the man. "We're taking your truck, and you're going to start walking down the mountain. Are we clear on this?"

The man nodded his head. "Please just let her heal me first."

Patrick turned to Lily. "It's up to you."

She knew that pleading look. She'd seen it thousands of times. "What is your name?"

"What does that matter?" Patrick wanted to hurry and get to the cabin before more cars came along.

"Fred Brown."

Now there was a name easy to remember. "What did you do for a living, Fred?" She asked, ignoring Patrick's annoyance, focusing her attention on Fred.

"I'm a retired carpenter."

"Huh," Lily smiled as Patrick tucked his gun behind his back, and his demeanor changed.

Fred stood a little straighter, squaring his shoulders as he spoke with pride. "I worked about 10 years in California. I rebuilt homes."

"Okay, that's impressive," Patrick replied with a slight grin. "Heal him and let's go." He wasn't going to admit that he was happy Lily was healing him. Fred was probably a good man. A hard

31

worker and someone who deserved to enjoy his retirement. California had suffered a devastating earthquake that left more than half the state in ruins. At the time there was a huge shortage of workers who knew carpentry. Carpentry was a highly respected field and was sought after for the reconstruction of California.

"Give me your hand." The moment she touched him, she could feel the energy. The strange sensation of unknown waves passing between them that told her abnormal cells were growing in his body. She closed her eyes, willing her own energy to build. She could feel her body warming. Soon she would be light-headed from the exertion. The healing always reduced her own metabolic energy.

She touched Fred's tattoo of a heart surrounded by roses, with a cursive name and birthdate in the middle. "Who is Dorothy?"

"She was my daughter." Fred's face seemed to soften ten years. "She died."

"I'm sorry."

"We wanted to take Dorothy to you. You were in Arizona at a healing gathering. But she was too sick to travel, and we couldn't get an airline ticket in time. It's hard to live with that."

"I'm sorry," Lily whispered. She stared into sad, clear blue eyes. "I'm healing you, so you're going to live a lot longer now."

Fred's throat grew tight with the emotion of gratitude. "Part of me wanted to die, but seeing you now, I realize I don't. I want a chance. Maybe the good Lord had me run into you for that chance. I have a wife I need to live for. She needs me." He hadn't been feeling well, and left his wife for a few days to do some fishing and catch up on sleep. Now he felt like the luckiest man alive, running into the one and only person on earth that could cure whatever was wrong with him. "I'll be forever in your debt."

Lily gripped his hand tighter as she felt the tingle of energy seeping from her body.

"Whoa," Patrick grabbed her arm to steady her as she began to sway. "What the hell," he muttered, noticing how red her face was getting. He glanced at Fred, who stared at her dumbfounded.

32

She let go of his hand. "I'm sorry I couldn't save your daughter, but you'll live now. Just get away from the plant, and head as far north as you can." Her head began to spin, so she leaned into Patrick.

"Thank you. Oh, God, thank you!" Fred looked from Lily to Patrick. "You're protecting her, right? Don't let the government take her. You know they'll kill her, like they did her sister. Don't let them get her!" he insisted frantically.

Patrick pulled Lily closer to his side. "I'll take care of her. Now go."

"Yes, yes, I'll go." Fred backed away. "You're so much more beautiful in person. On TV your eyes look brown, but they're not. They're gold, like the streets of heaven. You look like an angel. God Bless you, Lily McCallister! Stay safe!"

Even as Patrick helped her into the truck, he could hear the man shouting, "Lily, you're my angel!"

He hated leaving his Navigator, but he could always run down and retrieve it later. He anticipated possibly running into further trouble at the cabin. Fred walked away happy, but Patrick wondered if he wasn't the only driver who'd sped up the road at the sound of the alarm. People were panicking and searching for shelter. The SUV would block other cars from coming up the road. He glanced at Lily, resting her head against the door. "Are you okay?"

"I will be."

"What did that do to you?" The media showed clips of her healing people, but she never appeared red faced and weak, the way she did now.

"At first, it didn't require effort to heal people. But now…" She sat up a little straighter in her seat and looked at him. "It drains me. The scientists did things to me." She closed her eyes as she remembered the horrible solutions they made her drink. The needles didn't leave scars, but on normal people they would. "Even before the horrible experiments, I felt I was overusing my ability, healing too many at once. That's why I stopped holding large public sessions.

There were too many in need." She leaned back against the headrest, feeling exhausted. "But I haven't felt the same since the tests."

"Is that why you left?" The news reported she was uncooperative with the specialists studying her.

"I didn't leave, Patrick. I escaped."

He took his eyes off the road for a moment to raise an eyebrow at her. He was relieved to see she was recovering.

"The media lied. Everything they said was false. I was a prisoner, held against my will. When I asked to leave, they wouldn't let me. When I refused certain horrid procedures, I was forced. They wouldn't let me see my sister." She couldn't talk about her twin without crying, without getting angry. "I didn't even get to attend her funeral."

"I'm sorry," he finally said after a few moments of silence.

"No you're not. You have no clue."

"Enlighten me."

She glared at him. "How about I just tell you the least horrific things they did. Like forcing me to drink some blue chemicals that burned my throat and blistered my tongue to where I couldn't swallow. So they strapped me down on a cold hard metal table, shoved a tube down my esophagus and poured it in. It didn't matter that I felt like I was drowning, or that the pain made me want to die. All that mattered was seeing how my insides handled the acid while I was strapped under an X-ray machine." Anger kept her tears from flowing. She liked that when he glanced at her, his face showed the impact of her words. "Or how about when they used a scalpel to peel away pieces of my flesh, so they could track how long it took for it to repair itself. And no, I wasn't given pain meds. How about when they broke my—"

"Stop!" He felt sick. His hands tightened on the wheel. "Jesus, I get it."

From his pained expression, she knew she'd made her point. She stopped and drew a shaky breath.

"Why didn't you tell me this before? What they did is torture,

34

and illegal."

"Apparently, the rules don't apply when it's in the name of science. They called it, 'study' and they felt both entitled and justified to do whatever they deemed necessary for the sake of the human race."

He shook his head. "I'm sorry, Lily. You're right, I didn't know." Why hadn't he considered what the doctors would do to her? He'd watched his wife suffer from endless needles and sickening medications all in the hopes of saving her, and that was traumatic for both of them. But what Lily went through…. He thought about what Fred said. Enough people seemed to know the truth, why hadn't he?

"You probably don't believe me," she said crossing her arms.

"I do believe you." He set his hand on her arm. He wanted to say more, but as he approached the cabin he noted the sky-blue electric car parked on the grass. He'd made a huge mistake not realizing the truth. Now he wanted to make things right, but he didn't know how. All he could do was ensure her safety. "I need to check the cabin first. Whoever owns that car might be inside." He slipped the handcuff back on her wrist, hooking the other end to the steering wheel.

"You really are a Prick," she muttered as he left. The sun's rays shone through the trees, casting shadows over the cabin. Patrick glanced down at the gravel for footprints. A few sets ended just before the porch. If these were people fleeing the meltdown, they'd also be seeking food and water. Maybe they'd want to stay at the cabin.

He went around the side of the house to look through windows first. He glanced back at Lily, placing his finger to his lips.

She shook her head. "Yeah, I'm going to sit here quietly, Prick," she whispered to herself. She watched the way he moved and held his gun. He was definitely a cop, except no longer sworn to serve and protect, at least not her. She wanted to hate him. Just as she began mentally listing all the reasons why, her door suddenly opened.

"Don't be afraid, Lily! We're here to save you."

35

Chapter 5

Lily stared at a man crouching beside the truck. He held a large set of wire cutters, and cut the handcuff chain. "Don't be afraid, I'm a friend of Alex's," he told her.

The mention of her brother's name eased her anxiety. "Alex sent you?"

"No, Danny did." The man held his hand out. "Get out of the truck."

"How did Danny find me?" She asked, letting him help her down. Something about the man's face made her nervous. She could read people, and something didn't feel right.

"We were following Sage. We let this guy take you, and then followed. The warning sirens went off before we could get to you."

"We have him!" another man shouted.

Lily looked over the hood. "Oh, don't hurt him!" she cried out. The man near her grabbed her arm. Patrick's lip was cut and bleeding, and his eye was starting to swell. His hands were bound behind his back, and the large man behind him kicked him down into the grass.

"Lily, run!" Patrick shouted, before the big man kicked him again.

"We won't kill him… yet."

Lily turned to the man who claimed he was a friend of her brother's. "Who are you?" He wasn't anyone her brother or Danny ever mentioned. With his short, military haircut and black clothing, he looked more like a Marine. She couldn't be sure the man was lying, though. Alex had many friends, and Danny used all kinds of contacts. It was how they helped her escape the testing facility. Both Alex and Danny were part of a coalition.

"Lily, your brother wants us to take you to him."

She glanced from the man to Patrick. What did Patrick know that she didn't? He said to run. "Stop hurting him!" she shouted as Patrick was kicked again. Her mind raced, as she tried to pull away. If they'd been following her, how did they get to the cabin first?

"We're here to help you, Lily. Your brother is waiting."

She stopped struggling and stared into the man's eyes. "Okay, what's the password?" Alex told her if anyone was ever sent for her, they'd be given a password.

"This is my password." The stranger twisted Lily's arm behind her back until she cried out in pain.

Lily turned to see Patrick roll over and kick the big man in the groin. Then, like a gymnast, he sprang to his feet and landed a roundhouse kick that sent the man flying back. She cried out again as she felt the pain surge to her shoulder.

"Don't hurt her!" Patrick stood up straight, and was glad to see the man he'd just fought wasn't moving. "Look around, buddy, this isn't going to end well for you. Just let her go, and I'll let you keep breathing."

The man holding tight to Lily smiled at Patrick. "Oh? And how are you going to do anything with your hands tied?"

"Do you not see what happened to your friends?"

"I'm slightly impressed, but... she's coming with me."

Suddenly the pressure was gone from her arm, and the man dropped to the ground. Lily raised her head and saw the knife sticking from the man's eye. Before she could react, Patrick wrapped her in his arms, her face pressed against his chest.

"Don't look." He covered the side of her face softly. "Are you hurt? Is your arm okay?"

"I'm fine." Her body already healed any torn ligaments.

He walked her to the cabin, his eyes scanning the woods. "We can't stay here." He checked the pulse on the guy he'd kicked in the neck, and knew the man was dead. "Did you know them?" He set his hand on her cheek, and gently turned her away from the body.

"No, did you?"

"No. But I knew they weren't good men."

She wondered why Patrick was suddenly looking at her strangely. "What?"

"Weren't you in need of a certain feminine product?"

"I lied."

"Of course you did," he grinned. He didn't like how pale her face was, or that her hands trembled. "Those men didn't work for the government, Lil. Do you have any idea who they may work for, or with?"

"No." She walked into the cabin. "I need some water."

Patrick followed her. He could see she was shaken, watching as she approached the sink, turning on the faucet. She placed her racing pulse under the cool water while he grabbed a glass. "Here."

"That man knew that Danny and my brother are helping me." She took a long slow drink. "He told me Danny sent him, but claimed he was a friend of my brother's."

"Could they have been?" He reached out, wiping a small piece of grass from her cheek.

"I don't know. I honestly don't know what to think anymore. Everyone's after me. I'll never be safe, and I'll never be able to stop running." Her stomach felt queasy.

He regarded her a moment. "I have camping gear in my Navigator. We'll take the truck back to it, grab the pack and head out on foot. It's not safe here."

She chuckled. "Oh, and it's safer backpacking through the Appalachians, with radiation and nuclear debris in the wind?"

"You'll be safe."

He was standing close to her, and she studied his eyes a moment. He seemed sincerely concerned for her. "Are you still planning to take me back to the testing facility?" she asked him.

"I'm not sure." The moment the words came out, he regretted them. Why not just tell her the truth? He knew the facility would continue abusing her, and there was no way he'd let that happen.

She crossed her arms over her chest. "What do you mean, you're not sure?" Was he going to let her go?

"I mean I haven't decided."

"What is there to decide? It's your job. Don't you have to take me back?"

"You trying to talk me into it?"

"No! But I'd at least like to know what you're planning to do with me."

His eye was throbbing, his muscles ached, and he felt exhausted. He didn't know what to say to her. There was no way he was turning her in, but he also wasn't willing to let her go. He looked her up and down, before turning toward the fridge. He began to take out jelly and a loaf of bread. "Stop burning a hole in my back, Lil. I need you to go take a fast shower and put some clean hiking clothes on. It might be a while before you have the chance again." He hoped a shower would help relax her and maybe soothe her nerves. He set the food on the counter and opened the cupboards above the sink. "Where's the peanut butter?"

"Don't call me 'Lil'. Only my friends and family call me that." She took the peanut butter from the pantry and tossed it at him on her way to the stairs. She'd take her shower, and decide what she should do next. She needed a moment to think, and the thought of hot water easing her tension outweighed the desire to run outside with no gear, and no protection.

"Oh, and Lily…" He waited for her to turn. "You have exactly ten minutes, or I'll drag you out in whatever state I find you in." He glanced down at his watch and pressed a button.

She rolled her eyes at him, before climbing the stairs two at a time.

Chapter 6

As soon as she was up the stairs, Patrick opened the back door. He didn't want Lily to see the other three bodies in the backyard. He was left no choice but to fight and kill, and since he'd used a knife, the scene wasn't pretty. He quickly found the gun he had kicked away while he fought the three men. He checked the chamber and slid it behind his back before searching the men's pockets. The first wallet had no ID and a ten-dollar bill. Patrick took the money. The second man had no wallet and no ID, but he did have a nice hunting knife in a leather sheath, which Patrick tucked in his jeans. He found nothing but a stick of gum on the third man. He checked his watch. Lily had three more minutes, and he hoped she wasn't trying to escape.

Back in the house, he heard the water shut off, and the creak of the floor above him. He made four sandwiches and packed them in a paper bag. Sitting at the kitchen table, eyes on the window, he glanced at his watch as Lily came down the stairs. Her hair was wet, and braided at the side. She looked fresh and clean, wearing khaki cargo pants and a white V-neck t-shirt. The look suited her, and he thought of Fred's words. Lily was angelic looking, with a beauty, he decided, was quite stunning. "I'm impressed." She was exactly one minute late. He wasn't really going to enforce the ten-minute mark, but his threat worked. "We have to go."

"Aren't you going to shower?"

"No."

"You should clean your cuts, and your eye is swelling."

"I'm fine. I'll bathe in a stream tonight, once I know you're safe." He stood up, swung the backpack over his shoulder.

"I'm not going with you."

"What?"

"I don't think you'll hurt me, and I don't think you want to hand me over to those monsters that used me like a lab rat." She hesitated a moment, feeling calm. "I called my brother, and he's on his way to get me."

Patrick kept his face neutral, as he leaned against the wooden table. "You're lying again, Lily. There's no phone here. I checked your clothes, and the only phone was in your pack, which I have, and I removed the battery."

Lily held out a thin glass phone. "It was well hidden."

He was careful not to let his anger or worry show. He should have told her he wasn't turning her over to the government. He realized he left her no choice. "So you think your brother is really coming here to get you? How's he going to get past my car? I'll be pissed if he knocks my Nav off the road."

"He's already here. He's been living in the mountains." Alex loved camping and hiking, and as kids she and Kate spent every weekend exploring the wilderness with him. He knew every trail in the Appalachians.

"Damn." Patrick approached her, and she stepped back.

"Please, Patrick. I don't want to hurt you."

He hesitated. Just what was she up to? She had a phone, so maybe she had a weapon as well. "Would you?"

"If it means my survival. If I go back, they'll kill me. I can't go back!"

"Look," he met her morose gaze with understanding. "I'm not taking you back. You have to trust me."

"It's too late. I can't afford to." She pulled a stun gun out from behind her back. It was another well hidden item. "You're just like everyone else, believing the government's lies!" She pointed the stun gun at him. "I let them perform their tests, but there's no way to duplicate what I have. I gave them my blood, I endured immense

41

pain, and it was never enough!" Her hands shook. I suffered in the hopes they could find answers."

Patrick offered her a sincere apologetic look. "I know, Lily. You can trust me."

"They began testing my sister. My twin! She didn't even have the ability to heal! They tortured her for nothing!" She couldn't stop the emotions flooding to the surface. She was exhausted, her nerves shot, and she wanted to trust him.

"She didn't have my ability," she continued, as tears gathered in her eyes. "And yet they continued with their experimenting until she became too weak. They took too much blood allowing her to get sicker and sicker. It's because of them she got the deadly infection. They killed my sister!" Her voice broke. "She was my best friend, and half my heart! I escaped before they killed me too." She wiped a tear from her eye. "I wanted to help save people, but your stupid government couldn't find what they were looking for." She lowered her arms as Patrick approached her. "So I can't trust you, or anyone else."

He wrapped his arms around her, relieved that she let him. "You can trust me, sweetheart," he said softly and kissed the top of her head.

Before they had met, he believed what he'd been told. They said she refused to help, and was uncooperative. Many people who distrusted the government believed she had every right to refuse. He didn't agree until now, until he heard her side, learning the truth. He thought about Fred, how she'd shown him compassion. He believed she gave of herself because that was simply who she was. She wasn't a rebel refusing to help the world; she wanted to survive. "I'm sorry."

"Isn't that sweet," said a dry voice.

Patrick quickly pulled Lily behind him as he faced Jeffrey, his commander, at the front door.

"I knew you'd screw this up, Prick. We warned you not to let her looks throw you."

Two men stood behind the commander, but Patrick noted that

Jeffrey's gun was still holstered. "Look, just give me a few minutes, Jeff. You can see she's upset. Let me explain things to her."

"Did you call them?" Lily asked, from behind his back.

"No," he told her flatly, and his chest tightened at the fear in her voice.

Jeffrey stepped forward. "Ms. McCallister, you may as well come willingly. There's nowhere to run, we have you completely surrounded."

Lily wiped her tears away and whispered, "Please, Patrick, don't let them take me."

Patrick found her hand and squeezed it. She didn't have to ask. He had no intention of letting her go.

Jeffrey smiled, taking another step inside. "You know, those doctors are telling us you aren't human. We know the man who raped your mother wasn't from this planet."

Patrick glanced to his right at the federal agent standing outside the window. Suddenly, another man wearing a red ball cap came up behind the agent and covered his face with a white cloth. The two agents behind Jeffrey simultaneously fell to the ground. Patrick took the stun gun from Lily, quickly turned it on the commander.

He didn't wait for Jeffrey to hit the floor before grabbing the backpack and pulling Lily out the door. As soon as he stepped outside, the man wearing the red cap took a swing at him. Patrick pushed Lily back out of harm's way and ducked the blow. It still landed on the side of his face, but it only took him three moves to lay the man out cold.

"Do you know this guy?" he asked Lily.

She shook her head. She hoped he wasn't a man her brother sent. Alex hadn't mentioned anyone else. He told her he was coming himself. She wanted to wait for her brother, but Patrick was pulling her through the woods.

"That guy could have been with the first group of men from the cabin." Either way, he'd helped them by taking out Jeffrey's men. "Maybe he was just a good Samaritan who saw what was happening and decided to help."

"Wait!" Lily pulled her hand free. She glanced back at the cabin searching for a sign of her brother. "Please, just wait."

"Lily, that man could wake up soon, and more men could be coming. We need to reach my Navigator and get off this mountain." He glanced through the trees, aware of the direction to head in. "Come on."

"But my brother will—"

"He'll see the situation, and know you're not there." He pulled her along. "You can contact him later."

A tree branch whacked her in the face and she almost stumbled. Patrick helped her regain her footing. He paused, pushing her hair from her eyes. "Lily, I know you don't have a reason to trust me, but I need you to right now. I won't let them take you, and I promise I'll help you find your brother." He set his hand gently on her shoulder, offering an affectionate squeeze. "Please… give me a chance."

There was such a sincerity and kindness in his eyes, she felt a trustworthiness that made her nod her head. She continued following him. By the time they reached his Navigator, she was out of breath. Her feet and shins hurt from stepping over branches and prickly plants that scraped her ankles. Although her body healed quickly, she still felt the pain that accompanies injury. Gladly she got in the car when Patrick told her to.

"This is too easy." He stuck the key in the ignition. "I don't like it." He couldn't believe they weren't being followed.

"You can't go down the mountain backward!" Lily panicked as he began to move in reverse.

"Watch me."

He didn't go too fast, but before she knew it they were down the mountain and backing onto the road. "I can't believe you just did that."

"Yeah, well, we're not in the clear yet."

"Where'd you learn to fight like that?"

"Compliments of my brother, who insisted we take all the

martial arts classes my mom could afford."

Lily stared at him a moment, before glancing out the window at the desolate road. "Where are we headed?"

"They'll be looking for this vehicle, but I want to get closer to the power plant."

"What?" Nobody in their right minds would head towards the radiation source. That's why the roads were clear. "Patrick you can't go anywhere near there!"

"It's the only way to keep them from following us." He'd screwed up once already, staying at the cabin too long, but now he had a plan. He looked up at a helicopter flying low above them. "They won't fly into the blast zone. They won't risk the radiation."

"It's suicide for you. You'll be sick in no time!" Lily gazed at the gray cloud on the horizon, knowing it wasn't a thunder cloud. "I don't know if I can heal that kind of damage. I don't even know if my own body can handle it."

Patrick swerved as a black military Humvee sped alongside them. He yelled at Lily to put her head down when the passenger aimed his gun, firing a few shots. They were being chased by one vehicle and a helicopter. Patrick swerved again, trying to prevent the Humvee from knocking them off the road. Lily's seatbelt tightened across her chest.

The light was changing, as if dark rainclouds suddenly swallowed the sun.

"I just have to get closer." Patrick glanced over his shoulder before slamming his foot on the gas again. "Just keep your head down!" More bullets splayed the side of his car.

"Watch out!" Lily screamed as a deer leaped across the road twenty feet in front of them. Patrick veered again, hitting the side of the Humvee as he slammed on the brakes to avoid hitting the deer.

Patrick smiled at the near miss, but looked up hearing the sound of metal scraping metal. Checking the side mirror, he saw the helicopter closing in again. "Don't worry. I've got this under control."

She closed her eyes, praying his confidence was enough to save them. Bracing her hands against the dash, Patrick continued to swerve away from both the chopper and the vehicle following closely on their tail.

"Finally." Patrick stared at the review mirror.

Lily turned back to see the helicopter circling away, and the Humvee turning around. "I guess the government doesn't pay enough for those men to risk high levels of radiation." She looked at Patrick, picturing him sick. He seemed so unstoppable, it was hard to imagine. "How close are we to the plant?"

"Too close." Patrick was disappointed the men didn't turn back sooner. He pulled off the side of the road, watching Lily as she laid her head back against the seat.

"Now what?" She wondered where her brother was. She'd love to tell him she was okay, but doubted there'd be a signal on her cell. The thought of her brother breathing radioactive air made her stomach turn. The silence and the gray ominous light increased her eerie feeling. "Maybe we should turn the radio on, listen to what's happening at the plant." She reached her hand out, but Patrick took hold of it.

"It doesn't matter." He knew the plant had exploded and radiation was filling the air. He didn't need to listen to the news to know how grave the situation was. Television constantly ran clips of the bombings. This was just a repeat of what took place over a year ago, another exploding power plant releasing deadly radiation, and one more section of the United States that would be uninhabitable for years to come.

Forest lined both sides of the road, and the world seemed empty. Lily thought about the family who owned the motel. Were they far enough away to be safe? Did they have a bomb shelter? Would they have enough food and water, and be able to survive if their motel was completely vacant? She imagined few tourists would travel this way anytime soon. It was heartbreaking to think of all

46

the people who loved to backpack through the Appalachians. The mountains offered beauty and recreation for so many people. Would it ever be the same again?

Patrick rested his hand on Lily's, wondering what thoughts were going through her mind. She looked so unhappy. "Hey, don't worry. None of Jeffrey's men will come this far, and I've got a plan to get us out of here." He offered her a reassuring smile, and took the keys from the ignition. "Come on."

Chapter 7

The Virginia power plant was built in a low valley surrounded by mountains. It supplied electricity to half the state. Even though it was built with state of the art technology, nothing could have prepared it for a terrorist attack. Safety measures were implemented to prevent radiation from escaping, should the plant explode. Lily hoped that meant most of the radiation was still being contained. As they made their way through thick, unyielding forest, Lily kept a close eye on Patrick. He didn't appear to be slowing down and he said he felt fine. She noticed how he tried to keep branches from hitting her in the face.

"There should be a trail up ahead. It will be easier in a minute." True to his word, the forest opened to a clearing and a smoother, more obvious dirt trail. "Are you thirsty?" He stopped to unzip the side pouch of his backpack.

"Yes." She watched him, finding herself staring at his broad shoulders and arm muscles. He appeared to be a man much at ease in any situation and very self-assured.

"Take a few small sips. It'll be awhile before we get clean water again."

She drank slowly and deeply before handing back the bottle. "I feel like we are all alone in the world. There isn't a soul for miles."

He tipped his head at her. "Is that good or bad? I'm thinking it's good, but you don't sound pleased."

"I just hope my brother is safe. He'll be worried about me."

"Call him." He handed her his phone.

She stared at it. "You knew there'd be no signal."

"No, I had hoped there would be." He wanted to see her smile. "I'm on your side now, Lily. I promise I'll do everything I can to take you to your brother."

"Why the sudden change of heart?" She didn't know if she should trust him, though it occurred to her that she already did. "Back at the cabin you were still trying to talk me into giving myself up."

"Look," he said as he swung the pack over his shoulder, "I say stupid stuff sometimes. I'm pig-headed and I don't like to be wrong." A wide smile stretched his face. "What can I say...? I'm a Prick."

She set her hand on his arm. The apology wasn't great, but it was good enough for her. "Hold still a minute." She reached her hand up, and gently laid her fingers over his swollen eye. "I'm tired of looking at this." His eye was swollen and red, and already a deep bruise was forming in the corner. She felt the energy building inside her. She could keep her eyes open and watch the raised, red skin slowly recede back to normal, but she was using extensive energy to heal the wound, so she focused with her eyes closed.

The pain dissipated as Patrick stared at Lily's face, watching the flush rise in her cheeks. Her eyes were closed, and he wondered what it felt like for her. In a few brief moments the pain in his eye was completely gone. He wouldn't need to touch it to know that the swelling and cut were also gone. Even his throbbing jaw was now no longer sore.

She opened her eyes, and for a moment they just stared at each other. She cleared her throat and glanced at his lips as the cut closed and the swelling disappeared. He was quite handsome when he wasn't all banged up. "Does it still hurt?"

"No." He was mesmerized by her. It was almost surreal to comprehend that she truly had the ability to touch someone and heal them. It appeared supernatural, and yet she was so simply human, petite and fragile. He felt some slight tingling in his face. He hadn't thought about the fact she could heal more than cancer. With the country's destruction from radiation, and millions of sick people, the focus was always her ability to heal cancer. But being able to heal wounds, close cuts, and God knows how much more, her worth easily exceeded the value of anything remaining in the world.

Her hand was soft and warm. He'd taken in her flawless features, first noticing her smooth skin. There wasn't a single blemish. He hadn't noticed how long and dark her eyelashes were. Probably because what he did notice were her full lips, and her unusual eye color. He recalled what Fred Brown said. Lily was truly beautiful, with the look of an angel, and she just completely healed his wounds.

"Thank you." He took hold of her arm to steady her, noting she was weak again.

"You're welcome." She took a deep breath and tried to steady herself. "What exactly is your plan, Patrick?"

He guided her to a fallen tree lying horizontal with the path. "Sit for a minute." He eased her down on the large round trunk.

She was relieved to sit. "I'll be fine."

"We're going to get a new vehicle and drive to a place where I think you'll be safe." His buddy lived in Kentucky on a ranch. A secured location, and no doubt his friend would welcome Lily with an ice cold beer. "Once we reach someplace that has a signal, you can call your brother to come meet up with us."

She glanced at her surroundings. "Okay," she said, feeling deflated. They were in the forest, but she didn't know which part of the National Park they were in. There wouldn't be a soul in sight for miles because no one would be anywhere near the nuclear plant and she doubted they'd just stumble upon a car. She wore comfortable hiking shoes, but didn't feel like hiking. She was tired and hungry.

Patrick hunched forward, looking contemplatively at her. He bent down to her level, reached in the side pouch of his backpack, and handed her a Cliff energy bar. "Maybe this will help. Are you starting to feel… normal again?" He wasn't sure what the healing did to her, but it was obvious it took something out of her.

He smiled when she gave him the 'are you serious?' look. It was the same look she'd given him when he cuffed her to himself. He was learning her facial expressions, and delighted in how transparent her thoughts were. "Listen," he said placing his hand on her knee, "you might be relieved to know that when I was watching you this week, I hid a car about…" He glanced down at his watch and pressed a button that displayed a GPS, "three miles from here. I knew you might try to run, and I like to be prepared having more than one exit." He shrugged his shoulders. "I figured if you got away from me on foot, another car in the mountains might not be a bad idea." Having it parked close to the plant meant no one would find it.

"I see." She took a bite of the Cliff bar. "You were watching me for a whole week?" How had she been so careless, and more importantly, how come he hadn't called in reinforcements the moment he'd found her?

"Why do you think my pack is fully stocked? I've already spent plenty of time in the woods."

"That explains why you stink," she said with a smirk, and watched as his smile widened, revealing his deep dimples. "Why didn't you turn me in the moment you found me? Why the long stakeout?"

Patrick's smile instantly vanished, and he stood straight. "Let's go," he told her abruptly.

At first she assumed Patrick was merely a nice guy, willing to hear her side of things. But perhaps she was missing something. She stood, crossing her arms over her chest. "I'm not going anywhere till you tell me what it is you're trying not to tell me. Answer the question, Patrick."

On a long sigh, he rubbed the back of his neck. He wanted her to trust him, so he figured he owed her the truth. "The government doesn't want just you. They want your brother too. They want everyone and anyone who's helping you. I was watching to see if Alex would show up. The plan was to catch you both."

51

For a moment Lily's heart sank. Just hearing those words made her sick. "They already killed my sister. Now they want my brother too?" She watched him carefully, wondering if she'd been foolish to trust him. "Alex and Kate don't have any abilities. They can't heal, and the government knows it. Why?" she asked him, feeling angry and hopeless. "Why do they want him?" She wondered how differently things may have gone if her brother had shown up to the cabin.

Patrick felt his gut turn at the despair on her face. "I honestly don't know, Lily." He was truly at a loss. He'd believed in his mission. "I thought the government had good reason to bring you both in, but I don't anymore. I didn't know what they did to you. I didn't question things enough to have more answers for you." He didn't want to think about what she'd told him they had done. He wanted to comfort her, but felt they'd already wasted too much time. If he was going to keep her safe, they needed to leave. "Are you able to walk?"

The remorse in his eyes was sincere. She believed him, and was relieved that at least now he was on her side. She took a step forward and felt lightheaded.

"You're still weak, Lily." He steadied her with both his hands on her arms.

She was as emotionally drained as she was physically. "I'm okay," she replied softly, as she stared up at his eyes. He showed real concern for her, and she noticed how his demeanor could quickly change from strong and self-assured to gentle and caring. "Let's get to the car. It's not safe here." The men chasing her turned back out of fear of radiation contamination. She didn't like that Patrick was being exposed.

"You just read my mind." He grabbed the backpacks and walked alongside her. "We shouldn't be too far from the car."

The only sound was the wind. No birds were chirping, no sirens were heard, and Lily found the quiet of the forest alarming. Occasionally there would be the slight noise of a small animal scurrying under the brush. Those poor animals didn't know their part of the world was now contaminated. They had their little holes in the earth and homes in the trees. How sad to think that science had created a form of energy that couldn't be stopped; a powerful force with the potential of destroying all life on the planet.

She hated that the world had chosen to go with nuclear energy. There was a time when nuclear plants were shut down because all the disasters from past accidents had finally opened people's eyes. Chernobyl and Fukushima made such an impact that other countries closed many of their plants, shutting down reactors. Then the earthquake in California caused a power plant built right on the fault line to leak radiation. That nuclear disaster had caused considerable damage before they could repair it. But even after all the disasters, it was somehow decided that more nuclear plants were needed. Countries began to replace the world's fossil fuel power plants with nuclear reactors as a way to solve the problem of a warming planet. Most people were convinced thermal power was the only real way to eliminate climate change. Lily never understood why people ignored the impacts nuclear waste and disasters had on the world, but people sure were paying attention now.

"How are you holding up?" Patrick asked, interrupting her thoughts. He liked that she kept a steady pace alongside him. Part of the trail they were on was rugged and she hadn't complained once.

"I'm fine. It's beautiful isn't it?"

He cocked his head, one eyebrow raised. "You really enjoy traipsing over fallen trees, roots and rocks, feeling this muggy heat, and swatting away bugs?"

She laughed. "Is that how you see it?"

He smiled, remembering those were the words his wife once said to him when they'd hiked together in northern Michigan. "Not at all, but it's how some women would," he told her. His wife had complained about everything, and he realized being outdoors wasn't enjoyable for her. She preferred cardio at a gym.

"I love the forest. I grew up hiking and camping, and there's

53

really no aspect of it I don't love." She laughed again "Except mosquitos, but who doesn't hate mosquitos?"

"My wife hated mosquitos, all bugs in general, and wasn't a fan of hiking."

His response took Lily by surprise. She'd almost forgotten he'd been married once. "How long ago did your wife die?"

He stopped to retie the shoelace on his hunting boot. "Three years ago."

"How long were you married?"

"Five years."

"It must be hard… missing her."

He adjusted the backpacks. The large one he carried with both straps over his shoulders and hers he slung over his shoulder with one strap. He wouldn't let her carry it. "Seems like another life." He wiped sweat from his brow, and picked up the pace. "Megan was a sweet woman. She was a school teacher, and loved kids. She had a great sense of humor." That was one of the things he'd loved most about her. "She was easy going." He glanced at Lily, and a small smile touched his lips. "You remind me of her in that way. You would have liked her. I think you guys would have gotten along well. Except you're enjoying this hike, and she'd be complaining."

"Glad I can remind you of your wife."

"You don't," Patrick said, with a tone that surprised him. Was he irritated? Lily was easy going and sweet at the same time, but Patrick didn't think of Megan at all when he looked at her. Lily seemed to have those qualities, but with so much more. "You're different."

She felt a strange twinge in her belly at his words, which sounded like perhaps he was insulted. Suddenly, her defenses were up. "Why… because I can heal people? Because maybe I'm alien offspring? Or is it because I'm not normal?" Her lip curled in disdain.

He'd seen that fire in her eyes once before, when they'd been talking about the government. "Hey, that's not what I meant. You're the one who keeps bringing up the alien thing, not me." He remembered reading an article about her and Kate. Apparently their mother was in a mental institution because she believed her own twin daughters weren't human. There was an incident where she'd tried to hurt them, and that's when the state put Alex in charge of the girls. He recalled what Jeffrey said. The government claimed to have proof she wasn't human. "I don't believe in extraterrestrials. I don't believe in conspiracy theories, and I don't find you different just because you can heal people." He ran a hand through his hair in frustration, as her eyes were throwing daggers at him. "Look... I think you're different in a good way. You're strong as hell, and emotionally you hold it together better than most people I know. A lot of women would have fallen apart by now. You didn't lose it when I killed those men, and you didn't freak out when the helicopter was practically on top of us. Our circumstances are less than ideal right now, and I haven't heard you complain once. You're probably braver than half the men I work with." He stepped toward her, realizing he'd struck a sore spot. "Lily, I admire you. More than I have any woman."

She regarded him a moment, before looking down at her hands. They were soft and delicate in spite of the tremendous power they held. "I guess I'm a little sensitive." She knew how special she was. "If my father was an alien, I don't want to be viewed as non-human. My mother is human, and Kate was human. I'm not a science project."

"I know." He stepped toward her, wanting to pull her close, but she continued to walk.

"My mother was never able to talk about the rape. She pretended it didn't happen. Alex told me the doctors said it was her mind's way of protecting herself from the pain. She made herself forget, and she was able to create a fantasy world in which my father was a Marine who died in battle. She could describe him in detail." A sad smile formed on her lips, as she pictured her mom. "She'd sing a lot, and dance around the house. Kate and I thought she was wonderful." She could understand why doctors felt her behavior wasn't a danger to her children. Nobody believed she'd one day snap. "I remember her giving us baths, and making us laugh." Lily pictured the mother she loved and adored. "There'd be times her eyes would drift off, and she'd stare into space. I wondered what went through her mind in those moments, but then she'd suddenly smile and act like everything was fine."

Patrick encouraged her to continue. "What happened?"

"One night she just snapped. She must have remembered, and it resulted in a total psychotic break. She…"

Patrick stopped when she did, and seeing the emotion on her face, he said, "It's okay. You don't have to talk about it."

"I've never told anyone. Alex made Kate and me promise to never tell."

Now his curiosity was peaked. "She hurt you."

"Yes." For some reason, she wanted to share it with Patrick. Maybe because he apparently believed she was human, and he'd said he admired her. She wondered what he'd think. Would anything she said change that? She went ahead and told him the story about the fire.

She gave every detail, right down to the fact she'd healed herself and Kate before the ambulance arrived. No one, including her, had known about her ability to heal until that night. Alex amazed her with how quickly he'd accepted her extraordinary ability. He'd known right away it needed to be kept secret.

As they walked, she continued telling him how Alex petitioned the courts for guardianship, and he'd taken them to visit their mother in the hospital. He'd filled the role of both mother and father, and she and Kate were grateful for him.

"He sounds like a hell of a guy."

"He's the best. He's everything to me. Kate was too." The pain of losing Kate almost killed her.

A squirrel jumped down from a tree, startling them both. "We should be coming to the car soon," Patrick replied, glancing at his watch.

Lily wondered what he was thinking. He was a good listener and it felt good to talk about her past with him. If he was shocked or appalled, he didn't show it. He hadn't asked any questions either. Maybe she'd given too much detail. She'd even explained how hers and Kate's nightgowns burnt off their bodies, and how Alex put them in clean clothes. He'd told the paramedics that their mother attempted to light them on fire, but he'd gotten there in time. Only the bed sheets burnt.

"Do you have any siblings you're close with?" She asked Patrick.

"I do. My brother and I have had a good relationship. We don't see each other much, because I work all the time. He lives in my house with my parents. He lost his job when the nuclear plant in Indiana was blown, and he had to leave his home." Almost all of Indiana had been evacuated. It was now a radioactive wasteland.

"Your home is safe?"

"Yeah, I guess so. It's in northern Michigan, far enough away…I hope."

He checked the GPS on his watch again and realized there was a chance his location could be found through his watch. They were close to where the car should be, and he was feeling antsy to reach it.

"Look," she pointed to a tunnel of aspen trees. "It's so beautiful."

Just as Patrick was about to respond, they both looked up at the sound of the helicopter. "Damn it." He quickly took her hand to hurry her through the woods. "Where the hell is the car?" he vented, glancing over his shoulder at the sound of dogs barking. He should have known Jeffrey wouldn't have given up that easily. While fear of nuclear radiation made them turn back temporarily, he knew they'd return ten times more prepared. He was again angry at himself.

The helicopter spotted them, and was now circling low to the trees. Lily looked up to see some men in white hazmat suits slide down cables dropped from the chopper. "They're so close!" Her heart pounded as Patrick gripped her hand.

"There it is!" Patrick yelled, relief evident in his voice. The car was just up ahead. But he turned as Lily's hand slipped from his as she was falling down.   "No!" Panic gripped his chest.   They'd shot her with a dart.

Lily felt the pain in her shoulder, and her vision blurred as her knees hit the dirt.   She reached out for Patrick while he tried to help her up.

"I'm sorry, Lily," he said, catching her around the waist.   His vision blurred as another dart entered his chest.   He'd failed to protect her.   They'd been so close to the car when the darts struck them both.   He held her head in his lap.   "I'll find you, Lily."   His body went limp next to hers.

Chapter 8

Dr. Nathan Palmer stared at his reflection in the glass as he adjusted his tie. He allowed a woman to dab powder over his face before he brushed her hand away. "Is this stupid thing working?" He glanced down at the microphone attached to the lapel of his fancy suit. As the administrator of the facility, it was his job to speak publicly, so he wanted to make sure everything was perfect.

"It's working, sir," a woman replied. She had white hair with streaks of black in it. "Are you ready?"

The doctor walked past the shiny glass wall and opened the front door of the Hope Medical Facility. He instantly shaded his eyes from the sun as someone handed him a pair of black sunglasses. "Good afternoon," Nathan said.

A crowd numbering in the hundreds immediately quieted down. "As I'm sure you're all aware, Lily McCallister arrived at our facility yesterday. I am pleased to report she is safe and in good health." Nathan waited while the applause and shouts from the assembly of people died down again. "I'm also happy to report that Ms. McCallister has agreed to help us with the healing of those on the REL." Once again the crowd went wild with applause as Palmer smiled and held up his hand. When everyone quieted down he continued in a smooth voice. "Because of the hard work of some extremely dedicated doctors, we are now very close to replicating the magnetic molecular wave force that we believe Ms. McCallister's body produces. It's because of this extraordinary woman that we expect to have a fast and easy cure for both radiation poisoning and cancer."

A loud voice from the crowd yelled out, "Lies! It's all lies he's telling us!" The man was booed, while the crowd grew restless and agitated.

"We have proof!" Palmer held his microphone closer to his mouth to sound louder. It barely penetrated the noise from the crowd, but suddenly people turned their focus back to him. "It's my intention to allow Ms. McCallister to begin curing people on the Radiation Exposed List. The REL has already been made and will be posted soon. We have nothing but her best interest at heart. We assure you, she has given us her complete and full cooperation."

"Is she an alien? Where is the rest of her kind?" another man yelled out.

Palmer raised his hand again to silence the crowd. "I know you all have questions, but all I can tell you at this moment is that there is real hope for a cure. And in the meantime, lives will be saved." He flashed a wide smile at the people.

The crowd became more stable as people glanced around at each other. Heads were nodding in approval. Some people were crying while others were clapping. "We want to see her!" a man shouted from somewhere in the middle of the crowd.

"You will," Nathan replied in a reassuring tone. "I must ask you all to return to your homes. Turn your screens on and you will see Lily being filmed live. Those of you on the list will be called at home to notify you of your appointment time. All information on where to go and how the healing will take place will be listed on the social media sites." Nathan watched as people immediately began to disperse. Police officers were there to guide people safely to their vehicles and direct traffic. Only a few reporters remained standing to ask questions.

"Did she turn herself in? Are you forcing her to do this? Is she human? What other powers does she have?" came a few shouts.

Nathan smiled at the men and women. "Ms. McCallister is being treated with the utmost respect. The President himself is on his way here now to meet with her. If you return to your homes there will be a Presidential address in a few hours. Your questions will be answered at that time."

Amy was the head nurse at the Hope facility. She was a middle-aged woman who had decided years ago to avoid any and all chemicals in the hope of staying healthy. Her hair was streaked gray and she wore not a stitch of the makeup which would have obscured the dark circles under her eyes. She walked beside Dr. Palmer as he headed back inside the facility. "That went surprisingly well," she told him.

"They are all so eager for good news," Palmer mumbled under his breath as he walked briskly down the hall. "I want more officers patrolling the grounds, and get me the head of security. I don't trust that this building is secure enough." He dismissed her with a wave of his hand.

"Yes, sir." Amy walked away just as the doctor tipped his head to an officer. The officer stepped aside as Palmer opened the heavy steel door and walked into the room with a smile.

Lily was sitting on the bed watching a flat screen TV embedded in the wall. She didn't look at Dr. Nathan Palmer because his presence always made her sick.

"Did you enjoy the show, Lily?"

The walls of the ten by ten room were solid stone, painted a light beige. Only a twin bed and bedpan were in the steel-doored room. Not only was the room depressing, it was very familiar to Lily. "It will never work," she replied, scooting her back against the wall.

Nathan chuckled softly. "Sure it will. We have your brother, Lily."

Lily felt the blood drain from her body as she tried to keep calm outwardly. "So what," she shrugged her shoulders.

"Come now, Lily. I know you much better than that." He sat on the bed beside her. "Your father was alien, how do you feel about that?"

"You don't know that."

"Ahh... but we do," Nathan smiled. "All those tests we did. They weren't so we could learn how your ability to cure works. They were to test your DNA and you're definitely not human, Lily."

The room seemed to blur as Lily turned to set her eyes on him. All those horrible things they did to her and it wasn't even for the good of mankind? "So you're not close to finding a cure for radiation sickness and cancer?" She'd hoped that at least that part of his speech was genuine.

"We don't want to cure the world of cancer." As a major stockholder in the lucrative pharmaceutical industry, he was making enormous money off the sick, which probably accounted for the present condescending smile on his face. "Everyone knows there aren't enough food and natural resources left to sustain the amount of people now on this planet. Population reduction is imperative. When people are dying it instills fear... and fear makes people look for a savior. The government will be that savior, with your help of course."

"You're the one who isn't human! Where is your compassion?" It made Lily sick to hear him speak as if he didn't have a care in the world. He could have been discussing the weather with how careless and casual his tone was.

"Oh, I have plenty of compassion. That's why the focus will be on your healing power and the hope that gives people instead of on what you are and where you came from."

Lily felt bile trying to shoot up from her stomach, but she swallowed hard. She could barely speak, she felt so repulsed. "What did you do with Patrick?"

"Do you like him?" Nathan brushed a piece of lint from his suit. "Because when we have your cooperation... and Lily, we will have it... then maybe you can see him again."

"I don't care to see him, and I don't care anything about him. He was going to bring me here." She kept her eyes level with his. "I'm only curious if you kept him alive."

Palmer let out a small huff. "You're a very good liar." He

stood up. "The people you care about will be unharmed as long as you do as you're told. If not, well… your brother wanted me to tell you that Danny is dead."

Lily couldn't wait for him to leave. It was hard trying to maintain a poker face. "I don't believe you." He was a liar. Please be lying, please be lying.

"We found his base of operation. He wasn't supposed to be killed, but sometimes accidents happen." He opened the door, and glanced from the guard back to Lily. "You will be given your orders tomorrow."

Once the door was shut, Lily lay down on the bed and continued to keep her face from showing the pain and turmoil she was feeling. She knew that the TV in the wall was also a video camera, and they'd be watching her.

Chapter 9

The President of the United States, Clive Beckman, shared a few pleasantries with Dr. Nathan Palmer before getting down to business. His time was extremely valuable, and he wasn't comfortable being in the state of Michigan. He was a handsome man, with a tall, lean body. His good looks had undoubtedly helped him win the office, because apparently Americans had valued someone who looked presidential above all else. He was tall, strong in stature, with a distinguished businessman appeal.

While Michigan had been far enough north to have escaped the brunt of the radiation, the president still preferred the safety of his elaborate bunker in the mountains of Wyoming. Hope Medical Facility was built in the Upper Peninsula, a mostly rural area that also happened to hold the world's most notorious alien.

"I'm ready to meet her, Nathan," the President said, handing a folder to one of his agents. He'd just finished reading a brief description of the capture.

"Yes sir." Dr. Palmer led the President down the empty hall.

"How are you treating her?"

"You can see for yourself, sir." Palmer opened the door and dropped his smile.

Lily was strapped to the bed, her wrists and ankles tightly secured to a bed railing. Her thin blue gown was pulled up to her thigh, showing her thin muscular legs.

"Damn," he muttered. Lily wasn't supposed to look like that. He hadn't ordered restraints, and she was supposed to have makeup on to hide the shadows under her eyes.

The President turned an angry glare toward Nathan. "What's wrong with her?"

"I can see you're upset, sir, but this is not how she normally is." Palmer was already on his cell phone giving orders to nurse, Amy. "They tell me she was very uncooperative today." He knew that any explanation he could make up would offer little help.

He stared at her still eyes, and smiled. Lily was quite a clever creature. He knew she had purposely made herself appear this way.

"Can she speak?" The President pulled her gown down, and tapped her on the shoulder. "Lily McCallister, can you hear me?" Lily's eyes remained fixed to the same spot on the wall. "I'm very unhappy, doctor. This is completely unacceptable." He moved his hand over her arm. "You obviously have her on heavy medication. I need her alert and functional." The President crossed his arms and glared at Palmer. "This alien being is the hope for our nation. If we can't use her, then we'll have to use the twin sister."

Nathan kept a close eye on Lily. "Kate is even more uncooperative. She can't be controlled."

"I want to see her. Does she look like this one?" The President swept his hand over Lily. "She better not. I'm not impressed with what I'm seeing here. You're in charge of this place, and I hold you personally accountable for what goes on."

The doctor felt a twinge of panic. "I understand, sir. Kate is alive and well, and right down the hall. I'll take you there immediately."

The President walked to the door where an armed officer immediately opened it for him. He glanced back at Nathan Palmer. "Get this one fixed up, Doctor. If she remains this way, you and your staff will be lucky if I don't replace you all. I want her not only alive, but alert and well to cure the people who need curing." The rest of the world could die, however certain high profile people would need to be kept alive. "I'm also going to insist she cure me, just in case I have anything." He didn't think he had cancer, but he'd use Lily to make sure.

"Yes, sir, she will be good as new next time you see her." Palmer waited for the president to walk out of the room before he turned to Lily. "Nice little performance, Lily. You're going to pay for this," he whispered. Then he placed a kiss on her forehead and left.

Lily let out a deep breath, and then slid her hands through the straps. She'd strapped her own feet and hands to the bed, so she quickly untied the foot restraints. Every nerve and muscle in her body was alerted to the news that Kate was still alive. Part of her wanted to cry, while the other part wanted to scream.

Her plan to make the President angry with Hope Medical Clinic had worked. She'd fooled him into believing she was catatonic. She knew Palmer hadn't fallen for the ruse, but at least he hadn't tried to convince the president that her behavior was an act. He was up to something, and there was no doubt she'd pissed him off. Her stomach churned with the knowledge they had her sister. Could it be true? Could they have faked her death, and kept her alive for a year? Lily couldn't bear to think that poor Kate had been held captive in such a horrible place for so long. Yet, the hope and joy of believing her sister was still alive was overwhelming.

The tile floor felt cold on her bare feet as she stood up. She didn't care that she felt cold, or hungry, or weak. All that mattered was that Kate was alive! She felt certain they didn't have her brother, because she'd refused to cooperate until she saw him. It was becoming obvious to her that if they really had Alex, they would have already shown him. It was after all the most important leverage they had.

Lily stared at the bed sheet she'd managed to tuck into the cracks around the television. She knew no one was watching her now, and no one would see her fall to her knees and clasp her hands together in prayer.

She hadn't been raised religious, but she believed in God, and right now she felt a powerful need to close her eyes and pray. "Please, God, let Kate be alive. Let us both get out of here. And please let Danny and Patrick be alive too" she begged.

Chapter 10

Time never moved as slowly as it did during her time in solitary confinement. Lily had lost track of how many weeks it had been since they moved her. She'd been taken to a smaller room with baby blue cement walls, no TV, a mattress on the floor and an old toilet. Lily wondered if she wasn't being kept in an old prison that had perhaps been turned into a clinic.

She felt like a prisoner, although she'd have preferred the room to have bars rather than the blue steel door. If the room was meant to punish her, it was working. Day after day of staring at the same blue walls and blue door was torture. She would welcome a needle in the arm over the solitude of confinement. She was no longer finding it easy to sleep. They weren't feeding her much, and it was hard to sleep on an empty stomach. Lily stared at the slit in the door where her food tray was delivered. She laughed when someone tried to push a roll of toilet paper through, because it did not fit. Someone then told her to stand against the wall, while the person in a white lab coat quickly opened the door, tossed the roll of toilet paper at her, and then closed the door.

"Whoever you are, you know it's wrong to do this to me!" she had yelled. There had to be people working in the hospital who knew she was there. Someone had to feel some sort of sympathy for her. They wouldn't all just lock her up and never look back, would they?

Headaches and stomach pains were becoming more frequent as she continued in worsening malnourishment. She carefully tried to stand up, and felt the room spin. She'd been tearing off tiny pieces of toilet paper to mark the days, but without sunlight, she had to base the days on the trays of food she'd been given. However, yesterday she was only given one tray, which she assumed was given in the morning. Later she was simply given water.

The tiny pieces of toilet paper in the corner of the room were lined up in rows. Dropping down in front of them, she began to count the twenty-one small pieces that moved as she let out a long sigh. For three weeks she'd been confined to the same four walls, only getting out one time when she was allowed to shower. A man dressed in military clothing had escorted her to the shower stall and had stood outside the curtain while she was given five minutes to wash her body. He hadn't spoken a word to her, and at least he hadn't tried to hurt her.

A person could go crazy being kept in the conditions she was being kept in. Was that their goal? Dr. Palmer had visited her once to inform her that she wasn't really needed anymore. What game were they playing?

When Lily closed her eyes, she imagined Patrick. She'd often think about his face and the conversations they had during the one day she had known him. Was he still alive? Where was he?

There were voices outside her room, so she quickly crawled on her hands and knees to the slit in the door. "I know you can hear me! Please! Please let me out!" She was surprised when tears clouded her vision and the sound of her voice was weak. "I'll help you! I'll do whatever you need, just please don't leave me in here!" The hall fell silent, and all she could hear was the sound of her own sobbing. It was too much. She couldn't take being alone with only her thoughts. She desperately needed to see sunlight, and she needed to see anything but that damn baby blue steel door!

She began hiccupping as her breathing slowed. Nothing wrong with a good cry, she told herself. Her body could still produce tears, so at least she wasn't completely dehydrated. Starving maybe, but she'd been replacing meals with more water. The light faded from the crack in the door. Had they just turned off the lights, and gone home for the night? She stared at the door, until her vision blurred. She imagined the door turned into a blue pond, and then suddenly she was barefoot, wearing shorts and a t-shirt, getting ready to jump in. With her eyes closed, she could see Patrick standing on the other side of the pond, his reflection mirrored in the water as the sun shone down, warming her skin. Patrick really was a handsome man, and he was looking at her in a way of intense study. She always wondered what he was thinking. He was smiling at her, and in that moment she wanted to jump in and swim over to him.

Lily opened her eyes and stared at the blue door. I am going crazy. Is this what happened to my mother? She couldn't take the pain anymore, so she imagined a better world for herself? "I won't stay in La La Land," she spoke out loud and stood up. She raised her hands above her head, and used what little energy she had to do a brief stretch. Then she began to pace around the room, reaching for toilet paper to blow her nose. "I'll be okay," she whispered. Maybe they were going to keep her locked up, but she had faith that eventually someone would come for her. Someone would need to be healed and they would require her again.

She was a healer. There was a reason she had this amazing ability and that she was a strong person. She remembered times when she felt her gift was really a curse. How very different her life might have been. But deep down, she was fulfilled healing people and was thankful she had possessed the power to cure the burns that would have killed her and Kate.

Pacing the floor helped to warm up her body. She began to do jumping jacks, but it made her head ache, so she stopped and went back to pacing the room, counting the number of times she slapped the wall with her hands.

After a brief attempt at sleep, Lily woke to the sound of laughter. She sat up on the mattress and listened. "Hello!" She hoped someone would hear her. "Please let me see Dr. Palmer. I need to talk to him," she tried to shout, but her voice cracked.

The voices stopped and her food tray was slid thought the door. This time, there was only a very small piece of bread and butter, barely three bites of ham, and two long carrots. She wanted to laugh. Yes, they were trying to starve her. She listened as the footsteps faded away while she tore another small piece of toilet paper off and added it to the row on the floor. She assumed this was her breakfast, her one meal for the day. Eyeing the pieces on the floor, she counted twenty-six days. If she allowed herself to think how short a time twenty-six days was compared to a year, she would cry. The twenty-six days had felt like eons, and yet it was nothing. She knew it would be a very long time since she'd get to eat again. Part of her wanted to consume the food fast. The ham looked fresh and delicious, but so very small. It was cruel of them to tempt with something tasty but in such a minuscule portion. It will be enough.

The hospital gown she was wearing was dirty. For a moment she wondered if she'd be given a new gown after a month. Would someone tell her to stand against the wall while they tossed her a new gown, the way they had the toilet paper? Perhaps she'd die in the gown. If she ever got out of there, what could she do with the gown? She could make curtains out of it. After all, it was a simple blue gown. Blue, blue, blue. Everything was blue. "This ought to be my favorite color. Why isn't the tray blue? That is just an ugly brown color," she laughed. "When I get out, I'll paint my toenails blue. Now I'm talking to myself again."

Lily stretched out on her mattress, grateful that at least it was soft. She set the little cup of water beside the bed after slowly washing away the salty taste of her ham. She closed her eyes, and for some strange reason images of Patrick popped into her mind again. She wondered why she thought about him as often as she did.

A blast sounded and something hit the top of her head. She was sleeping on her belly when the ceiling came down. Her ears rang, and she began coughing from smoke. She tried to move, but something heavy was on her legs. She touched the back of her head and felt wetness, but never opened her eyes.

A loud siren went off and she heard her name being shouted. Another explosion sounded, and for a moment she was convinced she was dreaming. She tried to roll over, but she couldn't move her legs. It was dark, and the smoke was stinging her eyes.

"Lily!"

She knew that voice. "I'm here," she said but her voice was just a whisper. "I'm here!" she called out again as her head throbbed and the smoke was choking her.

She coughed and turned her face into the mattress. Closing her eyes she thought this is just a dream.

Chapter 11

"How do you know she's okay?"

"Because I know."

"She could be hurt, damn it!"

"She was hurt, but her body has already healed itself. She's just unconscious from being hit in the head. She'll wake up in a minute. Quit leaning over her, you're getting your damn blood on her."

"I don't think she cares. She'll be happy we are all in one piece and there's nothing for her to glue back together."

"I hear that. You're lucky you didn't get her killed."

"I didn't see you coming up with a better plan, and if her body didn't heal itself our plan probably would have killed her."

Lily heard the voices and smelled that familiar scent, mixed with blood. She tried to open her eyes. "I guess you never got that shower," she whispered, and felt her lips curl up.

"Lil," Alex sighed heavily in relief, taking his sister's hand. "God, it's good to have you back."

Fighting the fatigue that was swamping her, she tried to speak louder. "They had Kate. Did you find Kate?" Lily waited for her eyes to adjust to the light.

"What?" Patrick asked in surprise.

Alex felt his heart sink, knowing his poor sister was confused. "Lil, Kate is gone," he said gently. "You're safe now."

Lily shook her head at her brother. "No. I found out she's still alive. They lied to us. They lied to everyone. Kate was there." Her voice sounded faint and hoarse. "I need water."

Patrick held a glass out to her. The top of his hand was covered in bloody scratches. He had a cut at his left temple and blood was dripping down the side of his face. Alex didn't look much better with blood splattered across his gray shirt.

"Are you sure, sis?" Alex helped her to sit up. "We didn't see anyone else inside. We checked all the rooms while we were looking for you."

"The place is blown to bits," Patrick added.

Alex threw him a dirty look, "Way to go, Prick."

Lily wanted to smile at the way her brother used Patrick's nickname, but fear for her sister had her stomach in too tight a knot to smile. What if Kate had been killed during their rescue attempt? "They said she was alive and down the hall from me."

"She wasn't," Alex said. "She was nowhere on the floor you were on. If they had her in the basement, she could still be alive. We destroyed the facility to get you out."

"Maybe they moved her," Lily hoped.

"I'm so sorry it took us so long to get you out. It took us awhile to get the supplies we needed." Alex knew it had been worth the wait, when the first bomb went off, taking out the side wall of the building. They'd never have been able to get her out without the strategically placed detonators. Alex and Patrick had over thirty men flood the building, targeting the military personnel protecting the facility. Their goal had been to kill as few people as possible, by using hunting guns with sleep darts instead of bullets. Ever since guns had been banned, dart guns had become a popular and readily available commodity. The men and women helping Alex weren't soldiers. They were just people who believed in protecting the hope for the future. Lily was that hope.

"We have to find her!" Lily didn't have proof her sister was alive, but she believed.

"We will," Alex assured her, setting his hand on her cheek for comfort.

She set her hand over his. "I'm so glad to see you." She kissed

73

the side of his cheek as he hugged her.

"Don't." Alex took his sister's hand and placed it on the mattress. "I know you want to heal my wounds, but you can't. You're too weak right now." He smiled, and pushed a strand of hair behind her ear. "We look worse than we are."

"Do I get a hug?" Patrick was eager to switch spots with Alex.

"Does he deserve a hug?" Lily asked her brother. This time she did smile.

"He's the reason you're here, so yeah, I'd say he deserves a hug. But that's *all* he'll be getting from you."

Lily sucked in a deep breath. Her relief in seeing both Alex and Patrick alive was overwhelming. She knew she was safe, and the joy of no longer being in that prison of a room made her eyes water. She was in a house, in a child's bedroom. There were football stickers on the baby blue wall. She was lying on a twin size bed with a navy blue bedspread, and there were a white dresser and night stand under the window. Baby blue curtains the same color as her gown hung from the window. She wanted to laugh at the irony. She'd never look at the color blue the same way. "Thank you, Patrick." Her throat was tight with emotion.

"Hey," Patrick sat beside her on the bed and pulled her into his arms. He hugged her a little tighter and closer than her brother had, and his hand stroked her back. "I'm glad we found you."

She liked how easily she fit into his embrace, the way her head rested on his shoulder. "What happened? How did you get away?"

"It's a long story, sweetheart. I'll tell you all about it, later."

Lily looked at her brother. "They told me they killed Danny." She held her breath in the hope her brother would tell her differently. Instead he nodded.

"We don't know for sure, but it looks like it. His base was destroyed," Alex explained gently. "I'm sorry, Lil."

She felt her stomach tighten, and she knew she would mourn Dan almost as much as she had mourned Kate.

"We need to get cleaned up," Alex said, running a hand

through his hair and feeling pieces of drywall stuck to the short brown strands. "Let's let her eat and get her strength back." He set his hand on Patrick's shoulder.

Patrick cupped Lily's face, then gently rubbed his thumb under her eyes, noticing the dark shadows. "Did they hurt you?" He knew they'd obviously starved her, and he'd been out of his mind with worry that they'd been torturing her.

"No."

The knot in his stomach eased.

"Of course they hurt her!" Alex said angrily. "They didn't even feed her." He'd been shocked at her weight loss, her sunken cheeks, and the lackluster of her hair.

"It could have been worse," Lily said, shrugging her shoulders. But there had been times when the hunger pangs made her think nothing was worse than starvation.

"I'm sorry," Patrick told her.

"She wouldn't tell us if they had hurt her. That's why I didn't ask," Alex told Patrick in a cool voice. He remembered the first time he had rescued his sister from the hospital where they had been conducting tests on her. He knew she had endured horrific procedures, but she would never talk about it. She always tried to make it seem less terrible than it was in an attempt to shield him from knowing that horror for the rest of his life. His eyes turned gentle as he set them on his sister. "You're always about protecting... saving."

The pain in her brother's eyes and the look of remorse on Patrick's face was too much for her wearied emotions. "I'm truly fine," she told them. "I'll be even better when we find Kate."

"You'll be better when we fatten you up. We're going to get you fixed up first." Alex knew she'd ignore her own needs and wants while focusing all her energy on Kate. But this time she was in need of a lot of care.

A woman with short curly brown hair and bright red lipstick entered the room. She had some clothes draped over her arm and was holding a bowl. "You boys leave us women alone now." Lily

75

watched as the woman set the clothes on the bed. Then she turned to Lily and in a bubbly voice said, "I'm—"

"Connie," Lily interrupted. "I remember you." She was one of the many people she had healed. "How are you feeling?"

"I'm alive," Connie laughed. "It's just like you to ask how I'm doing."

"I told you she'd remember her name," Alex said happily, glancing at Patrick as if he'd just won a bet. "My sister asks the name of every person she has ever healed, and she remembers."

Patrick nodded.

"It appears you've not eaten much, so I made chicken soup. It should be gentle on your stomach." Connie waited for Patrick to stand up, and then she took his spot beside Lily on the bed. "You boys both need showers. Towels are already laid out and there is a first aid kit in the sink." She waved them away.

Lily watched Patrick follow her brother out of the room. Patrick was a good foot taller than her brother. He had brown eyes, while her brother had green. Why was she comparing the two? They were very different in every way, and yet…there was something about Patrick that reminded her of her brother. Perhaps the mannerisms were similar. They both carried themselves with an air of confidence. They were both strong and commanding, yet easy going at the same time.

"Will you help me with this?" Connie asked.

Startled from her thoughts, Lily glanced down. She hadn't even noticed that Connie had spread a paper napkin over her lap and was handing her the bowl of soup.

"Thank you," Lily whispered, taking the bowl.

"We'll start slow. Small gentle meals throughout the day, so you can gradually build your appetite back up. You will have meat on your bones before you know it."

"I must look awful." Lily knew her hair was a disaster. She too was in need of a shower, and since she hadn't looked in a mirror in weeks, she could only imagine how bad her face looked.

"You know something," Connie tipped her head, glancing up and down at Lily. "You're probably the only woman on earth who could go through a tornado, and still look drop dead gorgeous. I'm not sure how you do it. You're skinny as a carrot, and you've been through hell, but you're still pretty as an angel." She patted Lily on the shoulder. "Trust me… you've got nothing to worry about."

"Thank you, Connie," Lily blushed. She hadn't been fishing for a compliment, but she had to admit that Connie's sincere praise made her feel better.

Connie stood up, and cleared her throat. "They say you're an alien. They say on the news that your DNA is not human, but I don't care what you are," she put her hands on her hips. "You're kind, you save lives, and you're for sure human enough. You have a lot of people who want to help you."

"That means a lot to me."

"Humanity is in trouble. I'm sure the good Lord made you, because he knew we were in need of help. He probably knew we were going to blow ourselves up, since we seem to be so good at destroying things."

Lily smiled. She remembered the first time she had met Connie, all the spunk the woman had. She had stage four cancer, and had appeared frightfully thin and frail, but still she'd managed to speak her mind.

"Why would he stop at creating humans?" Connie continued. "If you're an alien, he made you too."

"Yes he did," Lily agreed. She was no longer sure of what she was, but she still appreciated Connie's attempt to make her feel better. Lily glanced out the window as the first pelts of rain hit the glass. The gray light that filtered through the window gave her a gloomy feeling. She took a sip of the soup and tried not to think of her sister. She pushed away thoughts of what might have happened, and what could still happen.

Chapter 12

Connie left the room while Lily continued to sip slowly. She was anxious to get her strength back, to ask questions, and to form a plan. The soup was delicious. She chewed the big chunks of chicken, savoring each bite, knowing she'd never take food for granted again. She had sipped the last of the broth when a knock sounded on the door, and Alex stuck his head in.

"Can you get dressed, Lil, and come watch the TV?" he asked. Lily knew from his voice, and the void expression on his face, that what was on the television was not good. She rose from the bed, and quickly tossed the hospital gown to the floor. Then she slipped on the black yoga pants that fit like a glove, and the pink tank top that had a glitter heart in the middle. The clothes obviously belonged to Connie's teenage daughter. Pink was Lily's least favorite color to wear, as she felt it clashed with her deep auburn hair, but Kate had always insisted pink looked good on her.

Lily stepped into the living room of the house, and just as she pushed thoughts of Kate from her mind, she felt the blood drain from her body when she glanced at the TV.

"Turn the volume up," Connie told her daughter, Anna.

Luckily Alex guided Lily to a chair before her knees gave out on her. "I can't believe this." There was no way to push back her tears or ignore the images on the television.

"We will get her back," Alex said in a tone of steel determination. He squeezed Lily's hand. "Right now I'm just so damn happy she's alive."

Kate was on the TV, sitting in a large plush leather chair, and holding a man's hand. Her hair was long like Lily's, instead of the short, cute, sassy style she normally had. She wore khaki pants, and a green striped shirt. It was the very outfit Lily had worn the day she tried to escape from Patrick.

"They've made her look exactly like you," Connie said, turning to Lily. "Those must be hair extensions."

Kate did look like Lily, except there was something wrong with her eyes. "What have they done to her?" Lily asked, wiping the tears from her eyes. Kate was holding a man's hand, the way Lily did when she would heal a person. Except Kate's expression was flat, and her eyes appeared lifeless. It reminded Lily of her mother's face, when she'd last visited her at the institution. Drugs had been responsible for the empty shell her mother appeared to be.

"She's alive, and that's what counts." Connie rubbed her sleeping son's head. Little Eric had fallen asleep on the floor in front of the television with his hand curled around a tattered mint green blanket.

Alex glanced at his sister with sorrow in his eyes. "We've been mourning her for a year." He squeezed the bridge of his nose with a shaky hand. "When I think of the pain you've suffered, and all this time they've had her alive." He felt a deep rage of hatred toward Doctor Nathan Palmer. Palmer had been the one to look him in the eyes and tell him that Kate had died of an infection. He'd been the one to lie to the media and the world, successfully convincing everyone that Kate was gone.

"I'll help you get her back." Patrick knelt down beside Lily. He wanted to comfort her, to ease the pain he knew she felt. "Whatever it takes, we'll get her back."

"There were protests outside the clinic." Connie hit mute on the TV. She knew her friends had seen and heard enough of the lie. "People need to believe Lily is healing people." She set her hand on Lily's knee. "I'm so sorry. I know how hard this must be for you."

Lily shot to her feet. Kate was alive, and that was all that mattered. She might appear to be a brainwashed robot, but she was alive. "Where is this healing taking place?" The sooner they could get her free from the government, the sooner they could help her.

"In the Square." Patrick set his hand on Lily's shoulder. "This is a trap, sweetheart. They will try to get you back. Since we bombed Hope Clinic, they will be ready for us, and the security around Kate will be tight."

"We have more men," Alex stated angrily. "We will kill every one of those bastards. We *will* get her back."

"No." Lily moved to stand in front of the television, and kept her voice low so as not to wake Eric. She bent down and shut the TV off. She didn't need to see her sister pretending to heal people; she knew what needed to be done. "I don't want more people to die. Those men who work for the government are just like Patrick." She glanced at him, and felt his regard toward her. "They are just men with orders to follow. They have families, and I don't want them killed." She wondered how many people had died during her rescue from Hope. "The world has seen enough death and injury, but what they haven't seen is the truth." People believed the continuous lies from the media, and the media wanted the world to believe that the government was altruistic. People believed Lily was in cooperation, and was sitting in the Square healing one sick person after another. Except it wasn't Lily, it was Kate. It was all a lie.

Patrick nodded.

"It's time for the world to start hearing the truth," Lily continued, glancing from Patrick to her brother. "We need the media. I need to get on the news and let people see what's real."

Alex's face brightened. "I've always liked your thinking, sis." He was already opening his laptop. "I'll take care of this, Lil." Danny had a good friend who actually worked for a news station, and Alex knew he'd be able to help. "I want you to go back in the bedroom and lie down, maybe eat some more food."

Lily couldn't explain to everyone why she wouldn't and couldn't go back in the small baby blue room. She was too tired to explain her need for daylight and fresh air. "I'm going to sit outside for a few minutes," she told them all, and headed toward the front door.

She expected her brother to argue, but he was already typing away on his laptop.

"Don't wander," is all he told her.

The sun was just above the trees, on its slow descent down. The leaves were already turning color, and Lily admired the golden yellow and bright red that shimmered in the sun's rays. She felt the cool air, and smiled as the wind blew strands of hair in her face. After being locked up for weeks in a tiny blue cell, the fall weather was an enjoyment beyond words.

Patrick stepped up behind her, and draped a jacket over her shoulders.

She jumped, "Oh, I didn't hear you."

"Sorry, I didn't mean to scare you."

"Thanks." She slipped her arms through the sleeves of his jacket. She hadn't realized she was cold until she felt the warmth of his coat. "What is today's date?" It dawned on her that she didn't even know what day of the week it was. It was difficult to push away thoughts of her captivity, but she was determined to forget and move on.

"Tuesday, September 20th." Patrick stared into her gold eyes, and felt that familiar tug in his gut. He wished he could ask her what she'd been through, but part of him wasn't sure if he could handle hearing it. Alex had told him not to bother, because she wasn't ever going to confess the truth.

Lily ran a hand through her hair, and felt the tangles. She should be in the shower now, rather than looking so dreadful in front of Patrick. "I'm sure I look positively hideous right now."

Patrick shrugged his shoulders. "Well, I never thought you were all that pretty to begin with."

She laughed, knowing he was kidding. "I guess I shouldn't worry then." She liked when he offered his teasing smirk. She'd pictured that exact smile many times over the last few weeks. "When

81

I first saw you, I thought you were fat and out of shape." At least that's what she had hoped he was before she had gotten to know him.

"Remember, it was dark." He dropped his playful grin when she suddenly turned serious.

"I can't believe you found Alex, and helped him rescue me."

"I told you I'd find you. I'm just sorry it took us so long to get you out." He took her hand, and was relieved when she laced her fingers with his. "I haven't had much sleep, worrying about you." Worrying wasn't even the right word. He hadn't been able to get the images of her being tortured out of his mind. His stomach had been in a constant state of agony. She'd painted a clear picture in his mind when they'd been driving up the mountain together. And ever since that day, all he could see was her beautiful flesh being peeled from her body, and blue liquid being forced down her throat.

"You knew me only one day, and you seemed set on taking me in. I didn't think you cared." She really liked the way he looked with a five o'clock shadow, and his hair combed back from his recent shower. She would have liked to heal his cuts, but they weren't that bad after he'd cleaned them. His tight black jeans and clean white shirt gave indication that perhaps he'd lost a little weight, leaving only defined muscle.

He took a step closer to her. "I screwed up." How many times had he beaten himself up for how he'd misled her? The fear he must have caused her, in making her believe he was going to turn her in. "The truth is, you've grown on me." How pathetic he thought his words sounded, when he felt so much more.

Lily felt her stomach flip. He smelled clean for the first time since she'd known him, and the scent was so appealing, she stepped a little closer to him. His lips looked soft, and his eyes were suddenly searching hers. She was almost dizzy as he slowly lowered his head.

"Hey!" Alex shouted, and Lily learned back in surprise. "Lily, Connie has a bath ready for you, and Prick, I need to go over my plan with you." His eyes glared at Patrick.

82

"I was just…" She didn't know what to say. Her brother had made her feel like she'd done something wrong. Like a teenager caught messing around with a boy. "I don't—"

Alex set his hand on her back, and his voice sounded gentler when he said, "Please go in the house now, Lil. Connie is waiting for you."

Lily glanced at Patrick, and he nodded at her. "Okay," she whispered, and walked toward the house.

As soon as the front door shut, Alex turned to Prick. "I knew it," he said emphatically, and his nostril flared. "You're after her." He would control his temper, because he definitely owed Patrick. So it wouldn't be right to punch him, but on the same hand, he wouldn't ignore what he saw.

Patrick's first impulse was to deny his words, but he couldn't. There was something strong pulling him toward Lily, and it was making him feel mixed up and frustrated.

"You told me you were just feeling guilty, but I knew there was more to it." Alex kicked a stick that was by his foot. "Look, she's not like other women, Patrick, and I'm not talking about her ability to heal. She hasn't had any experience with men. She doesn't—"

"Spare me the big brother speech, Al," Patrick interrupted him, trying to control his own temper now. "I know all about your sister's innocence. I'm not planning to take advantage of her… in any way." He rubbed the back of his neck. What could he say, when he didn't even understand his own feelings? All he knew was that he'd not been able to stop thinking of her for more than a minute the entire time she was captured. He hadn't expected to have the reaction he'd had when he hugged her. "I can promise you this, Alex. On my life, I will never hurt her."

"Damn right you won't." Alex's steam wore off as he caught the sincerity in Patrick's face. "I don't want you complicating things for us. We just found out our sister is alive, and getting Kate back is the most important thing to us right now. I need help, but I don't need you throwing Lily's focus off. She needs to rest, and get her

83

strength back." He jammed his hands in his pockets. The problem was he genuinely liked Patrick. They'd spent three weeks together initiating their plan. Patrick had proved himself to be a smart, assertive, likable guy. He had qualities Alex respected. He figured if his sister felt the same way about Patrick, perhaps it wasn't such a bad thing, other than the fact that Patrick was older and much more experienced than Lily. "Look, it's been my job to watch out for Lil and Kate since they were babies. I'm not ready for her to be... I don't know if she's ready to have a relationship yet."

"She's a grown woman, Alex." Patrick felt a raindrop and looked up at the sky. "She's going to do what she wants, and I'm not going to push her."

Alex believed Patrick, but he'd still keep an eye on them. "I've contacted some people who can get us a media network, so in a couple hours we need to leave. We've already been here longer than I wanted. I've used my laptop and I'm not sure how secure that is. If it was traced..."

The rain started to fall harder, as Patrick turned to walk to the house. "I've got some ideas to run by you, too."

Chapter 13

The Square was New York City. It had become known as the Square when surrounding cities were damaged by dirty bombs, and hospitals set up camps in the middle of the old Times Square, where New Year's Eve used to be celebrated. Instead of Times Square, it became known as Safety Square, and now just the Square. Patrick knew that the Square would be surrounded by military. It would be very difficult to rescue Kate, but if the people of New York City were on their side, there would definitely be more power in numbers.

If Lily could get on the news and inform the world of the truth, maybe more people would want to help her. Maybe the bastards holding Kate believed what Patrick used to believe: that their government was good and trustworthy, and that it's job was protecting the people of the nation. Both Alex and Patrick felt sick when Lily told them the doctors hadn't even tried to replicate her ability to heal people. They lied about being close to having a cure, when they were never interested in that to begin with. Lily could win anyone over, if given the chance. Patrick liked Alex's plan to get her on TV, and Alex liked Patrick's plan for rescuing Kate from the Square. In addition, both men agreed that Lily needed to be hidden someplace safe while they put their plan into action.

Connie made a fruit salad, and packed a small cooler full of grilled chicken, rolls, muffins, and beef jerky. Grocery stores were finally just beginning to restock their shelves, and carry more food, so Connie had taken full advantage. Lily had been enjoying the special treatment from Connie. She was sad to leave, but she knew the sooner they left the sooner they could rescue Kate. Connie's six year old son, Eric, cried when Lily kissed him goodbye. "I'll come visit you when I can," she told him. She kissed the side of his big brown eyes. "I hear your dad will be home tomorrow, and won't that be wonderful to see him after all these weeks?"

Eric sniffed. "I like having you here."

"I liked being here." Lily turned to his fourteen year old sister. "Anna, you be good to your little brother now."

Anna nodded. She hadn't spoken to Lily much, but she knew that Lily had healed her mother. She knew that Lily was very important, and it made her feel good having her around. She'd also enjoyed having the men in the house. With her own father being away working for the CCC it was nice feeling safe with Alex and Patrick. And both men had been fascinating to watch.

Lily turned to hug Connie goodbye, but Connie took her hand and led her outside. "I have something to tell Lily in private," she told everyone. "We will be right back." Connie led Lily out the door and into a small patch of woods on the side of the house.

"What's wrong?" Lily asked when they were away from the house.

Connie glanced down at the ground. "I just learned this morning that I'm pregnant."

Lily felt instant joy. "Congratulations that is wonderful… isn't it?" She realized Connie did not appear happy.

"I don't want the kids to know before I tell their daddy. This came as a complete surprise to me. I didn't think I could have any more children." Connie cleared her voice, and looked straight at Lily. "My cancer is back."

Alarmed, Lily grabbed her hand. "I'll heal you."

"No. You need all the strength you can get. I'm not going to have you heal me right now." She pulled her hand away. "I do have a favor to ask of you, though."

Alex glanced down at his watch. "What's taking them so long? Connie knows we need to leave." He was about to go get the women, when Patrick grabbed his arm.

"You hear that?"

"No, what?"

Pulling his gun out, Patrick pointed to the back of the house. He slowly walked toward the kitchen. He saw the first man out of the corner of his eye, and ducked in time to miss the bullet. "Run!" he yelled.

Alex heard the warning, and tried to grab the kids, but it was too late. Shots were fired as Alex dove on top of Anna, because she was right next to him. He yelled for the kids to get down, but when he glanced over at Eric, he wasn't moving, and a splatter of blood covered his cheek.

Outside, Lily and Connie heard the gunshots, and Lily quickly grabbed Connie's arm as she was about to run toward the house.

"My babies!" Connie yelled, yanking her arm from Lily's grasp and running toward the house. Lily was starting to run after her when Patrick came stumbling from behind the house. He grabbed Connie around the waist and tried to pull her back, but she screamed and elbowed him in the ribs.

Patrick released his hold on Connie so he could stop Lily from getting closer to the house. "Get back!"

More shots were fired, and Lily screamed in protest as Patrick covered her mouth and dragged her into the woods.

All Patrick could think about was that Lily needed to be hidden. "Lily, you have to run! You can't go in there!" He lifted her from her feet, grabbing her around the waist and running with her further into into the woods.

"Patrick, please!"

There was a cluster of thick bushes he immediately headed toward. More shots were fired, but Patrick kept running, ignoring the pain in Lily's voice.

They were in the middle of a bush when a branch swept across her face, making a small cut… a cut that would disappear in moments. Tears streamed down her face when he finally loosened his hold on her.

"Lily, you have to be quiet." He pulled bullets from his pocket and reloaded his gun. Just as he clicked the chamber, he heard sounds of feet crushing leaves, trees snapping. Patrick knew men were in the woods looking for them. "You have to stay here," he whispered, pulling a knife out from his boot. "Promise me, Lily, you won't move."

She nodded, trying to pull herself together with deep slow breaths. She didn't think she could move if she wanted to. Her body was shaking, she felt like she was going to vomit. Many shots were fired, and the thought of her brother and the kids being shot was more than she could handle.

Patrick moved as silently through the woods as he could. He didn't know how many men there were, but if he could take them out one at a time, he stood a better chance of protecting Lily.

The rain began to sprinkle. If it became a downpour, it would be harder to hear movement. Luckily, he heard the first man break a branch a few feet from where he was hiding. He was behind a thick oak tree, crouched down before he peered around it. One man in a solid green military uniform was walking with his gun held at his side. Patrick waited till the man passed the tree. It couldn't have been a more perfect opportunity, since he was able to sneak up behind the man and twist his neck. Just as the man fell to the ground, Patrick noticed another soldier. This one held his gun aimed, and was ready to shoot. Patrick threw his knife as hard as he could, breathing a sigh of relief when it landed in the man's chest before he could pull the trigger.

Patrick hid behind the tree again, glancing around for more men. When the forest got too quiet for his peace of mind, he ran off toward the cluster of bushes where he'd left Lily. He wasn't surprised to see that she wasn't there, but panic had him running fast toward the house. He stopped short when he got to the yard and saw that Lily was holding Eric in her arms. She had her face against his neck, and he could see she was crying. There was blood all over the little boy's shirt.

Alex came stumbling out of the house. His tan pant leg was streaked with dark red, and he was holding Connie in his arms, with a sobbing Anna directly behind them. Patrick ran over to help Alex with Connie. They both gently laid her on the ground beside Lily.

"What happened?" Patrick asked. He could see Connie had been shot, as blood soaked the front of her blue shirt. Alex ripped it open.

"She's been shot below the collar bone." Alex grabbed Anna's shaking hand. "Anna, your mom's going to be okay. She still has a pulse. I need you to run inside and get the first aid kit." Squeezing her hand a moment longer, he thought about the carnage inside, the men who ambushed them. "Do not look around. Go straight for the kit and *do not look*." He waited for her to nod in understanding, before he released her hand.

Anna stumbled to her feet, and ran into the house.

Alex glanced at his sister. "I think he's gone." He tipped his head, as Patrick moved to Lily's side.

"Lily," Patrick slid his hand along her arm. "Honey, let me see the boy."

"I'll heal you," she whispered, sending every ounce of her energy into Eric. She'd felt her entire body warm with the need to put life back into his tiny body. "I'll heal you," she repeated. She couldn't feel her legs, and her head felt light and dizzy. She knew she was pushing herself harder than she ever had before, but it had to be enough. She believed she had gotten to Eric in time before his heart completely stopped. "You'll be okay, you'll be okay."

Patrick picked up Eric's hand, trying to feel for a pulse. His heart ached at the thought of such a sweet, innocent child dying. He didn't think he could feel a pulse. "Lily," he said softly, "Honey, he's gone." He rubbed the back of her head when she tightened her hold on Eric. He didn't like how red her face was, and felt alarmed at the heat radiating from her body. "You have to stop now."

"No, no, no," she sobbed and rocked his body, squeezing him

to her chest. She continued to push every ounce of energy and strength she had. The weight in her chest was crushing, and the heat in her body was almost unbearable. She could never live with herself knowing a precious child was dead because she failed.

Moments passed, and Patrick glanced over at Alex who was using a pair of tweezers to remove the bullet from Connie's flesh. Anna was sitting beside her mom in the grass, holding her mom's hand and watching Lily. She was quietly sobbing, her face soaked from tears.

"You took out the two men in the back, but two more came through the front. Eric was shot, but I was able to shoot both men." Alex was replaying the scene in his mind, trying to decide if there'd been something he should have done differently. He pulled the bullet out, and dropped it in the grass. "The other guy had terrible aim. I swear I don't think that man had ever shot a gun before. He must have missed us ten times." Alex wiped sweat from his face with the sleeve of his shirt, and then took the needle and thread he'd used from his earlier stitching of his own cut to sew the bullet hole shut.

"I don't think these men really wanted to kill anyone." Patrick glanced at the house and the woods that surrounded it. "I think they were ordered to." They'd managed to kill a lot of men but lost Eric and almost Connie. "We need to hurry up and get out of here. Will she be okay?" he ran his hand over Connie's pale cheek.

"She's strong. I don't think the bullet did too much damage. It went in just below her collar bone." Alex pulled the last stitch in place, and then glanced at Lily. "Lil, we have to go." He felt a tight squeeze around his heart, looking at his sister holding Eric so tightly. "Patrick, go pull the car around."

Patrick took a step, when he noticed Eric's hand twitch. "My God!" He crouched down beside Lily, who was still holding him to her chest. Eric's eyes fluttered and then opened. "Lily, you did it! You healed him!"

Alex moved to Lily's side, setting his hand on her shoulder. "He's alive," he said in awe. One glance at Lily and he knew she

90

wasn't going to stay conscious. Her face was beet red, her shoulders slumped, and he knew she was struggling to keep her eyes open.

It wasn't until Anna began to laugh and smile that both men smiled too. "Thank you, Lily!" Anna kissed her brother's head. "Thank you!"

Lily couldn't move when Patrick brought the car around, so Alex lifted her up in his arms. "You're on fire sis," He said with concern. "You really outdid yourself this time." He carried her to the car and set her down gently in the front seat. Patrick picked Eric up and sat him on his sister's lap in the back. Anna kissed her brother, cradling his head in her arms.

Connie was still unconscious. Alex laid her beside Anna, before climbing in the back hatch. The car was small, and like most battery operated vehicles, only four people fit comfortably, but the trunk was open to the inside of the car so he could fit. Patrick pulled out onto the main road, yelling for everyone to keep their heads down as they passed what could've been a government vehicle. The speed limit was 55. Patrick kept that speed to not draw attention.

"Head east. We have another safe house an hour from here," Alex told Patrick.

Patrick glanced at Lily. She was leaning against the door with her eyes closed. "Are you okay, Lily?" He'd never seen her like this before. Her face was still bright red, and her heat was warming up the interior of the car. He wondered if she was conscious.

"She's very weak now," Alex replied, when Lily didn't. "Those bastards did things to her that have ruined her strength to heal." There'd been a time when Lily could heal as many as eighty people and still have enough strength to function normally.

Worrying over Lily was becoming a normal part of Patrick's life. Alex offered bottled water to Anna and encouraged her to try and get Eric to drink a little. Eric's eyes were open and he was asking for his mom. Alex was doing a good job of reassuring everyone that they would all be just fine.

Chapter 14

It was still raining when Lily opened her eyes. The room was dark, but she could hear the sound of raindrops hitting the roof, and a soft rustling of leaves. It didn't feel like she was in a bed, the surface under her was hard. She sat up, trying to let her eyes adjust to the room. She was next to a window, and the curtain was drawn. As soon as the blanket slipped from her body, she realized it was freezing. A small gasp escaped her lips, as she quickly pulled the blanket back up to her neck.

"Lily?"

She glanced next to her just as Patrick turned a lantern light on. "Patrick?" She breathed a sigh of relief. "Where are we?" She was lying on the floor in a sleeping bag, and Patrick was beside her in his own sleeping bag. She looked around the tiny room. "Is this a tree fort?"

"It's a deer blind." Patrick had never felt so safe in all his life. They were high up in a small wooden box that did resemble a little tree house. It would be very hard to spot, and he felt certain no one would find them in it. The only problem was that September in the Upper Peninsula was bringing a lot of rain, and the temperatures kept dropping.

"Where's my brother? Where are Connie and the kids? Is Eric okay?" Her mind was suddenly racing.

Reaching out, Patrick set his hand on her arm. "Everyone is fine. Your brother took Connie and the kids to meet up with Connie's husband. He's going to take the family someplace safe."

Patrick's warm hand on her shoulder, and hearing that the family was well, calmed her racing heart. "I wish I could've said goodbye and seen them for myself." She hoped Connie hadn't lost the baby. "Were Connie and Eric really okay?"

Patrick moved his hand down to hers. "They both kissed you goodbye, and they both were better than okay."

"We should not have split up. Why didn't we all go?"

"Honey, you have been asleep for two days." He hadn't left her side. "Guess you being the weight of a little stick came in handy, since your brother and I have had to carry you everywhere."

"Oh," her eyes widened in surprise, and her cheeks flushed as she felt slightly embarrassed. "Two days?" She didn't like the idea that she'd been a burden that long. He had that charming grin again, the one that made her stomach do a little flip. "I guess that explains why I'm thirsty."

"Here." He handed her a canteen, then reached into a small cooler and took out some beef jerky. "You need to eat, too. How do you feel?" He was happy to see her awake and find the normal color back in her cheeks. "Your saving that boy's life was a pretty awesome miracle, but Lil, you can't do that again." They'd been on the run for two days, and having her unconscious made it tough.

"I wouldn't have been able to stand it if Eric had died because of me. I can't let people who help me get hurt. I won't involve any more families, Patrick." She took another sip of water.

"That's why we're here, sweetheart. Wanna live in this house with me?"

Lily smiled at his mischievous grin.

"I'm surprised your brother left me alone in here with you."

"My brother likes you," she replied fondly.

She glanced around at the four wood planked walls. It was just big enough for three people to sleep. It was nothing but a wooden box with an open window, covered by a black faded curtain. "Will he be back soon?"

"Probably in an hour." Patrick wanted to see Lily stand. The

93

sooner she had her strength back, the sooner he and Alex could begin their plan. And if he could see her back to normal, maybe the knot in his stomach would go away.

"Don't you have anything better to do than run around hiding me?" She studied him a moment. They'd been on the run, yet he still somehow found time to trim his facial hair. It was short and gave him a rugged appearance that she found quite appealing. His gray shirt and black cargo pants were clean, and he smelled nice.

He gave her an amused smile. "Actually, I don't. I'm pretty sure that since I tasered my boss, Jeffrey, I've been fired. I'm probably wanted for murder now that I've left a few dead bodies along the way, and…" When a beam of sunlight slipped through the window and landed on Lily's face, Patrick was struck by how beautiful she was. The unique color of her eyes was vivid with the sun's rays on them. The yellow specks of gold almost shimmered the way a gold coin in the sun would. Her face was pure and flawless, her cheeks a lovely rose.

Lily assumed the look on his face, along with his pause, meant he was realizing for the first time the immense peril he was in. "I'm sorry," she whispered sadly. "Your life will never be the same because of me. You'll never work in law enforcement again, and you'll always be on the run." She placed her hand on top of his. "I've ruined so many lives. Danny died because of me, Kate's—"

"Stop it," he interrupted her tersely. "You're not responsible. You're not taking that on." He couldn't disagree with her more. He'd never felt so alive until he'd met her. If she hadn't still been frail and exhausted from unconsciousness, he'd have grabbed her and showed her just what he was feeling. But he knew now wasn't the right time, so he picked up her hand. "You're not to worry about me. I'm set financially, and I've always been pretty good at running." He didn't even need to use the sizable chunk of money his wife had left him.

"But what will you do with your life?" She placed her other hand on top of their joined hands. "I don't want you to end up in prison."

"I won't. I could disappear today, and live just fine, Lily, so stop." He didn't want to see that pain in her eyes. "I'm going to help you get Kate. I'm going to make sure the government never lays a finger on you again." That was all that mattered to him now.

There was a loud sound of a twig snapping in the woods. Patrick quickly moved to the window and peeled back the thick curtain just enough to see out. "Come look," he told her.

A beautiful buck stood just a few feet from the tree. His head turned toward the fawn next to him, and Lily could almost feel the love in the creature's eyes. "They are wonderful." Seeing a deer didn't constitute a great miracle, but it definitely gave her heart a needed lift.

Patrick turned to Lily and studied her beautiful face. He wondered if there would ever be a time when he could tell her what he was feeling. "It's stopped raining. Why don't you go down and stretch your legs." He picked a jacket off the floor and wrapped it around her shoulders, then pulled up on the square door in the floor.

She scooted over to the opening. "Too bad this cozy little house doesn't have a toilet." She wanted to stay and talk to him longer. There were still questions she wanted to ask him, but she needed to relieve her bladder.

"Do you need help getting down? I brought you up here over my shoulder, so I can take you down the same way."

"No, thanks. I can manage." She glanced down at the top board of the ladder. It wasn't a real ladder, just some two by fours cut short and nailed to the trunk of the tree. It couldn't have been easy carrying her up. "Are you coming down?"

"I'll put away the sleeping bags, and be down in a few minutes. I'll give you a little privacy," he winked at her. "Don't wander off."

"I think I've heard that before."

"Here." He held out a small revolver. "The safety is on." He turned the gun to the side and flipped a black metal switch, showing her how it worked. "Now it's off. All you have to do is point and shoot. Alex doesn't want you to be without this. I promised him I'd give it to you."

With reluctance, Lily took the gun. She hated guns, but at least this one had a clear safety switch on it. She started to put it in her coat pocket.

"No, Lil, not your pocket." He leaned toward her and took the gun from her hand. "Keep it in the small of your back." He reached behind her and lifted her shirt. Then feeling with his hand, he tucked the gun between her pants and warm flesh. "We will get you a holster for it." Looking in her eyes, it was obvious she felt the intimacy of his touch and from the way she was holding her breath and looking at him, he wanted nothing more than to touch her again. He brushed the side of her cheek with the back of his fingers, "I'm glad you're awake, Lil. You had us all really worried."

Lily felt warmth at the sincerity of his words, and the concern in his eyes. For a moment she thought he might lean toward her one more inch, and she felt disappointed when he sat back and glanced toward the sleeping bags.

"I'll be down in a few," he told her casually.

It felt good to walk, to breathe in the cool air that smelled of wet leaves and pine, and stretch muscles that hadn't moved in two days. Lily glanced around at the trees that grew closely together, and felt safe and at home. The stillness was a comfort. The hunting blind was up high in the middle of the Upper Peninsula's rich, thick forest. If it had been built bigger, and perhaps had a bed, Lily could imagine herself staying in it. Funny how she didn't need anything but the fresh air and the security of the forest.

There wasn't anywhere for her to go, and no discernible path she could follow, but she walked away from the tree so she could move, and have privacy. She didn't feel weak, as she squat low to the ground, and set the gun down. It wasn't working where Patrick had placed it. She didn't feel tired. But, Patrick had made her nervous. His closeness had made her heart beat faster. She glanced at her disheveled state. Her long red strands were frizzy from not having felt a comb in days. Her yoga pants were dirty with smudges of mud on the knees, her shirt was clean, but she'd love a warm shower. How could a person so small and meek save so many lives, heal so many people?

Her heart ached at the thought of Eric. Thank God, she'd gotten to him in time. If she'd stayed hidden in the bush, he might have been stone cold by the time she'd reached him. Connie and her family were safe, and once her brother returned she might actually feel happy. Happiness was a feeling she'd not experienced in a long time.

Her mind wandered to thoughts of her sister. Thoughts of how she could tell the American people that the government representatives were nothing but liars. And then her mind wandered back to Patrick. She glanced up at the tree, wondering what was taking him so long. She listened hard, and suddenly realized she heard his voice, but it was too faint to make out what he was saying.

She climbed the tree as quietly as possible. Halfway up, she stopped. She'd always had exceptional hearing, even after Kate had screamed in her ear the night they were set on fire. Her body might have sustained permanent hearing loss after that, if it hadn't the ability to repair itself.

"I'm still with them. They trust me," Patrick's voice said softly.

Lily felt an odd chill run through her body.

"It's hard to keep calling, but I'll keep you informed." There was a short pause, and then, "Yeah, I'll see what I can do about that."

Lily climbed down the tree, feeling as if an invisible hand just squeezed her heart. She leaned against the tree for support, a wave of panic swept through her. "No, please, God, no," she mumbled.

Patrick was climbing down the tree when Lily stepped back and raised the gun at him. She quickly glanced down at the safety switch, and turned it off.

"What are you doing?" Patrick didn't like that her hands were shaking, and stress and fear was etched on her pale face.

"How did you escape, Patrick?" She held the gun on him. Everything inside her hoped she was wrong. She'd trusted him, felt safe with him.

He felt a clench in his gut at the way she said his name. "Put the gun down, Lily."

She took a step back and set her finger on the trigger.

Patrick frowned at the move. She was serious, and he could see she was scared.

"Was this all part of their plan?" Lily pushed back the urge to cry. "You get close to me, protect me, and pretend to be on my side?" She tried to keep her arms from shaking. "It makes perfect sense. They didn't do anything with me at the hospital. All they did was keep me locked up." She wondered why they hadn't tried to use her to heal anyone. Why they hadn't tried performing more tests on her, or why they hadn't done anything but give her just enough food to sustain life. "They were waiting for you to get in tight with Alex. They knew what you were doing, because you were still working for them." She felt nauseous, and swallowed hard. "They knew you were going to free me, and then they could just recapture me and my brother. They'd have all of us with your help. No resistance would be left."

Patrick tried to ignore the heavy weight on his chest. "And just how have you come to this conclusion?" He already knew the answer, but he wanted to hear her say it.

"I heard you whispering on the phone. I happen to have excellent hearing. They trust me," she repeated his words.

Patrick sighed. He couldn't blame her for thinking the way she did. Her idea actually made perfect sense, and he felt a twinge of pride at how smart she was. "Will you let me explain?"

"Yes, explain fast." She glanced around the empty woods, wishing to God Alex would come walking up.

"I was on the phone with my brother." He was kicking himself for the uneasy way she stood there, her eyes pleading for a good excuse. "After I narrowly escaped being killed by my own commander, I knew my family wouldn't be safe. Jeffrey threatened that. I had them move to a secure location, being careful not to contact them, so my calls can't be traced to where they're hiding. I did get a chance to tell my brother a little about you. I told him you trust me, because he asked me how it is that you're keeping me around."

She remembered his words, 'It's hard to keep calling, but I'll keep you informed.' Maybe he was telling the truth. Maybe he was just keeping his family informed of what was happening. "How did you escape after they shot us with darts? You never bothered to tell me."

Patrick ignored her accusatory tone. "It's not like we've had a lot of time to chit chat and get caught up, Lily. It's been non-stop action since I've met you."

She couldn't argue with that. She'd had maybe ten minutes alone with him since she was rescued, and for two days she was un-conscious.

"After the sleeping dart wore off, I woke up in a van. Two men were driving it, and I was handcuffed, lying on the floor. I assumed they either had orders to take me back to headquarters, or they were driving to the place they intended to dump my body." He took his eyes off hers for a brief moment, as she slowly lowered the gun. "Remember how I handcuffed you to me?"

"Yes."

"Well, I still had the key in my pocket." A devilish grin crossed his face. "It wasn't hard to escape, Lily." He felt a little tension sub-side when she lowered the gun further. "I knew your brother was going to show up at the cabin at some point, so I went back there and waited for him. There were a few agents at the cabin waiting for you to return. Luckily for me, Alex saw me take them out. He'd already been there watching the place, in case you returned. You can ask him what he saw."

"How do I know that was your brother on the phone?" She desperately wanted to believe him, but why had he been so secretive? "Why didn't you just tell me you were going to call your brother?"

"I didn't want you or Alex to know my family was in danger, and I couldn't tell you where they are. It's just safer that way." He sighed, "Look…I'll reach in my pocket and take out my phone." He put his hands up to show her he was going to move slowly and cautiously. "I'll show you the phone, so you can see the last number I called. I'll call Paul again, and put it on speaker."

"Okay."

Patrick did what he promised, and when his brother answered the phone he said, "Hey, Paul, I forgot to ask you how Mom and Dad are doing?"

"They're good, but I already told you that. Is everything okay?" Paul asked with suspicion.

"Everything's fine." Patrick looked at Lily for confirmation, and when she nodded her head, he added. "Yeah, I guess I did ask that. I'm just making sure everyone is good."

"Stop worrying," Paul chuckled.

Lily dropped the gun at her side, as relief swamped her. She believed Patrick was talking to his brother, because there was no denying their voices sounded almost identical.

"Mom says just get a repairman to fix the toilet and she'll be happy," Paul added.

"I told you I'd see what I can do about that," Patrick replied, in a steady voice.

Lily had heard him say that when she'd been listening to his conversation the first time. Now the pieces made sense, as Patrick said goodbye to his brother one more time.

"I'm sorry." She felt tears swimming in her eyes, as relief washed over her. There was also a nagging feeling of guilt. This man who had done nothing but help her, and make her feel safe, didn't deserve mistrust. "I don't know what's wrong with me. I can't trust anyone. I can't…" Her eyes blurred as the tears dripped down her cheeks. "I should have trusted you. I'm sorry, Patrick."

"It's okay, Lil." He moved his hands to the side of her face, and tipped her head back so he could look in her eyes. "It takes time to build trust. You and I haven't had much time, and I haven't given you much reason to trust me."

His body was warm, and Lily felt a soothing ache at the gentleness in his eyes. It had always been his eyes that made her feel more at ease.

"That's not true, and my brother trusts you." She should have known Patrick wasn't secretly still working for the government. Alex would know, since he was an incredible judge of character. Better than her. "I should have trusted you. I shouldn't have doubted you."

"No." He rubbed his thumbs over her cheeks, wiping at her tears. "You're smart, Lily. You're incredibly brave and incredibly smart. Don't ever second guess yourself. You have to follow what's in your gut, and you were right to have assumed what you did. It was my mistake. I should have told you I was going to call my family. I shouldn't have been secretive about it."

The warmth he was creating made her weak. She moved her hands to his wrists, and held on. "I wasn't going to shoot you. Well maybe I would have shot your leg, but then I'd have healed it when Alex gets here."

"I appreciate that," he chuckled. "I'm sorry I put you in that position."

"You can tell me anything, Patrick. I want to know you."

He held her close. "I just thought the more I keep my family a secret, the safer they'd be." He also didn't want his own worries and issues to burden Alex and Lily. If they knew how concerned he was for the safety of his loved ones it might affect them somehow. "I don't want you worrying about my problems."

She accepted his words. It all made sense now. With his face mere inches away from hers, she could easily stand on her toes and lean in. Every part of her wanted to do just that, and she knew Patrick could see it in her eyes.

"I'm not able to resist this anymore." Patrick moved his hand to gently cup the sides of her face. Maybe if he'd kissed her all the times he'd wanted to, she'd have more faith in him.

Her mind emptied of all thought, other than how right the moment was. A sense of peace and tranquility washed over her. His mouth seemed to melt with hers, and the reality of the moment was so much greater than any expectations she had imagined. With the moment came a sense of belonging she'd never felt before. *Like she was home.*

Patrick was astounded by her. He'd never felt so overwhelmed with feelings, not even with his wife. Somewhere in the back of his mind, he worried if this was too soon. Was he taking advantage of her vulnerable state? But he realized he was the vulnerable one. He was the one consumed by her. He pulled away just long enough to catch his breath.

"What's going on?" Alex's voice said from behind her. "Geez, I leave you alone for a few hours…"

Patrick breathed deeply before rolling his eyes to heaven. "Your brother always has incredible timing."

Lily stepped back from Patrick as her brother pulled her into his arms. "I'm glad to see you up and about, sis. I was really starting to worry about you. How do you feel?" He kissed her on the forehead, setting weary eyes on Patrick. "Why has she been crying?" He could see her face was flushed, and her eyes were red.

"Just a misunderstanding," Patrick replied carefully. "We don't really need to report to you, Alex."

"You do if you make her cry." Alex folded his arms, and waited for his sister to reply.

"I'm fine, really. We were just sorting a few things out," she said, trying to steady her pounding heart.

"Yeah, well do me a favor… sort things out with your hands in your pockets." Alex glanced down at the gun Lily had dropped in the grass. "Why is this here?" He picked it up and did the same thing Patrick had done, carefully placing it in the small of her back, tucked in the waistband of her pants. "We'll need to get you a holster." He took the gun back. "Dumb yoga pant elastic won't hold this." He shoved the gun in her jacket pocket.

Alex had always been too observant and smart to lie to. He'd always known when Lily and Kate were up to something.

"Patrick and I were just talking about the gun. He wants me to

102

carry it, and I don't want to."

Alex gave her a look that said he wasn't buying what she was saying, but he'd accept it for now. "You have to keep it, Lily."

"I know." She didn't like having to lie to her brother, but she did like the wink that Patrick gave her.

Alex pulled a black backpack off his shoulder, and set it on the ground. "I've got three days of supplies, and more ammunition." He didn't like the looks Lily and Patrick were giving each other. "The kids and Connie were sorry they didn't get to say goodbye to you."

Lily recalled her last conversation with Connie. Connie confided in her that she was pregnant, and that her cancer was back. Lily had made her friend a promise. "I'll see them again soon." She'd make sure that in eight months, she'd see Connie again.

"Here." Alex handed Lily a Cliff bar. "I need to see you eating all the time. I don't care if it's just a bite or two, but I want you eating." He glanced at Patrick. "How long ago did she wake up?"

"Um, I'm standing right here, Alex." She hated when her brother went into father-caring-for-his-baby-girl mode. "I woke up about an hour ago."

Alex put his hands on his hips. He knew if he'd walked up one moment later, he'd have found his sister kissing the hell out of Patrick. Or maybe she already had. He wasn't sure what he was going to do about them, but staring at Lily with her arms crossed, he was reminded that she was in fact a grown woman.

"Did you get the details sorted out?" Patrick asked. Not only was Alex taking Connie and the kids to meet Connie's husband, but he was also meeting with the people who were going to help get them into Canada.

"Yes." Alex tipped his head toward the tree blind. "Get your things, because we have a day's walk. By this time tomorrow, Lily will be reading a little speech that'll be broadcast everywhere."

Chapter 15

Walking through the forest all day wasn't easy. Sometimes they were on paths, and other times they had to cross thicket and terrain that made her back ache and feet throb. Climbing over branches and trees was difficult because Lily still didn't have all her strength back. Her brother kept insisting they stop every half hour to eat and drink water.

The truth was, Lily loved being with her brother and Patrick. The only person missing was Kate. But Patrick helped with keeping her mind off her worries about her sister. She'd been enjoying getting to know him better. He'd been very talkative during their long hike. Most of the time, Patrick had taken her by the hand in a way that seemed natural and easy. He kept finding little ways to touch her, and make her laugh.

Alex noticed the gestures and rolled his eyes a few times, making Lily smile, but he hadn't said anything. Patrick shared parts of his childhood with them, and in return Alex shared a few stories meant to deliberately embarrass Lily.

After a while, Alex reminded them both that it was time to refocus. He wanted to go over his plan again in detail so that both Lily and Patrick understood what was going to happen. Lily was sorry she couldn't keep enjoying the pleasant conversation with Patrick. The more she continued to learn about him, the more she couldn't stop thinking about him. She was still thinking about him, when she sat down on a log to rest.

"Have you been listening to our plan, Lily?" Alex pulled some food from his backpack.

She heard the irritation in his tone, and rubbed the back of her neck. "Yes, why?"

"You seem distracted."

"I've listened to every detail, and I'm not distracted." Her eyes searched the woods for Patrick.

"He distracts you." Alex tipped his head in the direction Patrick had walked. The men were taking turns with their privacy breaks, so that Lily wouldn't be left alone. "Are you in love with him?"

Lily snapped her eyes from the woods to her brother's face. "Is that what you think?"

Alex shrugged, "There's definitely something between you two. Patrick is way more obvious about it."

"He is?" Lily had a lot she wanted to ask, but she knew Patrick would be walking back soon.

"You don't see the way he looks at you?" Why would she, he thought. She never paid attention to the way men responded to her. Alex was pretty sure that only Kate was aware of their impressive beauty. Lily didn't see it.

A branch snapped in the woods, and both Lily and Alex glanced over to where Patrick was walking briskly toward them. The conversation would have to wait.

"There's a big group of campers about thirty yards from here. We'll need to avoid that area." Patrick pointed in the direction.

Lily finished eating trail mix, and swallowed the last of her water. In another hour they'd be reaching Sault Ste. Marie, where their plan was to board a ship that would take them to Canada. Danny's original plan had been to use his network of helpers to smuggle Lily into Canada. Canadians hated the presidential administration ever since they'd rejected Canada's clean water plan; a plan that would have prevented pollution from harming the Great Lakes.

The fact that the Hope Medical Clinic was located in the Upper Peninsula had given them the advantage of not having to make Lily journey too far. And of course the rich Superior National Forest was an excellent way for them to travel. Staying off roads and away from populated areas helped ensure Lily's safety. There wasn't a person on the planet who didn't know who Lily was and most everyone believed in her healing ability. The government and social media had done a damn good job of brainwashing the world into believing she was not only the real deal, but would soon provide the cure for cancer.

The weather had been cooperative, other than a few light showers that hadn't lasted long. The temperatures were much colder in Northern Michigan than they were in Virginia, but Alex was well prepared with all the proper gear. Lily was no stranger to hiking and roughing it. In fact, being in the forest, any forest, was more comforting to her than any hotel or house. And the fact that both Alex and Patrick were safe from radiation was the greatest comfort of all.

Alex adjusted his backpack on his shoulders and zipped his jacket. He glanced at his sister, and was pleased that she'd been gaining her strength back. She'd been eating regularly, and she'd lost the pale, weak demeanor she'd had back at Connie's house. He didn't like the fact that she was so quiet, though. Granted, he'd monopolized the conversation discussing their next move, as well as his overall plan to rescue Kate. But Alex could see his sister was struggling with her own thoughts, and he was sure those thoughts centered on Patrick.

"You got another hour's worth of walking in you, sis?" Alex asked in concern.

"Yeah." Lily bent down to pick up a small handful of dirt. She felt the grain against her palm. Soil was such a precious resource now. Too much land had been destroyed by radiation. Clean land… clean earth was getting harder to come by. Scientists were trying to come up with ways to grow food mechanically. There were talks of how radiated land could be salvaged, and studies were being conducted for new underground living.

"You haven't said much." Alex set his hand on Lily's back as she followed behind Patrick. "How do you feel about our plan?"

Lily raised apprehensive eyes at her brother, before staring back at the ground. It was important to watch their steps, because all the branches and forest terrain were trip hazards. "It all sounds good, except for the part where I stay behind. I really feel I need to be there when you get Kate."

"No," both men said together.

"But…" Lily knew it would do no good to argue. Once her brother set his mind on something, his stubbornness left no room for change. "I don't like the idea of being on the air before you have Kate."

"I know." Alex wondered if his sister was going to pick up on the same concern and worry that he had. "There's a chance they'll decide they don't need Kate anymore, once the world knows it's been her pretending to heal, and not you. If they determine Kate is useless, they might just decide to kill her."

"I think we need to have Kate safe before I go on the air."

"There's no way to get to her." Patrick glanced back at Lily and Alex. "We need the outrage of the people, and the hope they'll turn against the men holding her, in order to get her back." The idea was for Lily to ask the American people for help. She had a huge following, and although she wasn't on social media anymore for her own protection, she knew millions of Americans were on her side. Patrick had his own plan to be as close to Kate as possible once Lily's broadcast hit televisions all over the U. S. He was hoping to be there in time to protect Kate and free her.

"I know." She'd follow their plan and pray that it would work.

"Get down!" Alex whispered, and pulled on Lily's arm.

Patrick immediately crouched in front of Lily, and listened, slowly pulling his gun from his back.

Lily heard the voices now and the footsteps in the forest behind them. She could hear multiple people talking. "Is it the camping group?" she whispered into Patrick's ear.

"I don't think so."

Alex gazed at their surroundings and was concerned there

107

wasn't enough thicket and tree coverage in their particular spot. If a group of hunters were headed their way, they needed to be more concealed. "You take Lily to the water," he told Patrick, and glanced at his GPS. "It's not far," he pointed in the direction they needed to go.

"No!" Lily whispered harshly. "We stay together."

"She's right, Alex. We can't split up." He already knew what Alex was thinking. "We don't know if they're strangers or government agents. They could be tracking us."

"I think they're probably just a group of hunters." Alex adjusted his backpack. "I'll buy you some time and throw them off the trail."

"No," Lily squeezed her brother's arm. "Don't be stupid. Let's just run." She didn't see why all three of them couldn't just run away.

The voices were getting closer. "They'll recognize you, but not me," Patrick told Alex. "I'll stay, and you take Lily."

Lily set her other hand on Patrick's knee. "I'm going to get up and scream, 'come and get me,' if either one of you tries to stay here. Now for once, do what I say and both of you follow me." She couldn't see the men yet, but she knew they would be in sight soon. It was now or never. "Run!" She picked up her bag and with all her strength took off toward the right. She made her steps as wide as she could and tried to avoid stepping on sticks or branches, but it didn't help. She knew they were making a lot of noise. There was no way to mask the rattle of their gear, nor the dried leaves being crushed by three sets of feet. But Lily didn't care. She was just relieved that both men were following her.

"Lily, stop!" Alex said, not wanting to shout.

Patrick grabbed her arm and pulled her to his chest as he moved them behind the trunk of a Maple Tree.

She hadn't realized how hard her heart was pounding until she stopped and was clutching the front of Patrick's jacket, barely able to catch her breath to speak.

"Your plan worked, babe." Patrick looked past the tree into the lush forest. There was no sign of the strangers, and the only sound heard was all three of them panting.

"Let's just keep going." Lily didn't want to take any chances, and allow that group of people to catch up to them. "I can keep going," she panted.

Patrick slipped his hand around the back of her head, his thumb gently caressing her neck. "Take some deep breaths, sweetheart. We're safe now, because you're one hell of a runner." He lowered his lips to her forehead.

Alex walked over to her, completely out of breath. "Okay, so it's safe to say you clearly inherited the running genes in the family. I had no idea you were so fast, sis."

"I'm glad you listened and followed me."

"Well had I known you could run like that, I'd have suggested it sooner." Alex never dreamed his sister would have the strength and stamina to run like the wind.

"My back's going to be killing tomorrow." Patrick leaned his forehead against Lily's. "Having to run with a forty pound pack on your shoulders isn't easy."

"My bag weighs more than yours, Prick." Alex smiled and adjusted his own pack. "It's sad that we were both outrun by a skinny little woman with short legs. And she too is carrying a backpack, so we can't even use that for an excuse."

Lily frowned, "My legs are not short!"

Patrick smiled down at her, "You never cease to amaze me," and this time he gently swept a kiss over her lips, not caring that Alex was standing right there. "Let's keep moving."

The kiss had been too swift and short, but she didn't say anything as she smiled at the grumpy look on Alex's face, and laced her fingers with Patrick's as he took her hand.

Chapter 16

The ship wasn't a ship. It was a small fishing charter. Mark Stevenson owned the charter and ten others like it. He happened to be the son of Gary Stevenson who worked for the United States Coast Guard and the brother of Kyle and Brad Stevenson who conveniently worked border patrol along the Sault Sainte Marie International Bridge at the Canada/U. S. border. As Danny always liked to say, 'getting things done is all about connections.'

"Welcome to Sault Ste. Marie, Ontario," Mark told Lily.

She accepted his hand with a smile. He was a handsome young man, with deep set baby blue eyes and a bald head. He'd already had several rounds of chemotherapy, and two surgeries. He wasn't out of the woods yet, and radiation treatments were scheduled to begin after Christmas. So far the tumors hadn't shrunk, and Mark wasn't feeling confident he'd beat the cancer. He was lucky to have received chemo treatments, even though it hadn't worked. Most people were on waiting lists for so long, they died before they could get care.

"I can't thank you enough, Mark." Lily said, patting his arm.

"It's me who can't thank you enough," Mark replied, bringing Lily's hand to his lips. He knew that by her healing him, she just spared him a tremendous amount of suffering, and guaranteed he'd live. "I hope you get your sister back, and can live in peace."

It wasn't hard for Lily to imagine Mark with a thick head of hair, and those baby blues charming the pants off some lucky girl. "Thank you." She laughed when Patrick tried to nonchalantly pull her away from the attractive twenty three year old.

Waves crashed along the sides of the charter, and Lily was grateful for the styrofoam cup of coffee that Mark gave her. She'd enjoyed the friendly conversation with him. It helped to take her mind off the cold breeze. Once they finally reached the Canadian border, Lily found Patrick once again dragging her away from Mark. She'd barely been given a minute to thank him for his help and hug him goodbye. Patrick led her to a black car. Once she sat in the back seat next to Alex, she smiled. She liked the thought that perhaps Patrick was jealous. Mark was a handsome man who'd showed her a lot of attention. And Mark's two brothers, Kyle and Brad, had also made quite a fuss over meeting the notorious and 'very stunningly beautiful,' Lily McCallister. She never understood why people found her so attractive, but the fact that three handsome men had said it, and were openly admiring her, made her feel quite special. Or maybe it was the obvious jealousy Patrick displayed that gave her a little jolt.

Alex handed Lily a Snickers. "I think you earned this," he smiled.

"Why's that?" she chuckled.

"You're a real trooper. I wouldn't mind celebrating right now with a little Scotch on the rocks." They'd traveled far, and managed to make it into Canada with no major problems. He also appreciated having a sister who wasn't high maintenance. He examined her a moment. "I'm glad you bounced back well after healing Mark."

Lily peeled the wrapper back on the candy bar. "Me too." She took a bite of the Snickers, as she returned Alex's smile.

Alex had enjoyed traipsing the wilderness and watching his plan of action take root. Of course he'd never have been able to do any of it, if it hadn't been for Danny. Danny was the one who uploaded all his contacts to Alex's computer. Danny was the one who'd managed to reach people all over the world who were willing and able to help them. Alex knew that if he did have a glass of Scotch, he'd make a toast to his old friend Dan. May he rest in peace.

"I'd join you with some whiskey and a Cuban cigar," Patrick said from behind the steering wheel. He glanced at Lily in the rear view mirror and swallowed the lump in his throat. He wondered if she really liked Mark, and if so, was it better for her to be with a man her own age? Patrick was eight years older and lacked the charm that many women look for in a man. His wife sometimes complained that he was too quiet and reserved. Perhaps his police training had something to do with it. He didn't like to let his guard down, and at the time of his marriage, he'd always had cases on his mind. Those Stevenson boys flirted with Lily something fierce. He appreciated the fact she didn't flirt back, but he could see she enjoyed it. Not that he could blame her really. The men were actually likable and sincere.

The road along the Lake Superior shoreline was scenic, but Lily only saw a few moments of it. After her candy bar, her head found its way to Alex's shoulder and she instantly fell asleep.

When Lily woke, she was in Patrick's arms.

"My brother is letting you carry me?" she snuggled her face in the side of his neck. His scent was a mixture of sweat and pine, which wasn't the least bit offensive.

"He's helping set up the cameras." Patrick held her close, wishing he could have more time alone with her. "You'll be on the air soon, Lil."

She knew what that meant. Soon Patrick and Alex would be leaving her, and the security and happiness she'd felt having both of them with her was going to end. She hated that she couldn't go with them to New York when they freed Kate. The thought of anything going wrong gave her anxiety, and so many things could go wrong. "Patrick, I…" She wanted to express her feelings to him. He couldn't leave without knowing what she felt. It was important that she tell him she'd never doubt him again.

Patrick set Lily on her feet as soon as he reached the front door. They were standing on a wide wrap-around porch of an old country style farmhouse. It was a secure location, with no other homes nearby, and a huge satellite dish in the front yard.

"We were letting you sleep in the car, but your brother has been inside for hours. These people are very nice. The wife is a little strange, but you'll probably like her," he smiled.

Lily felt her heart sink. "No!" she felt a twinge of panic. "I won't have any more families helping me. I won't put another mother and father at risk. Patrick, you and Alex promised me!" She glanced at the lovely looking home. Wind chimes in the form of little metal hand prints hung from the roof, potted mums gave purple and yellow color to the charming house that spoke of family, warmth and love. "I won't stay here!"

Alex yanked open the front door, and pulled his sister inside. "You have to keep your voice down, Lil." He tossed an angry glare at Patrick before taking his sister by the shoulders. "These people know the risk, and their son is the only one who can get you on the air. He's rigged the entire network system of the news stations. We can't make our plan succeed without the help of these people."

"You told me no more families would be involved." Lily scanned the open family room with the photographs lining the mantel above the fireplace, the cat curled up under the sofa table. "I can't put these people at risk. I just can't!"

Alex tightened his grip on Lily's arm. "No one knows you're here. Ian was a friend of Danny's, and has been part of the plan to help us since day one. He understands what's at stake, Lil."

"We feel privileged to help you," Ian commented upon entering the room. "I'd like to introduce you to my parents."

Lily reluctantly shook hands with each member of the Webster family before they settled into the dining room. Mr. and Mrs. Webster were just more kind people who were willing to open their home to her. There was obvious concern and worry in Lily's eyes as she watched the family gather at the dining room table. Mrs. Webster was a soft spoken woman who was trying to be a gracious host. She placed a bread roll on each person's plate, before seating herself at the large dining room table.

"Hey, it's going to be okay here, sis." Alex draped his arm over her shoulders, and squeezed her toward him. He was excited at how brilliant Ian's set up was. Ian had a strategy to hack the algorithm on social media platforms. It was crucial for millions of people to see and hear Lily's video, and with Ian's hack, millions would see Lily's video rolling across their phones and computers. It would alert the world even quicker than the television interruption. "This kid's absolutely brilliant," Alex whispered in Lily's ear with excitement.

Lily smiled softly and rested her head on Alex's shoulder. She felt slightly better hearing Alex's confidence. He was such a strong person, so sure of himself. Lily needed to borrow his strength and assurance. She wished she could absorb those traits the way she absorbed peoples' diseases. "I can't handle anyone else being hurt because of me." There were too many groups of people after her, and somehow, they kept finding her. She pushed back the memory of little Eric near death in her arms.

Ian overheard Lily's comment, and leaned toward her. "We live on six acres of private property. Our closest neighbor is half a mile away, and no one knows you're here." He straightened his shoulders, and lifted his chin. "I don't want you worrying about us. Danny died to protect you, and I will too if need be."

Alex rolled his eyes. That wasn't quite the speech he wanted Lily to hear.

"No one is getting hurt," Mr. Webster said firmly. He glanced at his wife, and asked her if she would like to offer a prayer.

Everyone bowed their heads. When Mrs. Webster was finished with the prayer, Lily glanced up to find Patrick's eyes on her. He hadn't said much since they walked in the door. She wondered if he was as worried about leaving her as she was about him and Alex leaving without her. She tried offering a small smile, but she could sense it was wasted on him. He knew how she was feeling, and in return he offered her a nod of assurance. He too appeared strong and sure. No wonder she liked him so much, he was just like her brother. Both men commanded the room.

Okay, Lily thought to herself, taking a deep breath. She would trust these two men who had rescued her, protected her, and gotten her this far. She would follow their plan and hold tight to her belief that God was watching over all of them.

The meal was a simple spaghetti sauce with linguine. Ian informed them that he was a vegetarian, and Grandpa Steve was allergic to seafood. Therefore, Mrs. Webster had a hard time planning meals. Ian resembled his grandfather more than his parents. He had his grandfather's thick black eyebrows, and deep eye sockets. He wore his hair shorter than his father. Mr. Webster insisted on being called Marty, and reminded Lily of a musician she'd seen playing on the streets for money. His hair was light golden brown, shaggy, and hung just below his chin. Ian obviously inherited his black hair from his mother and grandfather.

The mood in the room was quiet and somber. The plan so far had gone smoothly, but everyone knew the rescue was going to be difficult. Alex still had an appetite, and Lily couldn't help but smile when he reached for seconds. Perhaps the enormous helping of carbohydrates would help give him the energy he'd soon need.

"I planted a tree in the backyard in honor of Danny," Ian suddenly said, breaking the silence in the room. He glanced around at everyone. "I feel honored to have been his friend. I've never met anyone who helped people the way Danny did."

An image of Kate and Danny holding hands on the school bus popped into Lily's mind. That's how she liked to remember him. He'd always been sweet and affectionate with Kate. But Ian's words couldn't be truer, and Lily was happy that people would remember Danny in that way. Ian could have said Danny was a computer genius or that he loved the History Channel, which he always had playing, wherever he was. But instead Ian chose to remember him for his best quality, and that was a quality hard to find in people. It was because of Danny that Lily had managed to stay safe all these years. Being on the run would never have worked, had it not been for him.

"The tree is a cherry blossom, which is my favorite," Mrs. Webster replied. "It will look beautiful this spring."

Lily studied Ian's mother for a moment. Her name was Martha, but Lily decided she would address her as Mrs. Webster. There was something about her demeanor that somehow demanded re-spect. She didn't appear easy going. Her posture was stick- straight, and Lily imagined there was a tremendous will keeping her shoulders stiff. Her quiet mannerisms reminded Lily of an old fashioned bar-oness. Lily felt she was neither attractive nor unattractive, but simply plain, with dark circles under her eyes. Perhaps caring for her elderly father was exhausting work, leaving her nothing left over for herself.

"That's very nice," Alex replied to the comments about Dan-ny. It was still painful to think about his friend, and no one wanted to add sad thoughts to their mind, even though Alex understood that wasn't Ian's intention.

The broccoli was too mushy and overcooked, but the rolls were perfectly soft and delicious. Lily broke off a piece of bread and chewed it slowly. She wasn't surprised that the conversation died, and everyone began to clean up the table, carrying dishes to the sink. Soon, Alex and Patrick would leave. Ian would record her addressing the world, and then tomorrow morning, when Kate was pretending to heal people in the Square, Ian would run the video.

As Mrs. Webster cleared the last dish, she offered an apolo-getic look to Alex. "I'm sorry the meal wasn't better. It was a last minute throw together."

"We appreciate it, and your help. I enjoy pasta, in case you didn't notice," Alex winked at her.

Lily knew most women enjoyed her brother's charm. Alex was a handsome man, well built, and very polite. Lily regretted that her healing ability had interfered with her brother being able to live a normal life. He should be married with a few kids, and Lily was certain, it was her fault he wasn't.

"Lily, I'd like a word with you on the porch." Patrick handed his glass to Mrs. Webster before looking at Lily with a serious expres-sion.

Lily nodded and watched as he followed the other men into the kitchen. Mrs. Webster let out a sigh, and set her hand on her father's arm. Steve was wheelchair bound, hard of hearing, as well as unable to speak clearly, having lost his ability from a massive stroke. His words were slow and slightly slurred, and for a moment Lily wondered if she possessed the power to heal him. In the past her ability had never worked on degenerative diseases. It only seemed to work on fresh wounds and malignancies, not ailments of old age. She wished she could reverse the damage done to his brain, but that would not be possible.

Mrs. Webster offered to take Lily's plate, noticing she hadn't eaten much. "I can bring you up some of my homemade chili later. This meal wasn't very good, but I didn't have enough chili for everyone, so I had to improvise."

"I'm not that hungry." Lily handed her the plate. "You mustn't apologize, we are all truly grateful for your hospitality and kindness." The woman was too kind, and Lily wondered if worry and pain were what caused the creases on her pale face. She moved slowly, with that impeccable posture. Lily unthinkingly stood up and placed her hand on Mrs. Webster's shoulder. The woman winced slightly, and then stepped back. "Tell me what's wrong with you," Lily asked softly with concern.

"I have fibromyalgia. It's a severe case, and they tell me there is no cure." Mrs. Webster glanced down at the floor. "At least not for me anyway, but I try not to make a big bother of it, just try to get along as best I can."

Lily wondered if that really meant she wasn't able to get the medical help she needed, or if she'd tried and nothing had worked. Either way, she didn't know if she'd ever healed a person with fibromyalgia before. "I'd like to try and cure you, if you'll let me."

Looking at Lily, with slightly watery eyes, Mrs. Webster shook her head. "I'm sorry, Lily, but I don't believe in your power. I don't believe you can help me."

No one had ever said that before in such a kind way and Lily leaned back in surprise. The words were spoken sincerely and with kindness, not malice. Many times in the past she'd been confronted by people who did not believe she could truly heal. She'd been called

117

a fraud, a liar, and even the devil. But Mrs. Webster was kind, and her demeanor was different. It was an exhaustion that Lily now picked up on. "It's okay if you don't believe. You don't have to, and you don't need to do anything. I'd just like to hold your hand for a moment if you'll let me."

She wasn't sure if she could help this woman, but if she could heal first degree burns, severe wounds, and cancer, why couldn't she heal a disease that causes pain and tenderness in all the joints and muscles of the body? As Mrs. Webster reluctantly offered her hand, Lily closed her eyes and attempted to feel the energy in the woman's body. Lily tried to build her own healing forces, feel her unique heat waves and vigor flow from her hand. She pushed her power, feeling tingling in her hands and toes, and fighting the irritating fatigue that set in moments after she used her ability.

"I'm sorry," Lily whispered. She worried that her ability might be gone. The strength was no longer in her.

Chapter 17

Patrick cleared his throat, and Lily wondered how long he'd been standing in the doorway. Mrs. Webster picked another plate off the table, and then glanced down at her father in the wheel chair. "Dad, I'll take you to your room in a few minutes."

"I'll help you with the dishes."

"No, Lily. Please, go be with your family before they leave." Mrs. Webster offered her a warm smile, and then looked at Patrick. "The back yard has a lovely walking path."

If Mrs. Webster was holding back any disappointment she didn't show it, Lily thought, as she followed Patrick out the front door. He took her hand and led her down the steps to the side of the house.

"Here." He placed a piece of paper in her hand. "This is the phone number and address where my family is staying. I want you to hide this somewhere in the house, so if anything happens to us—"

"Patrick, nothing…" He put his fingers over her mouth to stop her from interrupting him.

"Lily, it's just in case. If anything happens, you can go there. You can stay with them, and my brother will keep you safe." He moved his fingers and pulled Lily into his arms. "I just want you to be safe."

Here she thought he would tell her to notify his family if he was dead… to maybe give them a message from him. But all along, all he'd ever done or thought about was keeping her safe. She pulled back, and stared into his eyes.

They both moved at the same time and at the same pace, seeking each other. "I don't want to leave you," he whispered against her mouth. "I'll come back for you, and I'll keep Alex safe."

She didn't want to think, cry, or beg him to stay. She wanted to be strong. The night air had given her chills, but now Patrick was keeping her warm. Being wrapped in his arms felt as safe as anywhere there could be in the world right now. Once again, she realized it felt like home.

He gave her a feeling that not even Alex or Kate could give. "When you come back, we're going to be together." She meant that in every sense of the word. "I want to be with you."

"Yes," he agreed.

"Why haven't we done this more?" Lily asked, as she pulled back just enough to look in his eyes.

"Your brother... need I say more?"

Lily groaned with the frustration of knowing exactly what he meant. Alex was always with them, watching, or more like patrolling. "He can't stop this, Patrick." Whatever it was they felt for each other, it was real, and growing stronger by the moment. "I'm going to tell Alex to back off."

"Hey!" Alex shouted from the front porch. "Where did you guys go?"

Lily leaned away from Patrick, and her eyebrows drew together. "He really does have terrible timing. I'm going to take care of this once and for all."

"No." Patrick took her face in his hands again. "We don't have time, sweetheart. We have to go now, the helicopter won't wait for us, and I'm not going to have you and Alex at odds right now. We'll solve this when we get back." He kissed her one more time, and then led her to the front of the house with his arm around her.

Alex frowned when he saw the look on both their faces. "Ian is ready to do the video. We will contact him when it's time to run the tape, and I'll try to call you, Lil, but if I can't, don't worry." He walked toward her. "We'll be back with Kate."

120

Any anger toward her brother vanished the moment he said Kate's name. No matter what, Alex always protected and loved his twin sisters. Lily knew he only wanted what was best for her. She hugged her brother tightly. "I love you, Alex." There was nothing more she needed to say. She already knew he would do everything in his power to stay alive and get Kate back.

"I'll take care of him, sis," Alex whispered in her ear.

Patrick put his bag in the trunk of the car and shut the door. Lily looked up at her brother, and touched his scruffy face. "Be safe," she told him trying to keep her tears in check. Then she walked over to Patrick and hugged him tight.

"I love you, Lily," he told her. His eyes darted toward Alex. He'd wanted her brother to hear the words, and know that he was done being careful. He wasn't going to hide his feelings.

Lily leaned back with tears in her eyes and a lump in her throat. He'd said the words first. "I love you, Patrick." And in front of Alex, they kissed each other long and deep.

"For crying out loud, this is too much!" Alex threw his hands up in the air and walked to the driver's side of the car. "Get in the damn car, Prick!"

Both Patrick and Lily laughed. "I'll forever be Prick now." Patrick's smile vanished as he sat in the car. As they drove away, he kept his eyes on Lily until he could no longer see her.

There was a bright halo around the moon. The sky was black, offering the view of thousands of stars. A gentle breeze blew strands of hair in her face, but Lily brushed them away along with her tears. She thought about Kate, about Mrs. Webster, Connie, and even Sage. She thought about all the brave women she had the honor of knowing, and how each woman had dealt with her problems. Connie lived strong and cared for her children while battling cancer. Martha took care of her father and her family while living with chronic pain, and still she managed to walk straight and tall. Kate had survived the harsh treatment inflicted on her by the government. So many women rose to the occasion in times of sorrow and pain. Lily would stay strong and do the same. She tipped her head back to stare at the moon. I'll stay strong, no matter what.

She walked back to the house, holding the piece of paper Patrick gave her. She glanced down at his handwriting. His brother's name was spelled out, along with a phone number and an address. Then at the bottom of the paper she read the words, "I love you, Lily. Not because you healed me, but because you heal me." She knew exactly what he meant. Her hands shook as she folded the tiny piece of paper. Walking over to the flower pot of mums, she gently dug a hole in the soil to bury the note. She felt like she'd been healed just reading his words. He loved her, and she'd told him how she felt. A weight was lifted, and her life was changed now. Because of Patrick she could feel hope.

Chapter 18

Ian was very precise with how he wanted to tape Lily. He'd made a backdrop of white cloth in the empty guest bedroom. Lily was to stand in the baby blue painted room in front of a white sheet and stare into the camera. She ignored the color of the walls which reminded her of the solitary room at Hope Hospital. Perhaps the blue room was fate, in that it helped add to her emotions… emotions she would need to show to the world. Her speech needed to be sincere to reach the heartstrings of the American people.

Lily took a seat on the high stool. "I'm ready."

"Okay, I'm going to count and you watch my fingers. When I get to one, you can begin talking. Remember to try and speak fast. I don't know how long the airtime will last, so you want to make your point right away." Ian hit a few switches, and then began to count. "5, 4, 3," then silence.

"My name is Lily McCallister, and I only have a stolen moment to tell you the truth. I'm not in the Square healing people, as you have seen on TV. The government has my twin sister, Kate, in their custody, and she's being forced to pretend. They are lying to you as they lied to me. My sister did not die and they are now making her pretend to be me. I need your help to rescue her. Please help me get Kate away from the people holding her hostage. I have helped many Americans, and now I'm asking for your help, because I can't do it alone. Please, if you are in the Square, do anything you can to aid in her rescue. I will heal as many people as I can on my own, but the truth is, the government doesn't want me to heal everyone.

They are only interested in using me for their own political agenda, and everything they say is a lie." Lily did not have to force tears; they came naturally streaming down her face. "Please help save my sister. I have always used my ability to help heal people, please, please, help me." Her words cracked with the last words, and Ian stopped the camera. There was nothing more she needed to say.

"I think that was good." Ian handed her a Kleenex. "I know people will see how real it was." He began pressing buttons on the camera. "I'll air this as soon as I get the word from Alex." He turned away and began winding up wire. "I wish Danny were here to see this. I think he'd be proud."

A part of Danny was there, because Lily felt him in her heart. She felt the same way and missed him terribly. Her heart ached with the need to hear that Alex, Patrick and Kate were safe.

"I'll get my stuff moved out and blow up the air mattress so you can get some sleep."

Lily glanced around the small room, with light blue walls and beige carpet. The inside door was even painted blue. "I'm sorry, Ian, but I can't sleep in here. Would you mind if I slept someplace else? I have a problem with blue rooms."

Ian looked at her puzzled for a few moments. "It's not a problem at all. I'll just put the air mattress in my room."

A knock sounded on the door, and Mrs. Webster stuck her head in the room. "Are you finished?"

"Yes. She did great."

Lily wondered why Ian was suddenly nervous. He had glanced away from her and was moving fast to put away the camera equipment.

"I was listening outside the door," Mrs. Webster smiled. "We didn't want to make you nervous by being in the room. You did well, Lily. I think the American people will all want to help you."

"Thank you." Lily walked to the door, eager to leave the blue room. "I hope it's okay that I've asked Ian if I can sleep anywhere else in the house. I can't stay in this room."

Mrs. Webster gave Lily the same puzzled look that Ian had given her. "Ian has a big room, and you will be far enough away from my dad's snoring. He can be pretty loud." She nodded to her son. "I'll show Lily to the bathroom while you set up the air mattress."

The bathroom was small and outdated, with a chip in the white porcelain sink and yellow striped wall paper. But Lily didn't care as she stared at her reflection. What would happen now? Would people see that the woman on the tape did not look the same as the woman in the Square? Kate might be her identical twin, but right now Kate's face was fuller, her hair wasn't as long, and her skin wasn't tan from the sun. Lily would go to bed and will herself to sleep, because the sooner she slept, the sooner morning would come. And the day when hopefully her sister would be rescued and the world would hear the truth.

With what seemed only a few short hours later, a soft pattering sound woke Lily. She opened her eyes and glanced around the bedroom. Orange and tan striped wallpaper covered the wall that Ian's bed was against. Two other walls were orange, and the closet wall was tan. There was a dresser, and an office desk, where Ian currently sat typing. When Lily sat up to stretch, Ian glanced over his shoulder. "Sorry, did I wake you?"

"It's okay, I heard you typing."

"Well I was about to wake you soon anyway. I know you won't want to miss the TV."

Lily shot out of bed. "Did you do it? Did you already air the tape? Did Alex call?"

Ian stared at her a moment wearing the same clothes she had on yesterday. She'd learned to sleep in her clothes in case she had to run at any given moment. He wondered how she'd ever have a normal life. He cleared his throat. "Haven't aired the tape yet, but I heard from Alex. They are at the Square, and they've located Kate in a hotel close by. She is supposed to be in the Square at noon, so I'm going to air the tape then." The idea was that if enough people could hear the message, then hopefully the crowd would help. A large mob

125

of people acting in support would aid Patrick and Alex in the rescue.

"So things are okay so far?"

Reading the worry on Lily's face, Ian wanted to offer her reassurance. "Everything is perfect so far. It's only eleven, so you have plenty of time to shower, maybe drink some coffee."

"Thank you." She wasted no time. She wanted to hurry, so she moved fast. Her pulse raced in anticipation of the plan, and she wished she could be there with them, but she knew Alex and Patrick couldn't focus on the rescue if they had to worry about her safety.

Connie's daughter Anna had given Lily a few of her outfits so that she could have clothes to wear for the week. While Lily appreciated having something clean to wear, she didn't feel comfortable in the tight fitting black leggings and pink shirt. It was simply not her style. When Mrs. Webster offered her some of her clothes, Lily accepted. The pants were a little too long, but she rolled them up and with a belt they weren't too baggy. The long sleeve shirt was actually soft and a clean crisp white. She ran a brush through her long hair, gently pulling the tangles out, and then brushed her teeth.

Ian answered his cell phone on the second ring. "She's in the shower," he told Alex. "I will." He set the phone down and then walked over to unplug the air mattress. He had everything put away when Lily came back in the room. "Your brother called while you were in the shower. He asked me to make sure you eat before I air the tape."

Lily was upset she'd missed his call. "Are you doing it in here?" She could see his computer was set up with four different monitors. There was a small flat screen TV on the wall, with plenty of electronics on the shelf below.

"Yes. You can sit on the bed if you want." He glanced at his watch. "Alex said to run the video at 11:30. So in five minutes…"

The windowsill was big enough for Lily to sit on. She liked being by the window, looking out at the sun's rays beaming through the tree branches. The street in front of the house was lined with big oak trees. The large lot offered peace and quiet from the distant neighbors. The sun was shining, and Lily could appreciate the clear beautiful sky. "Have you had any radiation in this area?" Reports had indicated that a lot of Canada was damaged by radiation blowing over from the United States.

"Not too much. We are safer here than some areas." Ian was preoccupied with typing on his computer. "The cancer rate is expected to increase, and sadly infant mortality rates are higher. There is also growing concern over the lack of fresh, clean water, but that's not really anything new."

"Yeah, it's scary what wars do to the planet." Lily sighed at the thought of all the massive destruction.

"It's not war, Lily." Ian turned in his chair after using a clipped tone. "Wars have been raging since the beginning of time. The difference is that back then when humans were annihilated, at least the planet remained intact. The soil could absorb blood, and the plants and trees would still grow healthy enough for animals to eat. Now the soil absorbs a chemical that kills all living things. This time when humans go down, we're taking the planet with us."

The thought sent a shiver down Lily's spine. She'd obviously hit a soft spot that Ian was passionate about. "I can heal people, but I can't heal this." She pointed to the window, and leaned her head against the glass.

Ian crossed his legs, and concern etched his face as he studied the famous healer. "Eventually it will all grow back. Earth will still be here, but it will be different. People will be different." It was one of the reasons he felt so determined to help Lily. She was beyond special, and the world was in desperate need of something special.

"Different." That was the word that described her life. The world changing drastically all around her made things different. Her life would never be constant… normal.

She thought of Kate, Alex and even her mother. But in her mind she had a clear image of Patrick. In a world that was always changing, only one thing could remain the same. "Love," she whispered.

"I'm sorry, what did you say?" Ian asked.

She stood up, and rolled her shoulders. "Nothing. It's hard to sit here and not help. What can I do?"

Ian shrugged his shoulders. "There isn't much you can do. I'm going to roll the video right now with a push of this button. It's as easy as that." He turned in his chair and set his hands over the keyboard. "It's rolling right now." He glanced at the computer screen on the left, which was muted, but showed a news station. Suddenly Lily's face cut through the current broadcast.

Walking over to the desk, Lily stared at the monitor. "That's too easy. I don't get it."

"I know how all this stuff works because I work in the industry, and I also happen to have some of Danny's computer skills." He felt pride in his ability to hack through a network. "It helps that I placed a wire feed at the news station months ago. They will find where the wire's located and cut it, but so far your words are reaching people." Ian stood up, crossing his arms over his chest. "I also have this going viral on every social media available. YouTube alone will reach millions." He watched as the screen suddenly went blank. "And now it's done, they cut it." He smiled at her. "Your entire message got out; they didn't cut it in time."

"Let's hope it works."

"I think it will. People need to know what's going on. Sometimes I wish I could just slap the entire nation and yell, wake up people! Pay attention!" He turned to watch Lily pacing back and forth in front of the window. He knew she was nervous. "You know… staying here and being safe is the best help you can give this planet. You're our—"

His words were cut off by the sound of Mrs. Webster screaming. It sounded as if the front door had been kicked in, and Mr. Webster was shouting.

"Stay here!" Ian whispered harshly before heading out the bedroom door.

Chapter 19

Standing by the window, Lily glanced out and saw the familiar face of the man she recognized from the cabin. He'd killed some of the government agents who were with Patrick's boss. He was the man Patrick knocked out cold. Her heart sank as she realized it was probably just one more group of people who wanted her for their own purpose.

More screams sounded from downstairs, a door slammed, and Lily could hear what sounded like shuffling on the floor. She heard Ian shout, "She's not here!" A gunshot followed, and then three more shots. Four shots for a family of four.

Blood rushed to Lily's head, pounding heavily behind her ears, and fear buckled her knees. She couldn't bear the thought of another family being murdered because of her. This wasn't supposed to happen. Alex promised her they'd be safe. "Safe." The word made Lily search the room, her mind scrambling for a place to hide. If Ian and his family were just killed, they died to keep her safe. She had to hide, and do everything she could to stay guarded.

There was no furniture in the room except Ian's bed, his desk, and a tall dresser.

Hearing the footsteps on the stairs, she knew they'd search all the rooms of the house looking for her. Suddenly her eye caught the cupboard of Ian's desk. It was probably just small enough for her to fit inside. Please be empty, she thought, as she pulled it open. All that was inside was a small box full of CDs. Her pulse quickened as she quietly set the box on top of the desk and folded herself inside the small cubbyhole. She closed the door, just as footsteps sounded in the hallway.

The man inside Ian's room first looked under the bed. There were a lot of boxes and bags under the bed, typical clutter one might find. Next he opened the closet door. Lily heard the scrape of hangers being moved across a pole. She tried to slow her breathing, praying the man would not think to look in the desk. It appeared far too small to fit an average size human being.

"She's not here!" shouted a voice from the stairs.

"I think we missed her," said the man from Ian's bedroom.

"We'll stay here, in case they come back."

"No. I don't think they stay in one place too long, and check this out." The men shuffled over to Ian's desk and stared at the computer screens. "Damn. They're in New York," said a hard deep voice.

"Let's go."

The sounds of footsteps faded and the house became silent. Lily released the sob she'd been holding. Though the cramped position hurt, Lily couldn't bring herself to move. She wasn't prepared to find the bodies of the family that had been kind enough to help her. If they were hurt, she wouldn't be able to heal them. She imagined Eric's little body in her arms, and how she'd used every ounce of her energy to save his life. It drained her, leaving her weak and unconscious for days. She wouldn't have enough in her for all of them, and she couldn't afford to be left in that state again, with no one there to watch over her.

Tears streamed down her face, as she pictured Ian, the 23 year old, with his entire life ahead of him. What was it he was going to say to her, before Martha screamed? 'You're our...' What? Death. I'm your death, Lily told herself.

She slowly opened the cupboard door. It hurt to stand up, her hands were shaking, her stomach felt nauseated. She walked over to the window and peered out. The trees blew in the soft wind, and the sun shone down on the quiet house. Part of her wanted to lie down in Ian's bed, pull the blankets over her entire body and stay there in the fetal position until sleep took over. But now there was another new threat to warn Alex and Patrick about. That man she'd seen at the cabin was somehow able to track them to the Webster's home. They were serious about finding her, and obviously had the means.

Ian had his cell phone on him, and that was the only way she could reach her brother. She'd have to be brave, find Ian's lifeless body and take the phone from his pocket. She took her backpack out from under the bed, and pulled out the revolver.

As much as she hated guns, she felt a wave of relief settle in her gut as her hand wrapped around the handle. If that group had left a man behind to wait just in case, then Lily wouldn't hesitate to shoot him. She proceeded to walk down the stairs.

The sound of her feet creaking on the stairway reminded her of the first day she met Patrick. He'd been the enemy coming to take her away, as his steps had sounded on the cabin stairs. That seemed like a million years ago, so much happened to them since that day. A shuffle sounded below her and she froze on the steps. Her heart leaped as she realized the sound was coming from the closet under the stairs.

With her fingers securely wrapped around the gun, Lily pulled the closet door open. Relief swamped her as she stared down at four faces. "Oh thank you, God!" she cried as she allowed the emotion to pour from her eyes. "I thought you were dead." She removed the gags from all four of their mouths.

Ian was the first to speak. "Get some scissors from the kitchen so you can cut these zip ties."

"Where did you hide?" Mrs. Webster asked.

"Make sure they're gone," Marty said, his voice sounding worried and hoarse.

"Hang on." Lily went for the scissors. The relief made her almost weak, and she couldn't stop crying. She uncut their zip ties, and pulled each one of them into a tight embrace.

Ian took the gun from Lily's hand. "I'll take this for now." She was too shaky and emotional to continue holding a gun.

Mrs. Webster held on to Lily. "I'm so glad you're okay. You truly *are* a gift from God."

Lily pulled back and smiled through her tears.

"It worked. You healed me." True happiness brightened Martha's face. "You've completely healed me." She hugged her tightly one more time, unable to express her gratitude. For the first time in her life, she felt not an ounce of pain.

"Where did you hide?" Ian wanted to know.

"Your desk cupboard." Lily wanted to hug Ian again, but he was already helping his grandfather to his wheelchair. "I'm so sorry I put you all in harm's way. You could have been killed because of me."

"You're worth the risk, Lily," Mrs. Webster replied and allowed her husband to pull her into his arms.

"I have to get you out of here now. Plan B is to take you to another safe house." Ian touched the screen of his phone. "Look at this." He handed Lily his phone.

She glanced down at the YouTube video of a mass riot in New Yorks Square. The news headline flashed, "Save the McCallister twins!"

"It's working! Go get your bag." He turned to his parents. "Take Grandpa and go to Aunt Isabelle's house and stay there. I'll call you when it's safe to return home. I've got another phone upstairs that you can use." It was a safe phone that couldn't be traced.

It wasn't right for them to leave their home, and Lily didn't want to put the family out. "Those men are headed to New York now. I don't think they will come back. I heard them say—"

"Lily, if they found us, then others can find us," Ian interrupted her. "I promised Alex and Patrick I'd keep you and everyone else in my family safe." He set his hands on top of his unkempt hair. "God, I failed them." He and his entire family could have been shot.

Ian's anguish made Lily's heart ache. "You haven't failed, Ian. You got me on TV. You did what we needed, and we're all alive."

"And I intend to keep it that way."

The cat leaped from the banister and jumped past Lily into Mrs. Webster's arms. As Lily climbed the stairs she listened to Mrs. Webster's soft words of comfort to her pet. Grabbing the backpack, Lily stopped cold when she glanced at the computer monitor. She was watching an image of fighting, and then a newscaster was saying something important. Lily quickly moved to the monitor and pressed the volume button up so she could hear.

"We have confirmed reports that one of the twins has been shot. We have not yet learned if it is in fact Kate McCallister or Lily. There is much chaos and confusion, as the American people want answers. We have another reporter at the Holiday Inn, where the shooting took place. Bill, back to you."

Ian ran into the room, and immediately began turning off monitors, and erasing hard drives.

"What are you doing? I want to hear that!" Lily tried to turn the monitor back on. "I need to see what's happening."

Ian blocked her hand. "I have to erase all the evidence. You don't need to see what's happening, because we won't know the truth until we talk to Alex." He didn't want her scared or losing hope, and right now he was eager to reach the safe house.

Lily couldn't stop her hands from trembling and forcefully grabbed Ian by the arm. "They said Kate was shot! There was shooting at her hotel, I need to watch the news!"

After the computer system was erased and wiped clean, Ian began unplugging the mainframe. "We have to get out of here. My parents are waiting to say goodbye to you." She wasn't listening, and he knew she was half frantic and out of her mind. He grabbed her hard by the shoulders. "Lily, my family isn't safe here. You're putting them in danger by staying here. Those men could come back, or some other group. Do what I tell you to do!" He knew that would get her focused. He finished the last things he needed to do.

Staring out the car window, Lily noticed autumn had already turned the trees from their glorious bright colors to the drab brown of dead

133

leaves. The sun was hidden behind the clouds, casting a gray gloomy light as they drove to an unknown destination.

"We're almost there," Ian told her. He glanced at Lily, but wondered if she'd heard a word he said. She was staring at the road, a look of empty despair on her beautiful face.

The Canadian radio stations were giving brief updates on what they knew regarding the possible shooting in New York of the famous twin. Ian turned the radio off. "I'm sure Alex will call, and we'll know the truth soon enough." He didn't know what to say to comfort her.

"It all went wrong," Lily mumbled. She felt numb. There'd been no word from Alex or Patrick. If it hadn't gone terribly wrong, one of them would have called Ian by now. But the fact was, Kate was shot, and she had no idea if her brother and Patrick were alive.

Ian pulled into the driveway of an old colonial house, located on a street with homes on either side. A few kids rode bikes down the sidewalk wearing hats and gloves, and an older man was picking up leaves from his yard. "Put this on, and keep your face down till we're inside." He handed her a baseball cap and sunglasses.

So this is where she'd hide while waiting to hear confirmation that everyone she loved was dead. Ian went around to her side of the door, and opened it for her. "Come on, Lily." He reached for her hand. Her legs felt heavy, and her eyes stung as Ian guided her through the front door of the house. As soon as he closed the door, she dropped to her knees and began sobbing. "I can't do this anymore." She had promised herself she'd be strong no matter what, but the pain was unbearable. She couldn't face losing her sister again, after knowing she was alive, and she'd never survive the pain of losing her brother and Patrick. Even as she rocked with tremendous grief, she could still feel Patrick's lips on her own. Her heart ached as if it were literally tearing apart.

She felt Ian's arms wrap around her, and somehow he was sitting on the floor beside her, gently rubbing her back. "It's too soon to start assuming the worst. Something may have happened with

their phones to prevent them from calling. I'm sure they're all right."
He continued rubbing her back all the while wondering, what on
earth had gone wrong?

Chapter 20

Two days ago, a man named Dave had held Kate's hand and cried. He believed that Lily McCallister used her healing powers to cure his radiation poisoning. He looked into the most beautiful red and gold eyes he'd ever seen, and felt the miracle he'd been granted. At age thirty-two he'd walked away feeling an improved state of health and a euphoria he could not contain. Lily McCallister saved his life.

Like most Americans, Dave believed Lily had the power to heal. With so many videos on social media of her extraordinary ability to close wounds, it would be hard to believe that Lily was a fake. There were thousands of testimonies, and doctors who re-checked cancer in people who'd been healed, and the proof was undeniable. The fact even the government was involved and had top scientists from the World Health Organization experimenting on Lily made it hard to doubt her. Dave wasn't sure if she was an alien, or somehow spiritually divine, but he believed Lily was a good person who truly had the ability to heal and wanted to use it for the greater good. He also leaned toward believing the conspiracy theory that indicated Lily's twin was killed by the government testing and too many cruel experiments. Many people questioned if the twins were under government control of their own free will, or if they were held captive. Either way, Dave didn't trust the government. Never had, and never would.

Now Dave stood outside on the cold street of New York, where the autumn wind whipped at his face. He pulled the collar of his jacket up and stared at the hotel he believed Kate McCallister was being held in. Security around the building and the Square was very tight. The twin was guarded by federal agents, and no one could get too close to her. It was no secret that each day an entourage of government agents escorted Lily to the Square to heal the long line of people waiting. Except, now Dave knew it wasn't really Lily. He saw the video that had gone viral just hours ago, and he believed it. He'd been duped. No wonder he wasn't feeling as well as he had the day he believed he'd been healed. He'd been riding on a placebo of happiness. But today, his symptoms were as strong as ever, and he knew he was dying.

His rage slowly simmered at the thought of Kate being forced to pretend. Lily's plea to the world was to help get her sister back and out from under the control of the government. Dave was dying, and he had nothing to lose. Now was his chance to help the most famous woman on earth and make things right. He'd been lied to, and given false hope. The government needed to pay for its crime. He thought of the other people who'd believed they'd been healed. Did they watch the video of Lily telling the truth, and were they as outraged? He wondered if Kate would be escorted to the Square today, or would they try to secretly transfer her to a hidden location? He was watching the building. He had a plan to get inside and keep an eye on her, but now he saw the angry mob of people approaching the building. Yeah, he wasn't alone. Americans wanted to free Kate. They wanted to help Lily.

A riot broke out in the streets when the desperate people waiting in line to be healed heard the news. The line stretched along sidewalks, and in front of tall glass buildings. People working in their offices who saw the news left their jobs to inform the sick what was happening. It was all a lie.

Everyone loved watching the famous healer on TV. It gave people hope. All the radiation-exposed and sick were going to be cured, and pregnant moms wouldn't have to lose their babies. The cancer rate would not annihilate half the planet and perhaps a real cure could be found thanks to Lily's DNA. But then Lily's video shocked and outraged everyone. It was all over the TV and social media. Ian had succeeded in getting it out there.

Kate was sitting at the table in her hotel suite, finishing her lunch. Three men sat on chairs positioned around the window, and two more stood by the door. The men were not allowed to have the television on because it was important that Kate always be kept in the dark about what was happening in the world. Outside the door, three more agents guarded the hallway. Today was Kate's last day to perform in the Square. Nathan Palmer had told her she was being transferred to another hospital. Apparently the Hope Medical Clinic was destroyed by a fire, but that's all Palmer had told her. Kate did her job, and now she was going to be allowed to see Danny. That's what the doctor promised her, and soon she'd be reunited with her sister.

The medications Kate was forced to take made her sick. For the past several days, she'd pretended to swallow the pills, but then flushed them down the toilet. Her mind was finally clear, though she knew it was important to appear medicated. It was another act she was tired of. She was weary of holding strangers' hands, staring into their hope-filled eyes and pretending. People would cry and reach for her, wanting to embrace her as they poured out their praise. They would swear they felt healed, but of course it was simply a placebo effect. The mind was incredibly powerful, and given that kind of hope and reassurance, it was more willing to believe. Kate suspected that half the people in line weren't really sick at all and the government had staged it. Kate hated having to lie.

She glanced over at one of the men who constantly watched her. She called him Creeper. His eyes were always on her, making her feel like she had no privacy. Creeper gave her a sardonic smile, making her anxious to return to the hospital, a place she never thought she'd want to see again.

Suddenly, gunshots sounded in the hallway. All the agents in the room stood at attention and pulled guns from their holsters. Creeper moved to Kate's side motioning for her to remain still. He smelled like cheap cologne and the Fritos he'd eaten earlier. The gunshots sounded closer, and she moved to stand in the corner of the room.

Chapter 21

The house was cold and quiet when Lily opened her eyes. She knew right away she'd cried herself to sleep with her head on Ian's leg. Bless his heart, he never left her side.

"Are you okay?" His voice sounded gruff and sleepy.

"Yes. I'm sorry." She took hold of his hands, as he helped her to her feet. "You must be very uncomfortable." They'd fallen asleep on the floor.

"My legs are a little stiff, but I'm good. You needed to sleep." He bent down to touch his toes and stretch his muscles.

Lily walked over to the window and peered out. "It looks like it's late in the afternoon. How long did I sleep?"

"Three hours." He glanced at his watch. "It's almost four. Another two hours and it will be dark. I hate that about fall. Winters are even worse." He turned on the floor lamp in the family room. There was very little furniture. A kitchen table and chairs, and one black rocking chair in the corner of a big empty family room. The walls were bare, so Ian wondered if the house had been abandoned or was in foreclosure. He'd been given the location to the house along with the key from Alex. Thinking of Alex, Ian pulled his cell phone from his pocket. "I'm going to try calling your bro… oh damn!"

Lily swung around quickly to face him. "What?"

"I'm so sorry, Lily. Somehow the phone turned off, and I have three missed calls." He pressed a button to redial the number and handed the phone to her. The phone just rang.

"Oh God," she placed her hand over her racing heart. "They

aren't answering."

Ian took the phone from her and tried again. Lily couldn't contain her anger and disappointment. "How could you let this happen? You know the phone is our lifeline to them! Ian, you should've been checking it regularly, and had it in your hand!" She couldn't believe he'd allowed it to be accidently turned off.

"Well, I'm sorry, but with your head in my lap, I couldn't very well pull the phone out of my pocket. I'm obviously not cut out for helping you!" She was right. He should've had the phone in his hand. He should be stronger, know how to fight, and be smarter like Alex. Maybe if he was more like Lily's brother, she'd look at him with more respect. He vowed to himself that after this moment he'd change, and perhaps ask Alex for training.

Lily glanced down at the hurt in his voice. "I'm sorry. It's not your fault... it's mine. The truth is, everything's my fault, and it's a weight that is almost too heavy for me to carry. My siblings, Patrick, your parents, and so many others wouldn't be in harm's way if it wasn't for me." Ian had only tried to comfort her, and of course if she hadn't been sobbing with her head on his lap, he could've held the phone. She sat down on the hardwood floor, and scanned the room. It was cold, empty, and brown... like the season that surrounded her. Empty and desolate. How many different places had she stayed? Would she ever have a house of her own? Would her family ever be safe? Why did the Hope Medical facility just starve her? What was the point of any of this? Maybe it would have been better if she had just died.

Ian sat beside her. "If anyone gets to play a pity card, it's me. You were right; I should've had the phone in my hand all this time. I'm sorry." He set his hand on her shoulder. "You might feel responsible for this, Lily, but you're not. The world has been headed down the path of destruction for a long time. But you're the hope. It doesn't matter why you have this power. It doesn't matter if you're half alien, or a messiah. You're the hope that the cure to illness can be solved." The passion in his eyes matched the conviction in his

141

voice. "You're loved, Lily… not because you have an amazing ability to heal people, but because everything about you is kind and good."

She appreciated his words, but knew he'd been just as brainwashed by the media as the rest of the world. "There's no hope for using me as a cure. It's not going to work, Ian," she said in a low voice. "I'm not the hope of salvation." She stared into his sincere eyes. His features were not what she would consider handsome, but there was a kindness about him that made him attractive. Lily didn't know much about him other than his computer skills and he'd been friends with Danny.

"That's not true. You're—"

"How did you and Danny meet?" She interrupted him, wanting to change the subject. People believed what they'd been told, and they trusted the science. The government convinced everyone they'd been close to breakthrough technology that could eradicate disease thanks to her. Ian wouldn't change his mind, and she knew arguing was pointless.

"We met at Wayne State University, and had some classes together. After the government took you and Kate to study, Danny reached out to me." Ian leaned back, placing his hands behind him on the floor. "I guess he was desperate to find as many people as he could to join his coalition."

Lily smiled. "Aw… the Save Lily Foundation." Her heart squeezed at the thought of Danny.

"I think he saw the big picture of what was going to happen to you, long before anyone else did. I wanted to help you, because I believed you were special." Ian cleared his throat. "You are special."

"Thank you for all your help, Ian."

The cell phone rang on the floor where Ian had set it down, and Lily quickly snatched it up. "Hello?"

"Lily, it's me."

"Oh thank God!" A heavy weight was lifted at the sound of Patrick's voice.

"Everyone is okay, we have Kate."

142

She could hardly speak with the sob of relief tightening her throat.

"Lily, listen. Kate is hurt bad. We need you to start driving to the bridge. We are in Detroit now, and will be at the Ambassador Bridge soon."

"Is she going to make it, Patrick? Where's Alex? Can I talk to him or Kate?"

Patrick paused on the line. "I'm sorry, you can't talk to them right now, but trust me, there's a chance for her only if we can get to you in time. Meet us near the bridge, just before you cross over, at the welcome area rest stop. I have to hang up now."

"Wait!" She gripped the phone wanting to ask more questions, but he was gone. She didn't even get to say I love you before he ended the call. She wrapped her arms around her waist, feeling as though something was wrong. Something didn't feel right, because Patrick didn't seem like himself. Detroit was far from New York, so Lily wondered how or why they'd ended up there. But she'd have answers soon enough. She wouldn't waste time analyzing things when Kate's life was at stake.

Ian had heard the conversation through the phone. "Let's get moving." He wouldn't let Lily or Alex down. He'd get her to the bridge in time for her to heal her sister.

Chapter 22

Kate held her brother's hand as Patrick wrapped gauze around the bullet hole in her leg. "You're lucky it went clean through," Patrick told her. They were lucky no one else was hurt.

"We need to get our hands on a cell phone so we can call Lil." Alex looked at the smashed screen of his phone, unable to hit any of the numbers through the shattered glass. His phone had been damaged during a fight, and Patrick had lost his. They were in the back of a van, and a man named Howard was driving them straight out of New York City. It was their unfortunate luck that Howard didn't have a cell phone on him. There were tools lying on the floor next to Kate's head, and every time the van hit a bump, the tools bounced. Alex laid a blanket down for Kate, since the work van's carpet was filthy. He glanced at Patrick. "Has the bleeding stopped?"

"Yes. Clean shot through the fat tissue." He smiled up at Kate, and found it quite disarming how she looked like Lily. She was fuller in the face and hips, but only because she'd been able to eat, where Lily had been starved.

"Lil will fix me." Kate squeezed her brother's hand. "Tell me everything I've missed. Tell me how everyone's doing, and do you think Mom is still safe?"

Alex shook his head. Kate was so much like Lily… always worried about everyone else. "Mom's still in the hospital, and as far as I know she's safe." They never had to worry about her because she was well cared for, and living in her own make believe world. "Lily is at a safe house, which we're headed to now, and I'm better than ever, now that I have you." He bent down and kissed her on the forehead. "You girls are going to be the death of me," he teased.

"No, Lily won't let you die. Like ever," she laughed.

Patrick liked Kate. He'd been told she was enjoyable and spunky, and that was proving to be the perfect word for her. He thought about Lily, knowing she must be worried sick. He wished he hadn't lost his damn phone.

"What about Danny?" Kate squeezed her brother's hand. "They're holding him hostage, but we can get him back right?"

Alex cast a frown at Patrick. "We can't get him back, sis."

Kate felt her chest tighten at the look on her brother's face. "What? Why?"

"I'm sorry, Kate." Alex shook his head, and the pain in his eyes told her.

"No." Tears filled her eyes as Alex pulled her into his arms to comfort her. "No. They told me they had him, and he wouldn't be hurt if I pretended to be Lily. They showed me a video of him." Kate couldn't believe Danny was gone. "How do you know?"

"He's gone sis." Alex held her while she processed what he was telling her.

Patrick moved to the front of the van to sit in the passenger seat. He wished he could call Lily. He'd lost his cell phone somewhere in the hotel, or perhaps someone had lifted it from his pocket. Regardless, it was gone, and they had no way at the moment of contacting her.

They would reach the helicopter pad in twenty minutes, and the same pilot who'd flown them into New York was offering to fly them back to Canada. He was a tour guide who had airspace permission from both countries so that he could fly his customers over Niagara Falls. It wouldn't be long before Patrick could hold Lily again. His mind wandered back to their goodbye kiss. He hated being away from her.

"I can't wait to see Lil, and take a nice long bath," Kate told her brother as they were pulling up to the Webster's house. Patrick looked at her in the rear view mirror. Her eyes were red and swollen from crying, and the chipper upbeat tone of her voice was gone, replaced with a somber one. She hadn't said much, and had slept part of the way from exhaustion. Everyone's nerves were on edge, but no one could complain. The rescue had worked, and Lily should be able to heal the gunshot wound on Kate's leg.

The drive to the Webster's house was dark, as the moon was covered by clouds. It was five o'clock in the morning, and had taken all day and night to return. They might not have made it back safely had it not been for the various connections Danny had given Alex. Patrick was sorry he'd never get to meet Kate's boyfriend.

As soon as they pulled up to the house, Patrick was the first to bolt through the door, and the first to see bullet holes in the floor by the stairs. The lights were on, but he sensed no one was home. He drew out his gun and listened to the quiet. His chest tightened at the worry that instantly gripped him. "They had trouble," he shouted to Alex who was assisting Kate from the car.

Alex told Kate to wait, since she needed help walking and he was already running into the house. He wasn't concerned just yet. Ian had been told to wipe the computers clean, and to leave him a message if they had to flee to the safe house. Alex ran up to Ian's bedroom and pulled back the bedspread. The note was there: 429, 3, 12, 5. He sat down on the bed, breathing a sigh of relief.

Patrick entered the room glancing at the paper in Alex's hand. "What does that mean?"

"It means they're okay. 429 is the safe house they went to, 3 means they left on Wednesday, and 12 is the time. 5 means all five of them are okay and have left."

"Nice." Patrick followed Alex back to the car and sat in the back beside Kate. He was happy not to drive, so he could rub at the tension in his neck. He'd never needed to see a person so badly in his life. Even after his wife died, he hadn't longed for her the way he was longing for Lily. He glanced at Kate, who was nervously twirling

146

the button on the sleeve of her red wool coat. Her beautiful features, so much like Lily's, didn't help calm his nerves. He needed to speak with Lily and to know she was safe. He couldn't believe they hadn't been in contact with her yet. The one chance Alex had to finally call her, and no one answered the phone.

"She'll be there," Alex said, noticing the look on Patrick's face.

"I don't understand why you guys don't have more cell phones," Kate replied, as if she'd read Patrick's mind.

"They can be traced. We use disposable, because we can't take any chances." Alex turned a corner and pressed his foot to the gas. "We're almost there."

"They aren't here," Patrick shouted again, when he bounded through the front door and up the steps of the safe house. There was no furniture except a table and chairs and an old black rocking chair. No notes this time. Alex quickly inspected the house looking for any clues as to where they could've gone.

"Now what?" Patrick didn't bother to hide the fear and turmoil he was feeling. He glanced at Kate as she opened the car door. He shook his head at her, watching her pained expression, before he whirled back to Alex, "What the hell were we thinking, leaving her with no protection? Damn it!" He ran his hand over his painfully tight chest. "We left her with a damn computer geek who's never shot a gun in his life, and an old man in a wheelchair, and—"

"We're in Canada, Patrick!" Alex cut him off. "I figured she'd be safe in Canada of all places! No one was supposed to know we're here." He ran his hand through his hair in frustration. He needed to think, and figure out where the hell they would've gone and why Ian hadn't left any clues.

"Well someone found her, and she could be anywhere!" Patrick moved to the staircase to sit down, just as Kate hopped through the door. She glanced around the sparse house, and shivered at the quiet emptiness.

Alex immediately grabbed the rocking chair and helped ease Kate down.

"Do you have a thing going for my sister?" she asked Patrick point blank, as he set his head in his hands.

"Yes, he's got a big thing for our sister," Alex replied. His tone sounded like regret. "You might as well hear the whole story now, sis." He proceeded to explain how Patrick worked for the government and was assigned to capture Lily. He gave details as to how he and Patrick worked to rescue her from the Hope Medical Hospital. He even told her about Connie and the kids, and how Lily healed little Eric who'd almost died. When Alex was done speaking, Kate turned to study Patrick.

She'd found him quite handsome. He had a tough, rugged look that she knew her sister would find appealing. She'd assumed Patrick was just another friend of Danny's helping them out, but now she knew he was much more.

Chapter 23

The traffic cleared, but the wind picked up. An ice storm was in the forecast, and Ian turned the heat up in the car. He wasn't ready for the chilly fall temperatures, especially since he hadn't brought a jacket with him. Lily had a light Zero Polaris coat that Alex gave her for hiking. He wondered if she felt the cold or was paying attention to the drive. "You've been pretty quiet, are you okay?" He asked her. He'd hoped that hearing from Patrick, and knowing her siblings were okay would have lifted her mood, but she appeared very depressed.

Lily kept her eyes on the night sky. The clouds seemed to move alongside the car, as if in slow motion, occasionally offering a glimpse of the moon. "I'm tired," she replied softly. Both physically and emotionally drained would have been a more accurate answer.

"Are you hungry? We haven't eaten in hours."

"I'm okay."

There was a sign for a gas station at the next exit. Ian decided he'd stop and grab a few snacks, and he needed to use the bathroom. He knew Lily wouldn't want to stop. She was worried about reaching Kate in time, and wanted to get there as soon as possible.

Ian pulled between two trucks, and shut the engine off. "I'm just going to run in real quick."

Lily couldn't deny him a bathroom break, but she wasn't happy about stopping. Truth be told, she could use one as well, but she'd wait till he got back. She lowered her head to remove her seat belt, and didn't notice the men in the truck who'd spotted her sitting in the front seat.

Suddenly the driver side door opened and a man jumped in behind the wheel. He was wearing a black baseball cap, a tan jacket, and jeans. "Don't move!" he shouted at her, and pulled her by the arm when she tried to open her door. He yanked her closer, as another man opened Lily's door, and pushed his way in beside her on the seat. She struggled, but the driver already started the car and was now heading onto the expressway. She found herself sitting on the lap of a slender man, with strong arms that were wrapped securely around her.

The man in the driver's seat glanced at her. "We need you, Lily, we need your help. Stop struggling, we don't intend to hurt you!"

"Please, let me go!" Lily tried elbowing the man holding her, but his arms locked tighter around her, and she couldn't move.

"Hold still, damn it," the man holding her said. "You're a strong little thing."

"Please, my friend will be worried about me. I'll help you if you take me back to get my friend."

"My ten year old son has radiation poisoning." Lily stopped struggling and stared at the driver. "My wife just died 7 months ago, and I can't lose him too. You have to save him, Lily, or I'll never let you go." The driver's nostrils flared.

How could Lily refuse such a request, even one made in such a threatening manner? Children were her weakness. She believed no child should ever have to die. She always chose to use her gift on children. It's what drew the attention of the government and brought more awareness to her fame. She'd visit children's hospitals and leave an entire wing of sick kids, completely cured. She knew she couldn't go anywhere, and the men wouldn't turn around for Ian. She was alone in this, and would have to figure out how to reach Kate. People were suffering and dying, and she'd never be free of the constant need to save a life. Her life would always be this way. "I'll heal your son, but only if you make me a promise."

"What?" Both men said at the same time.

"I was headed to the bridge to heal my sister. She's been hurt

150

and needs me. If you promise to take me to the bridge right after I heal your son, then I'll do it."

The driver visibly relaxed his body. "Yes of course. I'm sorry we had to do this. I saw you sitting in that car, and I knew you're our only hope. Is it true what they say about your sister pretending to be you?"

"Can you let loose a little please?" Her arms were hurting from his death grip. The man let go, and she wiggled to the side to get more comfortable, and was able to see the face of the man holding her. "Yes, it's true. We were able to rescue Kate, but she's been shot." The man appeared young, perhaps her age. He had a boyish face, with freckles over the bridge of his nose. His eyes were blue, and his lips were thin. He had a look of concern on his face, not hostility or cruelty. "What are your names?" She asked them.

"We're not telling you. We know you remember the name of everyone you've ever met. We don't want you turning us in," the driver said.

Grimly she chuckled. "I couldn't turn you in even if I wanted to. The police, the government… everyone, is after me. I'm completely at your mercy, so I'll trust you to help me after I heal your son."

"You've got a deal." Both men were quiet a moment while they looked at each other. Then the driver nodded his head and continued. "My name is Leo, and my brother's name is Allen. We live a few miles from here. My wife and son were visiting her parents in Indiana when the Power Plant exploded. Her parents brought my family back to me, but they were all real sick. My wife was out shopping too close to where the explosion happened. She was exposed to high levels of radiation. She was unhealthy to begin with, battling Lupus for years. My son was always real healthy, but for a year now he's been slowly deteriorating, and I've been told there's nothing can be done for him."

Lily didn't miss the catch in his voice, and felt remorse. "I'm sorry."

"We were on our way to a special clinic that's supposed to sell medications that help with radiation poison." Leo took his eyes off the road to glance at Lily. "I think my boy might be past the point of meds helping him."

"So is it true?" Allen asked her, releasing his hold on her.

"Is what true?"

"You're an alien who can really heal damaged bodies?"

Both men were staring at her, while Lily thought carefully how to answer. "My mother was human, and my twin sister is human. So no, I don't think I'm an alien."

"What are you then?" Allen asked.

"I'm…" What could she say, when she didn't really know? "I'm just a person trying to live."

"It's pretty messed up your president lied to everyone." Leo scratched his head. "Trying to fool people into believing they were cured by you. That's twisted."

Lily glanced at Leo. "People in Canada know the truth?" She wondered how far her video had reached. "Did you see my video?"

Allen chuckled. "Your video has over a billion views. Everyone knows Kate is still alive. Even after the riots in the Square, and the mass shootings, I think it's safe to say nobody in the U. S. is happy with your President."

"I need to reach Kate. She's been shot, and could die. You've got to promise to take me to the bridge."

"We will," Allen replied, as Leo turned onto a dirt road, and announced they were close.

The road ended as Leo pulled into a narrow gravel driveway. The house was a small square, with one picture window in front.

"Don't try running," Allen warned her, as they emerged from the car and headed inside.

The tiny kitchen barely had room for a table, and was connected directly to the family room. A beat up leather sofa, TV and coffee table were all that filled the room. The beige wall- paper with small lavender flowers was faded and torn in some spots. Two bedrooms were located off the narrow hallway that led to the only full bath. These people appeared somewhat poverty stricken, and that concerned Lily.

She wasn't sure if she could trust them not to turn her in to the government. Before Patrick found her, the bounty was over a million dollars. But what was also enticing was the promise of free medical care for life if she was captured unharmed. Lily knew she'd pass out after healing Leo's son, and they could easily hand her over. "Look," she said crossing her arms over the sick feeling in her stomach. "I'm just as worried about my sister as you are about your son. If you turn me into the authorities, I won't be able to heal Kate, and she could die." She hoped the fear in her eyes would appeal to their sense of compassion. "The government is lying to people. They don't want to use me to heal, they just…" she paused. What did they want her for? What was the purpose of using Kate, while keeping her locked up and starving? She didn't really know or understand what their goal was.

"Go on." Allen was interested in hearing what she had to say.

"All I know is that they can't duplicate my ability to heal. They told me they don't want to heal the sick. There are too many people on the planet and not enough resources. My point is… you can't trust them to give you anything in exchange for me."

"We know this," Allen said, placing his hands on his hips. "We hate the American government. Most Canadians aren't fans of the U. S. The President seems to think that just because you were born in America, they own you. I don't care if you're an alien, or the Messiah. You don't belong to them." Allen had watched a special documentary on the famous Lily McCallister years ago. It was when she'd just started healing people, and the documentary was proving her gift was real. "You saved a lot of lives." He looked at her fondly. "I understand you'll never be free, and there will always be people like me who need you. But you have my word that after you heal Jason, we'll take you to Kate."

"He's this way," Leo said, wanting to get down to business.

Were all bedrooms painted blue? She'd never noticed until now. The baby blue room appeared to be freshly painted and the navy curtains looked new. But what drew Lily's eye first was the small, frail body lying in the bed. "Was he left here alone?" She hadn't seen anyone else in the house, and it didn't seem right to leave a sick, dying child alone. "Why didn't one of you stay with him?"

"No." Leo guided Lily closer to the bed. "Allen's girlfriend is here. She's having a smoke in the garage, because we won't let her smoke in the house with Jason."

The boy turned his head and opened his eyes at the mention of his name. Lily sat beside him on the bed, and rested her hand on his forehead. "Hi, Jason." Her tone was soft and gentle. "My name is Lily." She watched as awareness crossed his pale features. His eyes were shaded with dark circles, and his lips appeared terribly dry and cracked. "How are you feeling?"

"He doesn't have much energy," Leo answered when his son stayed quiet. "Jason, this woman is going to heal you." He picked up his son's hand, brought it to his lips. "Please," Leo pleaded, his voice strained and gentle. His eyes begged Lily, "Please, heal my boy."

Lily's heart ached at the tenderness she saw in his eyes. This was a man who loved his son deeply and didn't want to lose him. The boy was near death and would require every ounce of her strength, and even then she wasn't sure she'd have enough to completely restore him. "What symptoms has he had?"

"His stomach hurts him all the time and he's lost a lot of blood in his stool and stopped eating a few days ago. We manage to get some food in him, but he's withering away."

Allen walked to his brother's side and set his hand on his shoulder in a gesture of comfort. There was pain in his eyes, too. Lily believed these were good men, and hoped they'd stick to their end of the bargain.

"Jason was always such a happy, active kid," Allen said sadly. "Please, Lily. See what you can do."

She took a long slow breath. "The government did things to

154

me that have weakened my ability. I can't be sure this will work, and I'll probably pass out. I might not be conscious for a long time, so I need to know you'll take me to the bridge. I'll need you to find my brother and sister." Patrick entered her mind, but she didn't say his name, only felt the familiar ache of wanting him.

Leo nodded his head with a somber, sincere look. "You heal my son; I'll owe you my life. I'll do whatever I can to help you."

And that's how it worked. That's why Danny had been able to form a coalition of people. Lily nodded her head, and placed her hands on Jason's arm. She closed her eyes, and willed her body to respond. The familiar heat began to build. She opened her eyes as the room began to spin. *Not yet*, she told herself. She had to keep the waves of energy flowing into Jason's small damaged body. He needed all her strength. Tingling sensations rippled through her. "When he feels better, make sure you give him lots of water. He's dehydrated and needs electrolytes." Those were the last words she spoke.

Chapter 24

Alex plugged in his laptop, and began emailing his various contacts. Patrick went to the nearby store to purchase disposable phones. At least now they'd have a way for other people to contact them, and he'd have an extra one in case one got lost.

The safe house was too cold for Kate's taste, so they'd returned to the Webster's home. At least there was plenty of food in the refrigerator, and furniture to sit on. Kate's leg ached as she lay on the sofa, but at last the bandage was clean. Although she'd lost a lot of blood, her energy was slowly returning.

It'd been a long time since Kate had watched the news, but now she wanted to see the footage she knew Lily may have seen. She didn't want Lily to think she was hurt badly and be worried. Almost every station showed clips of the riots and protesters in New York City. People were outraged, and wanted answers. The hotel where Kate had been staying was closed off, and cell phone videos caught footage of Patrick picking Kate up from the ground and carrying her to a white van. It was a good thing they hadn't stayed in the van long. Almost all the details of her rescue had been recorded by various people, and were flooding social media.

The President was addressing the nation, urging viewers to believe the video was a hoax. The President tried to reassure people that Lily was still in their custody and the video was made by a group of radicals. People who believed Lily was the Messiah, and called themselves Twin Seekers. So many lies were told it was a wonder if anyone could know a shred of truth. The sad truth was that Lily was missing, Kate was mourning Danny and feeling horribly depressed, and they were stuck in a stranger's home until Alex could figure out their next move.

Kate thought about her mother in the psych ward. Part of her was glad her mother wasn't living in reality, because reality right now was fairly grim. She thought about the people she'd pretended to heal, and felt a heavy weight of guilt. But most of all, she couldn't keep images of Danny from her mind. If only she'd married him when he'd first asked her. She'd wanted to wait, because Lily needed her. Lily's needs always came before her own.

"If you're not watching the TV, why have it on?" Alex asked, walking over to shut it off. He'd seen enough lies and chaos, too. "Are you okay?" He asked Kate, before glancing down at his watch. "You can probably have another Vicodin now."

Kate shook her head. "I was watching that."

"No… you were staring out in space." He stared at her in concern. "Are you in pain?"

"It aches, but I don't want to take anything yet." The medication upset her stomach and she had enough problems feeling sick from her emotions.

Patrick walked into the room carrying a serving platter with sandwiches on it. "How about some food, before the meds?" He'd overheard the conversation.

The light from the window shone on the silver tray and reminded Kate of a silver necklace Danny bought for her years ago. It reflected the sunlight the same way. "That looks good," she smiled, but her eyes didn't light up.

"Find out anything?" Patrick asked Alex. He hated waiting, almost as much as he hated not knowing where Lily was.

"No. But if Ian calls an emergency contact, I'll be notified." He reached for a sandwich, and grinned when he peeled back the bread to find it well stacked. "I appreciate you making this worthwhile."

Kate smiled at her brother, and turned to Patrick. "Alex would

157

call this a man sandwich. It has a little of everything you can find in the fridge."

"You got it." They engaged in polite, easy conversation, but there was no hiding the tension each of them felt.

The cell phone in Alex's pocket vibrated and rang at the same time. He practically dropped his sandwich, quickly pulling it from his pocket. "Hello," he said eagerly. He listened a few minutes as both Kate and Patrick set their food down and leaned over trying to hear the voice on the other end of the phone. "Oh, thank God. Okay, call me back if you hear anything more." Alex's lips curled up, giving both Patrick and Kate hope.

"What did you find out?" Patrick was impatient and ready to jump out of his skin.

Dropping down on the sofa next to his sister, Alex took his laptop out and began running his fingers quickly over the keyboard. "Ian called his father. He informed Marty that he's headed back home. Lily was taken at a gas station." He squinted at the laptop. "Ian waited there a couple of hours, because he didn't have a car and wasn't sure what to do. He figured she wasn't coming back, so he called an Uber. He had to use a stranger's cell. He's on his way here, so we'll get more info when he arrives."

"Oh God," Kate covered her face with her hands.

"The good news is that Ian said it wasn't government officials who took her. Just some local men getting gas that'd noticed her in the car."

Patrick rubbed his neck. "What makes that good news? And why the hell are you smiling?"

"Because we're damn lucky the government doesn't have her. It'll make getting her back a hell of a lot easier. The men who took her probably want her to heal someone, and soon I'll have a location on where she is." He glanced briefly at Patrick, who looked like he wanted to kill someone. "Ian didn't have a cell phone, because he'd left it in the car with Lily. Between the phone and the car itself, I'll have a GPS location in a matter of minutes."

Kate felt better with the confidence Alex displayed. Patrick on the other hand couldn't contain his fear. What if the men who'd taken Lily hurt her? The woman was so damn beautiful, and thanks to his past police work, he knew that no woman was ever truly safe from strangers. What if she couldn't heal anyone in her weakened state and they decided she was useless with an enormous bounty on her head?

"Got it!" Alex shouted.

"Let's go!" Patrick headed to the door.

"Wait a minute, buddy." Alex glanced from Patrick to Kate. "Ian should be here any minute, and we need someone who can stay here with Kate."

"Oh no you don't!" Kate pushed herself up. "I'm not staying here while you go get her. I'm coming with you!"

"I only have an address, Kate. I don't know how many men have her, or what kind of situation we'll be walking into. You've got a hurt leg and can't do anything but get in the way. You're staying here with Ian, and Patrick and I will bring Lily back."

Just as Kate began to protest, Ian walked in the front door.

"I'm glad you're okay, buddy," Alex said, shaking Ian's hand. "Tell us everything that happened."

"Make it fast," Patrick added. He didn't care what the hell happened. All that mattered was Lily's location, and they needed to get there immediately before anything bad happened to her. "We don't have time for this." He was beyond frustrated and antsy.

Alex knew how important details could be. He placed his hand on Patrick's shoulder. "We'll leave in a minute. I want to hear what happened."

Patrick noted Ian's disheveled appearance, his tousled hair, and the stress around his eyes, but he didn't care. As far as he was concerned the guy had no damn business being in charge of Lily or Kate's safety.

Ian looked confused. "We were on our way to the bridge to meet you."

"What? Why?" He had Patrick's attention now.

"The phone call," Ian stared at Patrick, his brows pulling together in puzzlement. "You called and told Lily you were in Detroit, and needed us to meet you at the bridge, because Kate was hurt badly and needed to be healed." He glanced at Kate. He was stressed that Lily was taken, but pleased to see Kate alive and well. Ian continued to explain.

Alex immediately figured out what had happened. "So whoever found your cell phone, Patrick, pretended to be you in order to lure Lily." Alex shook his head. "What I can't figure out is why Lily wasn't able to recognize that it wasn't your voice."

Ian took his jacket off, and responded. "The call was short, and Lily was distraught. I'd missed a call from you, so when the phone rang, I think she was only focused on knowing you were all alive. She wasn't going to question anything, knowing Kate needed healing."

Patrick took the blame and squared it away on his shoulders. "If I hadn't lost my damn phone, she wouldn't have been contacted." It was probably Jeffrey's men who'd found the phone and put two and two together.

"Right," Alex huffed. "You were only fighting off three men to clear a path for us, why you let your phone fall out of your pocket is just dumb. I mean my phone was only shattered, but at least I still had it."

Patrick ignored the sarcasm. "My phone, my fault." He grabbed his backpack off the floor. "We need to find her *now*."

Kate tossed a pillow at Patrick. "I'm the one you had to risk your lives for. If it wasn't for me, Lily would still be with you. She'd—"

"It's my fault. I should *never* have left her alone in the car," Ian said vehemently.

"All three of you stop trying to place blame. We've got an address where the car is located, and we're going to get her back!" Alex zipped up his jacket. "Ian, I need you to stay here and protect

Kate. The address is about 2 hours away. I have no idea how long we'll be, but this time we've got cell phone backups. If you have any problems, follow the same protocol as last time."

"Oh 'cause that worked out so well," Patrick mumbled. He didn't like the idea of leaving Kate with Ian.

"I'm going with you, and you can't stop me." She hopped to the front door.

Ian smiled. "You sound just like her. It's weird to see Lily's face and hear Lily's voice. I see why everyone was fooled by you." Kate frowned and Ian instantly realized his blunder. "I'm sorry, that was insensitive of me to say."

"It's true, we're too much alike. I just wish that Lil was normal like me, too."

"Hey," Patrick turned fierce eyes on Kate. "Lily's as normal as they come. The only thing that separates her is the fact she's got more strength and guts than ten people put together. Her heart is bigger than anyone's and she's got more compassion than I've ever known. But damn it, she's normal."

"Easy there, Romeo." Alex set his hand on Patrick's shoulder. "Kate didn't mean it like that."

Kate was too busy smiling to defend her words. She was thrilled that her sister had found herself a champion.

"I know how you meant it." Ian replied. "You were talking about her ability to heal."

Patrick rubbed the back of his neck. "I'm just tired of hearing that word *normal*. It's thrown around a lot. I'm on edge and anxious to get the hell out of here."

"I like you, Patrick." Kate limped over and kissed the side of his cheek. "I'll be in the car."

"You're not going anywhere, sis." Alex took her arm to stop her. "You and Ian are staying here." He handed Ian a gun. "This time, someone comes in your house, you shoot them."

The gun felt heavy in Ian's hand, but he was prepared to use it. "I won't let you down again. I'll guard Kate with my life."

161

Patrick rolled his eyes, and stepped over to Kate. He leaned down and whispered in her ear, "Protect Ian for us."

Kate laughed. "I'm going with you, and you can't stop me. I've seen what happens when we split up." Her leg was painfully sore, but she wouldn't let it stop her from finding her sister. She took the 9 mm Glock from Ian and checked the chamber with aptitude and efficiency. Unlike Lily, she wasn't afraid of guns, and Danny had taught her proficient handling. "If you try and stop me, I'll shoot you."

Patrick was impressed. Clearly she knew how to handle a gun. "Let's go."

Alex shook his head, knowing she was a hundred times more stubborn than Lily. She wasn't going to let him leave her behind, and truthfully he couldn't blame her. He glanced at Ian. "You know the difference between Kate and Lily?" He didn't wait for a reply. "Lily listens better, and has more sense."

Kate limped out the door, tossing over her shoulder, "Lily's a people pleaser... I'm not."

"Hang on, Kate!" Ian ran upstairs, and when he came back down he handed Kate a pair of crutches. "These were my grand-father's. You can use them. Be safe." He kissed her on the cheek.

Chapter 25

Allen removed the boiling soup from the stove, and glanced up at the small kitchen window. The rain had turned to ice, and was blowing hard against the glass. In a few more weeks it would be Halloween and more than likely Jason would be able to go Trick-or-Treating, thanks to the famous Lily McCallister who was still out cold in the other room. He hoped she'd wake up soon, and be okay.

Jason sat on the couch with a sketch book in his hand. He'd always had a talent for drawing comic book characters, and now he had enough strength and stamina to hold the pencil and glide it across the paper.

"How's she doing?" Allen asked, as Leo walked into the room whistling.

"She's still passed out, but her pulse is strong, and her breathing's fine." Leo had never been so happy in his entire life. He sat on the couch next to his son, and wrapped his arm around his shoulders.

"It's because of me," Jason replied in a voice that held not a trace of regret or sadness. "I'm going to live now."

Leo pressed his lips to his son's temple. "She'll be okay, and yes, thanks to her you're going to grow up to be an artist."

"No, I'm going to be a comic book writer." Jason tipped his paper toward his dad so he could see what he was working on.

"I thought you wanted to be a police officer?" Allen replied, setting a bowl of soup on the table in front of Jason, offering him a wink. "How long do you think she'll sleep?" he asked Leo. He was getting nervous because they hadn't yet taken her to the bridge.

As if Leo could read his brother's mind, he replied, "We'll take her to the bridge soon." He too felt guilty. So far they hadn't held up their end of the bargain. But Jason was only just beginning to get his strength back.

"If anything happens to her sister, because we failed to—"

"I said we'll leave soon." Leo sounded annoyed, but then his face softened. "I want to make sure her healing worked."

"It's worked!" Allen set his hands on top of his head. "Jesus, it's worked so amazingly well that I'm starting to think the woman *is* the Messiah. I want to help her, Leo." They owed her.

Leo frowned, glancing out the window. The weather was bad, but his brother was right. They'd already wasted a couple hours, and they'd made her a promise. He felt even guiltier when his son stared at him with light and hope in his eyes. "Okay. I'll carry her out to the car, and you grab some blankets and pillows for her." He ruffled the hair on Jason's head. "What do you say we go for a car ride, A-champ?"

Jason sprang from the sofa with the ease of a healthy child, and again Leo marveled at the boy's strength. Only a few hours ago, he'd been dying, with barely the strength to speak let alone move.

The door suddenly crashed open and a man with a gun barreled into the room.

"Nobody move!" the man shouted.

Leo quickly pulled his son behind his back. "Don't shoot; I've got my boy here!"

The back door was kicked in, and Allen and his brother heard another man shout, "It's all clear!"

"Where is she?"

Leo tipped his head. "In the bedroom… we didn't hurt her I swear. She healed my son, and then she passed out."

Patrick glanced at the boy peeking his head out from around his father's waist, and then he turned to see Alex holding Lily in his arms.

"She's okay, Patrick. I've got her," Alex reassured him. He

164

frowned at Kate as she hobbled into the house. "I told you to wait in the car."

"I heard you say it was all clear." Kate could see the situation was under control. Patrick had his gun aimed at the two men and a boy, and Alex had already checked the back of the house to make sure no one else was home. "What happened to Lily?"

"She healed my boy and then passed out," Leo repeated. "We were getting ready to take her to the bridge to meet you." He was pleased to see Kate was alive. Lily had wanted to be with her brother and sister, and now she was. "We planned on helping her get to you."

Patrick wanted to punch the guy for taking Lily in the first place, but the fact that he'd prevented her from going to the bridge was good. Whoever had found his phone, pretending to be him, was potentially way worse than these two men who simply needed her to heal a child.

The wind blew hard at Kate's back, and the cold chill made her step further inside and shut the door. She and her brother were wet from the icy rain, and balls of sleet clung to her long hair. It was scary driving in the hail storm, but they would stop at nothing to find Lily.

"You're welcome to dry off and stay. I've got food on the stove." Allen put his hands out in front of him to show he meant no harm. "We only want to help Lily."

Just as the words were out his mouth, Allen's girlfriend came up behind Alex with a revolver, and yelled, "Put your gun down, or I'll shoot him!" She'd been smoking in the garage and had quickly hidden, while watching the home invasion.

"No!" Allen cried. "Jane, put the gun down!"

"They need to put their guns down first!" The woman blew her long black bangs out of her eyes so she could see.

"Patrick, put your gun down," Alex said calmly. He wasn't going to risk some scared woman shooting anyone.

"No," Patrick said firmly. He wasn't giving strangers the upper hand. He slid his eyes toward Allen. "You guys were in the wrong.

165

You tell her to put that gun down, or I'll blow a hole clean through this man." He tipped his head to Leo, adding "and into the boy."

"For heaven's sake, Jane, put the damn gun down," Leo demanded.

Jane lowered the gun and glared at her boyfriend. "You're absolutely worthless. We've had a home invasion, and you'd let them rape me, and steal all our stuff."

Leo laughed. He never understood what his younger brother saw in that girl. Jane was as full of drama as she was air. "This isn't a home invasion, Jane. They came for Lily."

"Oh, for heaven's sake," Kate muttered. "Who *are* you people?"

Patrick lowered his gun. He'd heard enough. "Take Lily to the car," he told Alex. He glanced at Kate. "We're leaving."

Alex carried Lily outside, and carefully laid her in the car.

"Are you okay?" Allen asked Kate, as she turned to follow her brother. "Your sister was real worried about you. She'd asked us to take her to you at the bridge."

Kate glanced at Jane, who was standing with her arms crossed over her chest. She was wearing skin tight jeans that clung to her slender figure, and a V-neck T-shirt that showed ample cleavage. Kate wondered if she'd shoot her boyfriend when they left. "I'm fine," she replied dryly. "It's a good thing you didn't take her to the bridge."

In the car everyone practically slumped in relief, as Alex drove away.

"We're all together now," Kate said, with tears in her eyes, turning to take her sister's hand. She was sitting in the front passenger seat next to Alex, and Patrick was holding Lily on his lap in the back seat, brushing the damp hair from her face.

Kate felt overwhelmed with love. After a long difficult year, she finally had her sister and brother. The only person missing was Danny. She felt the grief and missed him terribly.

"Where are we going?" Patrick asked after a few minutes. He didn't really care, as long as Lily was in his arms, and they were safe. He finally felt at ease holding her close. He didn't care what Alex thought or anyone else.

Alex glanced in the rearview mirror. "We're being followed. Three cars back, a black Ecoshell." Ecoshell's were expensive cars that drove much faster than the car they borrowed from one of the strangers who'd helped them escape back to Canada.

Patrick didn't turn around. He knew not to draw attention. "Can you lose them?"

Alex let out a huff, "In this storm? Maybe if the roads weren't slick from freezing rain, and if the windshield wipers worked better, and I could see through the streaks."

"What are we going to do?" Kate squeezed Lily's hand. She'd never seen her sister so weak and frail.

Lily heard the worry in Kate's voice, and opened her eyes. "Kate," she whispered.

"I'm here, Lil. We're all here!" Tears stung her eyes. "I missed you so much."

"Is he alive?" Lily whispered.

Kate tilted her head in confusion.

Patrick knew. He knew Lily would want to know if the child was healed. He brushed his lips over her forehead. "Yes, the boy is well now. Everything's going to be okay."

"Except we're being followed now, and—"

"Not for long!" Alex turned his blinker on and slowly made his way to the far right lane. "I'm about to lose them in just a sec."

Again, Kate felt the pang of missing Danny. She could almost hear Danny's voice giving Alex commands. He would have already had a plan forming in his clever mind. She felt her shoulders sag as she turned back to face the road, offering Patrick the privacy to kiss Lily.

The traffic was moving slowly, thanks to the ice storm, but Alex knew the city was just up ahead. "It's going to be tough to run, when Kate's on crutches and Lily can't walk."

"We've done it before, we'll do it again," Patrick replied.

"I can walk." Lily tried sitting up, and fought the lightheadedness. "I'll heal Kate." She couldn't keep putting her family at risk, and she hated feeling weak and groggy.

Patrick kissed her softly, and hushed her. "It's okay, sweetheart, I have no problem carrying you. I prefer to hold you," he smiled. "Kate's leg will heal just fine, and she's a natural with crutches."

"Please, Patrick."

He hated hearing the pain and stress in her faint voice, so he changed the subject. "Did you miss me?"

"I didn't have time to miss you," her lips curved as she reached her hand up to trace the outline of his lips. "All I thought about was you."

Alex wanted to beat his head against the steering wheel. "Keep in mind, we can hear you!" He changed lanes, and watched the rear view mirror as the black car did the same. "Quit with the cheesy reunion, I'm trying to concentrate."

"Leave them alone," Kate scolded her brother, and glanced in her side mirror. "I think it's wonderful." What would Danny do if he were here, she wondered. "Let me use your cell phone, and I'll call Danny's friend Chris to see if he can help us."

"I'm going to lose them, right now!" Alex cut the wheel hard, almost hitting another car, but he managed to get off at the exit. He drove as fast as he could on the shoulder so he'd make it to the light before the men following them could see which way they turned. The men following were still trying to reach the exit. Alex gunned the car, making it fishtail on the icy road. Kate's seat belt dug into her shoulder.

Patrick held Lily tight, admiring the skill at which Alex was handling the car. He was doing everything right. "Pull into that McDonald's. There's lots of cars there, so we might be able to stay hidden long enough to switch vehicles."

"My thoughts exactly," Alex replied.

Chapter 26

Soft light invaded Lily's eyes when she opened them again. It was no longer dark outside, and rain wasn't hitting the car. This time she was in a warm, soft bed in a motel room. Patrick was lying beside her, and her hand was held in his. She leaned up to scan the room. Kate and Alex lay on the other double bed, Alex with his hand over his gun, and Kate on her side with her leg propped up on a pillow. Her heart soared. Her brother had obviously lost the men that were following them, and they managed to find a motel room. She must have passed out again, but she wasn't feeling weak and dizzy at the moment.

She couldn't remember the last time she was in a room with both her siblings, feeling content and at peace. You only know how much tension you carry once it's gone, she thought. The feeling was incredible. For once, the tension in her gut was at ease. Everyone she loved was safe in the room with her, and she'd give anything to keep it that way.

Patrick stirred before opening his eyes. He wondered what it would be like to wake up every morning to Lily's beautiful smile. In that moment, he was sure there was nothing better. He pulled her down and kissed her softly. For a moment he forgot her siblings were in the room with them.

"This has to stop, I can't take it," Alex said, sitting up, rubbing his hands over his face. "Patrick, I might have to shoot you."

Patrick just smiled. He figured Alex was getting used to his open affection toward Lily.

Kate woke with a grunt, feeling how stiff and sore her leg was. Alex glanced at her with concern. "We need to figure things out." He arose from the bed, turning the TV on so he could watch the news. Since he'd slept in his clothes, he was already fully dressed. He felt edgy and restless. Part of him wouldn't have minded punching Prick a few times in the face.

"I've got a cabin in the U.P." Patrick sat up, and pulled Lily with him, keeping her close at his side. "It's not listed under my name, so no one can find it. My brother and parents are staying there now, but I can relocate them easily enough." His eyes drifted from Alex back to Lily, "Might be a good place to lay low for a while."

Lily snuggled closer to Patrick's chest, setting her hand on his stomach. He wore a black t-shirt and jeans. "I love the forest."

Patrick kissed the top of her head, "I know you do."

Alex sent a sideways glance to Kate. "You'll stay with me," he told her.

"What? No!" Kate rolled off the bed and hobbled over to her sister. "I'm not ready to split up yet! I spent a year inside a tiny blue room with nothing to do but watch TV and read. I need to be with you." Now that Lily was awake, she needed to hug her sister.

"You need to use the crutches," Alex scolded.

"I'll heal you."

"No!" all three of them shouted at Lily.

"You have to get your strength back completely, and your healing days might just be over," Patrick said, sliding over to make room for Kate.

"I'm fine, sis. The wound is healing well." Kate masked the pain she felt by putting on a smile. Her wound was healing, but she needed to stop using her leg so much. She let Lily squeeze her tight. "Don't you dare try healing me."

Lily was overwhelmed with love. She wanted the energy to heal Kate, but it simply wasn't there. "We don't know who's following us, but if it's the same men who found me at Ian's house, then we know they're smart and have the means. They probably won't give

170

up, and we know the government never will. I need to know that your leg will be okay, so as soon as my strength returns, I'm going to heal you." Lily glanced from her sister to Alex. "I refuse to let us split up. You're going to have to deal with us, Alex. I just got you all back, and I'm keeping it that way."

"Right on!" Kate kissed her sister's cheek, then leaned back to examine her. "You look much better today. How do you feel?"

"I'm good." Lily felt overwhelmed and laughed. "I'm just so incredibly happy to have everyone right here." She stared at her sister. "I grieved for you for a year. I honestly thought I would die from the pain of it. I'm never going through that again." There were so many questions she wanted to ask. "Did they hurt you?" She needed to find out if the blue room affected Kate the way it had her. Lily only spent a few weeks in it, but Kate was gone an entire year.

"You two get caught up." Alex checked the chamber of his gun, and walked over to the door. "I'm going across the street to get us food… and coffee."

Patrick stood. "I'll get ice, and I need a word alone with you, Alex." He read the concerned look on Alex's face. "I'm only going down the hall, and my eyes won't come off this room. I'll keep them safe."

As soon as Patrick shut the door, he folded his arms at Alex's rigid stance. "Do you trust me?" He kept his voice low and even.

"You know I do."

"The weather is changing. We can't keep running. No more camping out in the woods. She needs a safe house where she can rest and gain her strength, and I've got a place."

The hall of the motel was quiet and empty, except for a low hum from the ice machine. The beige paint was chipping in spots. The building was old, run down, but mostly vacant. Alex understood what Patrick was saying. He wanted to be the one to protect Lily, and he wanted her alone.

"The next step was always to leave the country, and I don't

171

mean Canada." Alex crossed his arms and leaned against the wall. "Danny and I planned to take them to Australia." There were remote places in the Outback, where social media wasn't as prominent. "But things are different now that Danny's gone." He felt the heavy pain of his loss. "Kate will want to see Danny's parents, attend a funeral for him, and Lily won't want to leave us."

Patrick shook his head. "It's not possible. Do you even know where his body is? You know they'll use Danny's family to try and find us."

Frustration and need for caffeine made Alex's voice hard. "Listen, Prick, I've been protecting my sisters all their lives. You don't need to tell me anything." He instantly regretted his response when Patrick raised a brow. "Look. I'm sorry, man. I just need some coffee."

A door opened at the far end of the hall, and Alex tipped his head to the ground, as an elderly couple walked by. Patrick shifted casually to the left to shield Alex from view, until the couple passed.

"We have to stay together for a while." Alex wouldn't go against his sister's wishes, knowing how important this was to them. "Lily and Kate won't split up. You don't know what the twins are like. They have to be together."

That's what concerned Patrick. "They're grown women. They need a chance to live." And Lily needed to make a choice. All four of them couldn't remain living together forever. Everyone needed a life of their own.

Alex narrowed his eyes with irritation, "And what, Patrick? You just whisk Lil off to some cabin in the woods… the two of you alone in front of a fireplace? What life is that? She can't live up north. It's too damn close to the Hope Medical Facility, and all those people who worked there. The entire country isn't safe for her." He was feeling heated, but didn't want to fight with Patrick until he had his coffee. "I get that you think you're in love with her, but—"

"What the hell do you mean; I *think* I'm in love with her?" Patrick used a low harsh tone so no one could hear. "Don't think for

172

one minute that I'm confused about any of this. I didn't want to care about her. Jesus, my whole life has changed because of that woman. I didn't want to fall in love with her, but I *did!* She's my world now."

"Okay, take it easy, buddy." Part of him appreciated the candid display of love Patrick had for his sister. He was honest to a fault with his feelings, and Alex couldn't blame him. No one thought more highly of his sisters than he did. Kate and Lily were exceptional women, and Alex prided himself on that. He'd played the role of father, mother, and big brother, having a huge influence on them. He couldn't be more proud. If Lily was going to go off with a man, she probably couldn't do better than Patrick. And Alex had slowly taken the time to accept the fact that soon he'd need to let another man take over his role of protector. "Look, I'm going to go get us food. Get back in there, before they start to worry. Let me get some damn coffee in me, and then we'll make a plan for how we're going to get us all to your cozy little cabin in the woods." His sarcastic reply had the desired affect when Patrick grinned and shook his head.

Once the men had left the room, Kate immediately brushed off the questions Lily had for her. "Forget all that for a minute. I want to talk about what's going on with you and Patrick. You're in love with each other. Have you…"

"No!" Lily's face turned red. "Not yet." She ran her fingers through her hair. "It's all happened very fast, and we've barely had twenty minutes alone together. Alex watches us like it's his job."

Kate chuckled. "He's very handsome, and he's very sweet with you."

Lily blushed again with a small smile. "Yes, he is. And oh the way that man can kiss…" She knew Kate had to be grieving terribly over Danny. "I assume Alex told you about Danny? I'm so…" She paused when Kate held up her hand in a gesture to stop.

"I honestly can't talk about it yet, Lil. I'm just trying to hold it together." Kate couldn't handle the pain that came, just hearing his name. Wrapping their arms around each other, the sisters comforted one another. Lily wanted to absorb her sister's pain, but heartache

173

wasn't something she could heal.

With the sun shining high in the sky, one would never have known that there had been an ice storm the night before. The temperature had risen, melting any trace of winter. Birds chirped in the nearby trees, as if it were spring. Alex kept his face down, allowing his baseball cap to conceal his identity. He'd gone weeks without shaving, hoping his beard and mustache would make it harder for people to recognize him.

Before entering the small Coney Island, he glanced around at the small town of Mapleburry. It was located on the outskirts of the expressway, an hour from Windsor, Canada. Canadians paid less attention to people than Americans did, but still he reminded himself to act casual. Blend in.

A mother wearing a long wool coat pushed a stroller down the street, window shopping at a few of the stores that lined the strip mall. Her toddler clung to her skirts. If the mother had fears of potential radiation in the air, she didn't show it. Many kids were kept indoors this close to the United States. The destruction of the United States nuclear plants had affected Canada, but Alex wasn't sure how far it reached.

She can't cure the world, Alex thought to himself, as he glanced at the little boy wearing a winter jacket and boots. There'd been a time when Lily was able to touch hundreds of people and cure them, but that was before the government did their tests on her. That was before they almost starved her to death. Lily had been younger, too. She held healing conventions as a teenager. Now she was in her twenties, and perhaps her power to heal was diminishing.

Many such thoughts filled Alex's mind as he entered the restaurant. Patrick was complicating things. If it was just him watching out for his sisters, it'd be easier. He was used to devoting his life to protecting them, but now someone else wanted the job. It wouldn't be easy splitting up, but he knew that's eventually what Patrick wanted. And maybe that's what Lily deserved… a chance to enjoy love. It'd made him extremely happy to see his sisters hold each other.

They'd suffered great heartache believing Kate had died. Maybe it was time for Lily to start living, and find a little happiness.

Alex ordered a ton of food to go, and then glanced across the street at the dime-store. There was a fifteen minute wait before the food was ready. "I'll be right back," Alex told the man who'd taken his to-go order.

The dime-store had everything Alex needed, but the problem was going to be purchasing the items. The young man behind the counter might wonder why a man was buying many female products. If he paid too close attention, he might easily recognize Alex, and the reason for the products. Between getting the food, and buying what he needed from the store, he was taking a huge risk.

Then he saw her.

She was in the vitamin aisle. She may have been dressed young, with black fashion boots up to her knees, wearing leggings with a tight white sweater, but he could see she wasn't a kid. And he'd bet anything that she was bald under the pink scarf that was wrapped around her head. Her eyebrows were thin and perfectly arched. She had high cheek bones, and a wide mouth with full lips. Quite attractive, Alex thought.

He moved over to where she stood. "Hello," he offered casually. "I've a favor to ask of you."

It was then that her eyes met his with a quizzical look.

"I was wondering if I give you cash if you'd mind buying these items for me at the register. I'm in a bit of a jam." He watched as she became obviously nervous. "Do you recognize me?"

"No," she said carefully. "I'm sorry, I—"

Alex offered her a soft smile at the moment recognition kicked in. Now she knew. "I'm here with my sisters. You know we're hiding." He lowered his voice, glancing at the empty aisle. "Please don't make a scene. I need your help."

The woman nervously adjusted her purse strap over her shoulder and glanced at the pharmacy counter. "You're Alex McCallister?" Her voice was soft and pleasant. "The famous sibling of Lily?"

He relaxed a little, feeling she wasn't going to blow the whistle. "Yes." Now he'd cut to the chase. "What type of cancer do you have?" His eyes swept over her scarf before meeting her pretty blue eyes.

She reached a hand to her head self-consciously. "Breast cancer."

"How old are you?"

"Thirty." She couldn't take her eyes off his. Normally she'd have her wits about her to say, it's none of his business, but at the moment she was starstruck. She'd seen his face many times in magazines, and on the news. She followed him on various media sites. He had a fan club, and a huge following. It was a surreal moment to be talking to him. Once she looked past his reddish brown facial hair, she could almost picture him the way he'd looked clean cut. His eyes were more gray than green. Most women found him attractive, and now she could see why.

He was only four years older than her, but she looked younger. "Will you help me?"

His plea broke her trance. "What?" What had he asked of her?

Alex held out the basket of items. "I'm in a hurry, Miss. Why don't you buy these items for me, and then meet me on the sidewalk outside of the Coney Island." He tipped his head in the direction of the restaurant. "I trust you, Miss…" He waited for her to supply a name. When she just stared at him dumbfounded, he said, "What's your name?"

"Oh," she jumped a little. "I'm Sarah." She took the basket from him, and quickly stared at the items, not really registering what was in it.

"Sarah." Alex's lips curved when he repeated her name. "It's nice to meet you. Meet me outside, and I'll see what we can do about that cancer of yours."

Getting the food went easily enough. He'd been a little longer than

176

fifteen minutes, since he'd taken a chance on meeting Sarah, but the restaurant was busier now. They seemed eager to get the order out, and send Alex on his way. He was lucky no one took the time to notice him.

Sarah was standing on the sidewalk, holding two paper bags. She was slender, and quite a few inches shorter than him. Her nose was red, and she wasn't wearing a jacket. From the way her shoulders were scrunched up, Alex knew she was cold. "Thank you so much for helping me out." He took his jacket off and wrapped it around her shoulders, before taking the bags from her.

Pull yourself together, she thought. She was just standing there like a fool. Why was he so easy going and friendly? He spoke as if they were friends, and leaned in a bit closer to her as she held his warm jacket around her shoulders. "Sure," she managed to mutter.

"Come on. I'll introduce you to my famous sisters." He turned and started walking away, assuming she'd follow. He opened the door to the motel for her, but she hesitated a moment. "It's okay. You don't have to come in if you're… uncomfortable." Her eyes were wide and fearful. He shifted an inch closer to her. "Sarah, it's okay."

His reassurance eased her tension. His eyes were kind and gentle. The choice was hers, knowing she was free to leave. "I'm a little in shock still." She brushed past him through the door. All the information she'd ever read about the McCallisters told her she had nothing to fear from them. They were good, decent people. Famous, and on the run.

Chapter 27

Patrick had taken a shower so Lily and Kate could have more time to talk privately. He understood they needed to share a year's worth of things, and he knew what it was like to need time alone with Lily. The warm water soothed his muscles. Having Lily and Kate safe did wonders for easing the tension in his neck and the tightening in his stomach. Now it was a question of keeping them that way. What he feared most was the decision that Lily might one day have to make. It's like Alex said, 'she's going to have to choose. ' He wanted her to choose him. He hoped she'd want the chance to get to know him better. He needed to know that she trusted him completely, because it hadn't been that long ago she'd pointed a gun at him.

When Alex opened the door he heard laughter. Kate and Lily were giggling. A sound that instantly lifted the anxiety he'd been feeling. The room suddenly went quiet when Sarah walked in behind him.

"Everyone, this is Sarah." Alex swept the room. Lily and Kate were sitting beside each other on the bed. Patrick was at the table folding the clothes he'd slept in, and shoving them into his backpack. "She helped me get a few things." He tossed the two paper bags on the bed.

Kate reached for them first, offering a pleasant hello to Sarah. Lily wasn't pleased her brother had brought in a stranger, so she glanced at Patrick to his reaction. He simply held his hand out to her and introduced himself.

"Hair dye?" Kate pulled the contents from the bag. She

flipped the boxes over. "One of us is going blond and the other black?" There was red lipstick, black eye liner, thick lash mascara, a pair of scissors, and a few other items.

"It's time for you to change your appearance." Alex pulled a chair from the table and offered it to Sarah.

Lily picked up the black-framed reading glasses, and then thought the red pair looked nicer. "What color do you want to be?" she asked Kate.

"I've always wanted to be blond." Danny had once told her he liked blond hair, even though red was his favorite. She was always changing her hair, cutting it with various trendy styles, and he'd always noticed when she'd done something different with it. She closed her eyes, pushing back the pain.

"I should go," Sarah said, standing up. She felt uncomfortable, and out of place.

Lily stood. "What type of cancer do you have?" She was surprised her brother had brought in a person for her to heal. Hadn't they all said her healing days were over? No matter. Sarah helped Alex, and in return, Lily would heal her. It was simply the way things worked. That was the payment for a debt owed.

"Not so fast," Alex moved between Lily and Sarah. "She needs healing, but not right now." He turned to Sarah. "My sister's too weak to do it right now. We need to give her a little time."

Sarah hadn't even thought of her cancer or the chance to be cured. She'd been too caught up in the presence of famous people. Her mind had been going over the latest news events. Kate had been shot, and government officials were reporting that a radical group of people were trying to take Lily, and trying to convince everyone the government was using Kate.

"Was Kate pretending to heal people?" She found herself saying out loud. She was immediately embarrassed. "I'm sorry, that's what everyone's saying." Her gaze shifted to Alex.

"I was forced," Kate said.

"Everything you've heard in the past on the news and social

179

media was a lie. We're trying to get the truth out. We just want our freedom. " Alex let out a long sigh. "We just want to be left alone."

"There are so many conspiracy theories; nobody can know what to believe." She clasped her hands firmly together as Lily stepped toward her. "I... I don't need to be healed. I'm confident the chemo has worked." She was fortunate that her parents were wealthy, and they'd been able to get her the medical help she needed that so many other people had to wait for. "I'll be in remission soon." Her voice sounded hopeful.

"May I touch you?" Lily stepped forward, and Alex put his hand on her shoulder to stop her.

"I'm not going to use my ability. I just want to see if I can feel anything." She could usually sense how sick people were. Patrick winked at Lily from across the room.

"You're still pretty sick. I can sense malignancy."

The color deepened in Sarah's lovely face. "I'm scheduled next week to see if I still have cells in my lymph nodes, and I was anticipating good news." She couldn't hide the fear and disappointment now. "I can't believe you can tell that just from touching me." The world knew about Lily's special ability, and yet it was still very hard to believe.

"You still have some cancer cells. I can feel it."

Sarah was taken aback. She'd thought the chemo had worked. How could a person touch another and know what was inside them? "I have to go."

"Wait," Alex reached for her hand. "Sarah..." his expression softened when he looked into her glistening eyes. "My sister will heal you. Just wait, okay." He couldn't explain why it was important to him that this particular woman be healed, but it was. He'd make her stay with them until Lily had her strength back. Maybe she could use a little less energy and heal Sarah in small doses. Either way, he didn't want her to go.

Kate rose, and when she gasped, everyone turned to her. "I'm okay." She held up her hands. "It's just sore, and I moved wrong."

She placed the crutches under her arms. "I'm going to eat now, I'm starving." The food was spread out on the table next to Patrick... omelets, hash browns, French Fries, toast, and pancakes for Kate. She'd always loved pancakes.

Each person struggled with their own insecurities and thoughts, but no one wanted to break the lighthearted conversation. It was nice to escape the worry, and simply talk about normal things. When Patrick mentioned Halloween, Kate brought up the time she and Lily had dressed up as matching Bumble Bee's. They'd fooled everyone in their identical disguises and even Alex couldn't tell them apart.

Sarah joined the conversation, offering a few details of her life. She'd graduated from college three days before she'd been given her biopsy results. She was a certified accountant, who had turned down a job working for a medical supply company when she learned she'd need an operation and chemo.

Just as everyone was cleaning up their mess from breakfast, a knock sounded at the door. Patrick and Alex pulled their guns from behind their backs. Alex nodded to Patrick as he moved carefully to the door to look through the peephole.

"Housekeeping," a voice said behind the door.

"We forgot the Do-Not-Disturb sign," Patrick whispered.

Everyone looked around the room. "There isn't one," Alex shrugged.

Opening the door slowly with the chain still in place, Patrick thanked the maid, and let her know they didn't need service, but since her cart was right there, he asked for more towels. He waited while she reached in her cart to find a Do-Not-Disturb sign, and handed it to him.

Alex put his gun away. "We need to get out of here." He hadn't been on his guard enough. Too much reminiscing, he thought. It was time to get serious. "Lily and Kate, go color your hair now, and put on makeup. Do that smoky eye thing you ladies do." He waved his hand in the air. "I want to leave as soon as you're done." Reaching for the scissors, he handed them to Kate. "You like to cut hair,

181

so go hack it off."

"I'd like to help." Sarah offered. She was feeling more at ease now, having realized how easy it was to be around them. And there was something about Alex, which made her not want to leave. "I have a car, and I have lots of money."

Patrick raised a brow at Alex. "The Stevenson brothers are waiting to help us across the river again. All we need is a new car." Patrick recalled the way Kyle and Brad Stevenson had openly flirted with Lily. Now the young border patrol men could dote on Kate, and Sarah was quite stunning as well.

"Thanks." Alex downed the last of his coffee. "Will your car seat five?" Some battery-operated cars only had room for two in the backseat.

"Yes, and it's fully charged, too. It's parked behind the drugstore. I'll get it, and pull it up front."

"No, pull around back," both men replied at the same time.

She hesitated a moment. They were both examining her, obviously wondering if she could be trusted. A few giggles sounded from the bathroom before the water was turned on. "You can trust me," she told them.

"I know we can." Alex gave her a look of appreciation. "Do you have a passport?"

"I do."

"How soon can you get it?"

Lines formed between her eyebrows as she contemplated the question. "I…" Was she going to follow them back to the United States? Would she go? "I live fifteen minutes from here."

"Go get it, and pack a small bag, with a few changes of clothes." Alex glanced at Sarah's petite, slender figure, figuring she was close in size to the twins. "Can you grab some extra stuff for my sisters? Lily needs pants, and Kate needs some sensible shoes. She's a size 7."

"What luck. I'm a size 8, but Kate could easily wear boots one size too big. I'll try to hurry."

Chapter 28

Everyone was exhausted. Between little sleep, the stress of trying to stay hidden, the crisp air and travel had worn them all out. They'd traveled on foot back through the woods, the same lush forest they'd been in before. Next, they'd waited an hour in the cold for Patrick's brother to pick them up. At least the rain had held out. The sky was an ugly gray, the clouds thick and threatening.

Patrick's brother, Paul, had been quiet. Of course the introductions were made quickly, since everyone had been eager to sit in the car and rest. It was a short drive from the forest to Patrick's cabin, because they'd chosen to hike the forest rather than travel by road. By the time Paul was there to pick them up, everyone had food and sleep on their minds. Still, Patrick got the feeling that something was bothering his brother, but he'd need to wait till they made it to the house before he could find out.

As Paul drove, his eyes wandered to the rear view mirror. The three women were pressed closely together in the back seat, while Alex sat crammed on the floor.

"So Paul…" Lily broke the silence. "I like the nickname you gave your brother." She'd noticed his eyes on her and felt uncomfortable. She was curious about the quiet driver who'd grown up with Patrick.

"Yeah, he was a real prick when we were kids," Paul replied, teasingly. His lips curled revealing a smile with straight teeth similar to Patrick's.

Lily studied his side profile. As he spoke, she could see the family resemblance. Patrick had thicker hair, more unkempt and wild, whereas Paul's was short and buzzed in the back. His cheeks were a bit fuller, and while he lacked the hard, chiseled bone structure his brother had, Lily decided he was attractive in a cute way. Not sexy and rugged like Patrick. "Prick doesn't really suit him now," she replied happily.

"I wouldn't necessarily say that," Alex added from the floor.

Everyone laughed.

Patrick took Lily's hand as he guided her into the house. "Mom… Dad…," he called from the foyer.

The house was more like a cottage in the woods. It was concealed in a safe spot, since there wasn't a main road, only an overgrown dirt trail. Thick trees and brush surrounded the house. Unlike the cabin in the Appalachians, there was no lawn or property line. The house was surrounded by forest. A large weeping willow tree swept over the roof, as if hugging the house.

"Perfect," Alex murmured, as he took in the entire layout. "This is great." Patrick had assured him that the house wasn't in his name, and the government wouldn't find out about it. He liked that it was buried deep in the Upper Peninsula's rich forest. He glanced around at the interior… cozy and clean, with enough furniture for everyone to gather in front of the fireplace. The kitchen was small, but the open floor plan was nice. He'd be able to see all the doors and windows, which were covered with thick blinds. Turning to Sarah, he offered to help her with her coat.

Patrick greeted his parents with hugs when they rose from the kitchen table and walked over to greet everyone. "This is Linda and Jack Reeves," he smiled introducing them.

Lily was surprised when Linda pulled her close and hugged her. "We've heard a lot about you." She had Patrick's warm eyes, and long straight nose. She was a woman who'd taken care of herself through the years, and her embrace was strong, her body lean. She wore her natural gray hair pulled back in a ponytail, and thick bangs covered her forehead.

Jack, Patrick's dad, had turned from hugging Kate and said, "Now don't you two look beautiful with your new hair color. The black suits you, Lily." She felt the same forceful pressure when he embraced her. These people were strong, confident, and still young looking. It was obvious where Patrick got a lot of his traits from.

"She hates it," Kate replied with a chuckle. "She doesn't like the blond on me, either."

"I think you look great," Lily insisted, and felt all her tension roll away when Patrick put his arm around her.

"I love the black." Patrick reached up and held a strand that was cut short, framing her face. He'd been a bit shocked by how different she'd looked when she'd first stepped out of the motel bathroom. She'd gone from angelic and sweet, to seductive and racy. And Kate looked like a Hollywood movie star.

"Are you guys hungry?" Linda stepped into the kitchen. "I've got some bean soup on the stove."

The house smelled of the aroma, and the fire made it feel cozy. Paul had carried in more wood and set it on the hearth. There were pictures on the mantle and throw rugs covered the beige shag carpet. The walls were painted white, fresh and clean. Linda and Jack had made the house a home.

Lily, Kate, and Sarah sat at the kitchen table with their soup bowls. After they ate, they moved into the family room to sit on the large soft sectional.

This, Lily thought, was everything. She watched her family settle in. Everyone she loved safe and together. Everyone appeared content. If only life could stay this way. Patrick had his family, and she had hers. Alex was showing interest in Sarah, and Kate seemed to be doing okay, though grief would always come in waves.

"What's the big smile for?" Patrick asked Lily from across the room, though he had an idea what she was thinking.

"This is nice." She blushed. "I'm happy to be here." Her smile faded when she glanced at Alex. His face had dropped into a gloom she immediately recognized. "What's wrong?"

Alex set his bowl of soup on the coffee table in front of him, and looked morose when he pushed out of his seat. "Nothing. I'll be right back." He walked out the door.

"What's that about?" Kate asked, trying to find a comfortable position with her leg.

Sarah rose from the couch. "I'll go see."

"No." Lily set her hand on her arm. "I'd like to talk to him. Please." She found her brother leaning over the railing on the porch.

He glanced sideways at her when she shut the door. "You need a jacket," he said in a terse voice.

"I'm fine." She moved beside him, bumped him lightly with her shoulder. "Spill it, bro. You haven't been acting right since we left the motel in Canada. What's eating you?" He'd been quiet and moody. He'd had a few private conversations with Sarah, and he'd laughed a little with her, but the rest of the time it was obvious that something was bothering him.

"I hate not knowing."

The wind blew the short wisps of hair in her face, so she angled her body away from it. "Not knowing what?"

"What's going to happen? What are we going to do?" He was completely frustrated. "I love seeing you happy, Lil, but we can't all just live here," he tipped his head to the house, "one big happy family. We need to find a place we can live." He emphasized the word live. "I know you feel happy and safe right now, but this isn't living, Lily. This is hiding." He jammed his hands in his pocket and looked her square in the eyes. "Danny had made arrangements for us to go to Australia. He sent me an entire file with information on where we'd live, who'd get us the fake passports we need, what jobs we could each have." Feeling the need to pace, he moved away. "Lily we can't keep running and hiding. We have to leave the country. It was all supposed to be easy when Danny was alive. God, I miss him."

Lily felt the cold creeping along her arms. Alex was right. "I miss him too." The words were just a whisper, but her mind raced

186

with so many other thoughts. Would Patrick want to go with her? He'd have to leave his family. Could she really have a life in another country so far away? "What about Sarah?" Kate and Lily had really enjoyed getting to know her, and Alex had seemed particularly fond of her.

"Yeah, she's a problem too."

"A problem too?" Lily folded her arms across her chest. "Am I a problem, Alex?"

He drew a deep breath, and slowly released it. Man, he felt tired. "No, Lil. That's not what I meant." He sounded defeated.

Lily reached her hand up and set it on her brother's cheek. "I get it." All her love for him swam in her eyes. For years, he'd spent his life constantly on the go. He and Danny had worked together from the moment Lily and Kate had been taken for testing. His life had become all about her; always forming plans of escape, taking action to secure her safety, running, hiding, one thing after another. Danny was gone and the weight was all on Alex now. Except it wasn't just Kate and Lily anymore. There was Patrick, and maybe even Sarah to consider. And he deserved a break. It was time for him to live his life his way. "You're restless and uneasy without a plan." Their future was unpredictable, and perhaps he was feeling the hopelessness she had felt when she had cried herself to sleep in Ian's lap. "Let's all go to Australia. Let's form a plan for how we're going to be able to live. We need to find a place where you don't have to worry about us anymore. I want you to find peace and happiness for yourself."

"Really?" his shoulders lifted. He hadn't thought she would agree to go. He hadn't imagined they could somehow stay together while managing to have lives of their own. "What if Patrick won't go?"

Lily wrapped her arms around her brother's waist. "I'll deal with it." Alex had given and done too much for her, and now it was her turn to do something for him. If moving to Australia is what he needed and wanted, then that's what she'd do.

187

"I love you, sis." He squeezed her tight. "You girls have been one big pain in my ass since the first time I had to change your diapers, but I wouldn't change one second of it."

Patrick stepped away from the window when Lily had stepped into her brother's arms. He knew they were having a serious talk, and somehow he knew it was about staying in his house. He walked over to the refrigerator and grabbed a beer. His nerves were suddenly jumping. Would Lily stay with him, or would she leave with her siblings? Would he let her go, or follow her? Could she be happy staying in his little house? Was it fair for him to ask his parents to leave? They had their own home they could go back to, but he'd never know for sure if they'd be safe. Both his parents had said how much they liked living in the forest. He still needed to talk with his brother, because Paul hadn't seemed like himself. There was also the question of the mysterious men who'd been following them.

Kate's laughter broke his train of thought. She'd been in a deep conversation with Sarah. The door opened, letting in leaves and cold wind. Lily quickly shut the door.

"Is everything okay?" Kate asked, pulling a blanket around her shoulders.

"Yes." Lily smiled, but it didn't quite reach her eyes.

Linda walked over to Lily and offered her a sweater. "It's cold out there, come stand by the fire."

"Thanks."

Patrick held a beer out to Alex before he walked to sit beside Sarah.

"Listen to this," Jack said, turning up the volume on the television. The President of the United States was giving a speech. He was telling the American people that they had proof Lily was an alien being, and not of this world.

Everyone moved to gather in front of the TV. Kate slipped her hand in Lily's as they both stared at the President. "He's there," Kate whispered in a shaky voice… Dr. Nathan Palmer, the evil doctor who ran the Hope Medical Facility. The man who'd lied to the world telling everyone Kate had died from complications of the flu. The man who'd threatened Kate and forced her to pretend to be Lily. He'd performed hideous tests on each of them, and he was responsible for starving and confining Lily.

"I hate him," Kate hissed.

Lily pulled her sister close, feeling the same way. She listened to the President spew out more lies.

"We have DNA samples and proof that Lily McCallister is not human. We know that her power to heal comes from an advanced alien species we believe may be living on our planet." The President paused a moment to let his words sink in. *"There has been much confusion over the internet scam that took place a few days ago. But we can assure you that video of a supposed Lily pleading with the world to help her was not real. Lily has been taken from New York, and we are still searching for her. We ask that all Americans help us find her. Doctors were extremely close to replicating the alien's power. Breakthrough technology has occurred as a result of studying this unique alien being. Doctor Nathan Palmer is here with us today, to answer more questions you may have."*

The President glanced down and paused as if allowing his emotions to change. *"The truth is, no harm will come to the alien. It is our hope that there are others like her living on this planet that will be willing to heal more people. Our planet has been damaged, but we will continue to focus on re-building our nation and curing the sick. There is hope for our planet, because of Lily and her unique ability to heal. If Lily McCallister is watching this, I ask you… will you stand by and allow more people to die, when you have the power to save them? I urge all Americans to keep this notorious alien safe. Make her feel welcomed on our planet, because mankind needs her. Science needs her."*

Jack muted the TV. The room was silent but all eyes were suddenly on Lily.

"It's all lies." Patrick glanced down at the twins' hands laced together tightly. "He's emphasizing calling you an alien to make you appear less human. That's how he'll get American's to view you differently."

"It's his way of trying to get people to help capture Lily," Alex pointed out. "He plays on their fears and need for hope." Anger was

189

building and he wanted to punch something. "The sooner we get the hell out of this country, the better."

Kate turned to search the emotion on Lily's face. "Don't you believe it," she stated firmly. "You're not an alien. If you are, then I am too, and I know we're not."

"My DNA is different." Lily let go of Kate's hand, as Patrick's family watched her with guarded expressions. "I am different, and I'm okay with that." The fire licked at the logs, making crackling and popping sounds that barely sounded above the pounding of her heart.

"So what if your father was something from a different planet. Your mother is human." Linda stood placing her hands on her hips. "People were affected by that video you made, and they trusted you. Most people believe you could be an angel… that your powers come from God." Linda glanced at Patrick. "By saying Lily's an alien it strips her of any divinity."

"Nothing that liar said changes anything," Jack added.

Everyone had their own opinions, but Alex knew only one truth. "We aren't safe anywhere in America."

Lily turned to Patrick. "I've been ignoring the fact that my DNA is different. Your boss Jeffrey and Doctor Palmer both told me my DNA wasn't human. Now that the President of the United States has confirmed it, no one will look at me like I'm human."

"Stop." Patrick took her hand. "I want a word alone with you." He dragged her outside and down the porch steps.

"Where are we going?"

He didn't answer her as he gently pressed her against the side of the house and kissed her. His hands moved up under her sweater, touching her bare skin. "Do you feel this?" he breathed, sliding his lips to her ear. "You have a heart that beats like mine. You breathe like me, your blood is red, and your skin is warm." He kissed her again, before looking into her eyes. "It doesn't matter what your DNA says. There isn't one damn thing about you that isn't woman… that isn't human." He didn't let her speak. He hated that she doubted herself, and no way would he let her feel inadequate. He pulled away just enough to see his reflection in her eyes. "You're human, Lily, and I need you to trust me on this."

She realized as she smiled through blurry eyes, that she trusted him implicitly.

Chapter 29

The week slowly passed and the days became shorter with the sun setting after dinner. It was taking longer than Alex had anticipated acquiring the things he needed in order to leave the country. A few of the resources Danny had given him were no longer available. For one thing, Alex couldn't reach one of the pilots that Danny had given a phone number for. Then the boat they needed wasn't going to be available for at least four days. Alex was feeling frustrated, but it had helped to see his sisters happy.

His laptop needed charging, so Alex moved from the couch to the kitchen table where the cords would reach the outlet.

Sarah stepped out of the bedroom holding her jacket, and glanced at Alex with a smile. "Can you take a walk with me?" She'd been sleeping a lot, and had very little energy.

"Sure." Alex helped her with her coat before they stepped outside. What leaves still clung to branches were slowly letting go in the wind, to fly and twirl before landing on the ground.

"Lily says she's feeling better. Her strength is back, and she wants to heal me."

Alex took hold of her hand, and led her into the woods behind the house. "I know… she told me. I think she can handle it now. I'm glad you've stayed with us and waited."

Sarah decided she'd take a chance. It was now or never. She'd been trying to muster up courage for days. "Alex, is there something between us?" She needed to know if what she was feeling was one sided. Was he simply waiting for Lily to heal her so she could leave?

Or did he want her to stay for more reasons than that?

He pulled her over to a giant tree trunk that had fallen over and was lying sideways a few feet off the ground. "Let's sit here." He studied her face a moment unsure of what to say. "Even if I do have feelings for you, I'm leaving."

"You have feelings for me?" She leveled her hopeful eyes with his.

"I like you... a lot." Maybe he felt more, but he couldn't. *Wouldn't.* "My sister will cure you, and I'll be happy knowing you're going to live."

"So..." she clasped her hands together, "your sister heals me, I go back to Canada, and that's that?"

"Do you want to come to Australia with me?" He said it jokingly, as if the idea were absurd. But then her eyes widened, along with her smile. "Wait," he turned his body toward her, brought his leg up higher on the branch, and gripped her hand tighter. "Is that even a possibility?"

She bit her bottom lip and paused a moment before answering him. "I've always wanted to travel and see the world. Having cancer makes you realize how short life is. I've been living with the idea that I'd die before experiencing anything." She adjusted the scarf on her head. "I really like your sisters." She'd become practically best friends with Kate "And I really like you... a lot." She said the words the same way he had.

His pulse raced. "But you'll be in danger. Anywhere we go, anything we do has risks. I didn't think it was fair to put that on you." He had over a week getting to know her, with long talks on the porch, playing gin rummy with her by the fire, and long walks in the woods. She knew what his life had been like, and he'd mentioned all the future fears. She would know what she would be getting herself into.

"I'm well aware. It might not ever be..." she made the quote sign, "normal. But the truth is, I don't want to go home. I don't want to leave you."

"I…" He stood up. He hadn't been prepared for this. He figured after she was healed she'd want to return to the life she had. He paced the ground in front of her, stepping on broken branches, crunching on leaves. "I haven't had a girlfriend in a very long time. I don't even know if I know how to have one." He was suddenly nervous and stopped pacing when she stood up and reached for him.

Her eyes were alight with hope. "I don't know when the last time I kissed a man was, but I'm pretty sure now would be a good time."

He was laughing when he pulled her to him, and lowered his mouth to hers.

Chapter 30

Lily felt better than she had in years. Her skin glowed, she'd gained an extra ten pounds, and her nails were finally long and strong. She stepped out of the bathroom with a towel wrapped around her head. After she dressed and put on her makeup, she found everyone sitting at the kitchen table, chatting as normal and eating breakfast. Alex had insisted that Kate and Lily wear their disguises every day, because if they had to run, the twins needed to be harder to recognize. The smoky eye make-up, glasses and different colored hair had really altered their appearances. Alex wanted to keep it that way.

As Kate giggled at something Patrick had said, Lily's heart swelled. It was going to be very difficult to leave the house she loved. She adored Patrick's parents and Paul had finally warmed up more. She discovered that once he started talking, it was hard to get him to shut up. Today was the day she'd heal Sarah, and she felt confident she could do it without passing out for days. She knew Alex was ready to leave soon, and this cozy cabin happiness she'd been feeling was soon to end.

"You better get in here and get some pancakes before Kate eats them all," Patrick called to her. He was laughing when Kate threw a blueberry at him.

Lily took the towel off her head and towel dried her damp hair, as she smiled at her family. They'd all survived being under one small roof for ten days. They'd played games, taken walks together, watched old movies, and they'd all gotten along perfectly. Both Kate and Lily were enjoying watching Alex act sappy and romantic with

Sarah. She made him smile all the time, which filled Lily with immense joy. She and Patrick had many times to be alone, and intimate moments where he insisted on reminding her how human she was. But she hadn't asked him yet if he'd leave the country with her. And she sensed that he was avoiding the topic. Everyone knew Alex was making arrangements daily, forming his plans.

The week had gone by too fast, and Lily cherished the moments. She'd gotten to know Patrick very well, and she enjoyed watching him with his family, and hearing stories of his childhood. Patrick was respectful, kind and fiercely loyal. The past week her life had felt completely normal.

Alex rose from his seat, offering it to Lily so she could eat. "Have some protein, because I want you to have plenty of strength." He shoved a plate of spinach at her. "Eat your spinach so you can be strong to the finish."

The classic cartoon had become a joke between them since three days ago, when Linda put the cartoon DVD of "Popeye the Sailor Man" in the player and introduced it to them. Lily had watched a lot of old classics she'd never seen before on the old antique player. She didn't know what a DVD player was, and had found it to be a wonderful device. She couldn't understand why they became obsolete. She'd watched old movies from the 1980's that she'd never even heard of, like E. T. The Extra Terrestrial. It was a very old film, but she enjoyed the story line. She was able to laugh when Alex joked, "Hey sis, there's your kin."

"How do you feel?" Sarah asked.

Lily sat down, and Patrick leaned over to kiss her on the cheek. "Have some bacon."

"You all don't need to push food on me," Lily laughed. "I feel great, and I'm going to heal you Sarah. I can't wait for your hair to grow in so we can see what color it'll be."

"I told you I'm blond." Her tone had more excitement than normal. Lately she'd been too tired and drained to appear excited. When she spoke with her parents, they reminded her that she was due for her next round of chemo. Her parents weren't happy that she'd taken off on a missionary retreat. They understood she needed time alone to process what she was going through, but now wasn't the time to disappear with a church group. That was the lie she'd given them, and they'd believed it. Her next lie would be that she was going to another country and would receive treatments there with the new church group who were supporting and helping her. Sarah was giddy at the idea of one day returning home healthy and strong, with her hair grown long. She missed her parents, but she knew she'd return to them vibrant and completely healed.

"Blond hair and blue eyes." Alex bent down and kissed her. "The perfect combination."

"Or blond hair and red eyes are nice too," Kate added happily.

"Golden eyes," Patrick corrected her. "Your eyes are gold, with flecks of red."

"Actually they are copper red, with specs of mustard," Lily chimed in, and everyone laughed.

"We've got a problem!" Paul shouted suddenly, pointing to the window. "Everyone hide in the bedroom!" He moved away from the window and put his finger to his lips to be quiet. Patrick and Alex both moved to the door with their guns drawn.

"Two cops just pulled up in a car." Paul glanced out the window again, as the officers approached the porch. "Let me answer the door."

"No." Alex put his hand out, speaking quietly. "Let them think no one is home. They can't enter without a warrant."

Patrick told everyone to hide out of sight. The back windows had curtains drawn. From the outside it should appear unoccupied, except for the red car parked by the side of the house. It was his brother's car, listed under Paul's friend's name. His friend had given him the car and never transferred the title. If the cops ran the plate, they couldn't make a connection to Patrick and his family.

Everyone stayed perfectly still while the officers rapped on the door.

Lily's heart was in her throat. She glanced around at her family, and was once again reminded of the position she placed everyone in. It was her they were after, and this was how her life would always be. She could have weeks of happiness, days of feeling safe and secure, and then just like that, it could all change. What if they could never stay in one place for more than a week?

The knock sounded again, indicating they weren't going away. Lily couldn't keep making everyone in her life live this way. Alex deserved to have a normal life with Sarah. Kate would never be able to meet someone and fall in love if she always had to relocate, and Patrick deserved so much more. If she wasn't in any of their lives, they would all be left alone. If she died, the world would forget about her siblings, and Patrick would continue to live in the house with his parents and Paul. Turning herself in wouldn't work, because Alex and Patrick would just rescue her again. They'd never stop trying to keep her safe.

Tears stung her eyes, as she thought she probably couldn't even kill herself. If she slit her wrists, her skin would close and heal before she could bleed out. If she shot herself, the same thing would happen. Hanging from a tree was a possibility, since she was pretty sure going without oxygen would work. But she didn't believe in suicide, and the grief it would cause a family. She didn't believe it was right to take your own life, because where there was life, there was hope. But what hope did any of them have? It was a fact that they'd never have a normal life, and she'd have to make them see that they were all better off without her. She'd have to somehow convince them to let the government take her, and do with her what they would. Maybe there was a chance they wouldn't harm her. Either way, if she was out of the picture, her family could live in peace. Kate wanted children of her own, and she deserved the chance.

"Hey," Patrick bent down to where Lily was sitting on the floor. "Sweetheart, we're okay. They left." He touched her pale face. Her eyes were wet but fixed on the wall. "Lil, look at me."

She hadn't realized that the officers had left and everyone

moved from their hiding spots. She sat against the wall and tears blurred her vision as Patrick stared at her in concern. "It will never work," she muttered. "We can't be together."

"What are you saying?" Patrick glanced from Lily to Kate.

Kate shook her head and sat on the soft carpet beside her sister. "Lil, what are you talking about? We're safe now."

"No." Lily pressed her hand to her heart. She'd had almost two weeks of pure happiness and feeling safe. Now reality was smacking her hard in the face. "No. You'll never be safe. You'll never live a normal life with me around. You have to let me go. I have to leave you."

"Stop." Patrick's voice was hard, but didn't quite mask the concern. "You're talking nonsense." He leaned in to kiss her, but she pushed him back and got to her feet.

"No, listen to me!" She pushed Kate's hand away. "I don't want to be with you guys anymore. I'm going to leave, and you'll go to the police, tell them I'm missing, and you don't know where I am." The government didn't want any of them, so why would they keep them? "I don't think they'll try and use you again, Kate. People will be suspicious. Maybe you could have Ian make a video of you telling the world you're Kate and you're trying to find me." Her voice rose with the ideas that were popping in her mind. She kept moving away. "There are things you can do. You can be free of me!" She grabbed her backpack from under the bed that was always packed and ready to go in case of an emergency. She flung it over her shoulder, and pushed past Sarah on her way to the front door. "I'll make your lives better! You'll see how much better off you'll be when I'm gone."

Alex stood in front of the door.

"What's wrong with you?" Kate said, grabbing her arm.

Lily whirled on her, yanking her arm free. "You have to let me go!" she shouted right back. "I'm not staying with you. I'm not going to watch all your lives be ruined because of me." Anger and frustration dried her eyes. "I'm done putting everyone in harm's way. I'm done trying to live like…" she let her arms fall out in front of her, "like this. I'm not staying with you." She tried to push Alex away from the door, but he wouldn't budge.

"Get hold of yourself, Lily!" Alex looked at Patrick. "You just going to stand there?"

"Yup." It took all of five seconds for him to realize what was going through Lily's mind. He'd never seen her like this, and many times he'd wondered how she could handle the stress of her situation without ever breaking. "She's allowed to have a temper tantrum. Hell, she deserves one." He had no intention of letting her out of his sight. If she needed to storm out the front door and go running through the woods, he'd be right behind her. They were miles away from civilization, and she didn't have the key to Paul's car.

Anger now burned through her at the sound of Patrick's casual words. Lily didn't care if his parents were watching her act like a maniac. "A temper tantrum?" She shoved Alex again when he tried to touch her. Her eyes glistened with fresh tears and hostility at Patrick. "I've got news for you, Prick, that's not what this is. You're not listening to me! You are each going to find a way to live without me, and in time you'll see that you can. In time, you'll each have the life you deserve!"

"Ha! A life without you is what we deserve?" Kate's fear and concern had ebbed since she saw how Patrick was responding. He was right. Lily needed to blow up. She'd always held too much in.

Lily tried the door again, and when Alex blocked her way, she punched him. He caught her arms and pinned them to her waist. "Jesus, you're strong," he said, as she tried wildly to escape his hold. "I think you can definitely heal Sarah now," he laughed.

"I hope you're not going to leave before you do," Sarah said from the other side of the room. "I've waited a long time for you to do it."

Was that humor she heard in Sarah's voice? Lily went perfectly still and glanced around at the faces in the room. The worry and heated emotions she'd seen on their faces a moment ago were gone. They appeared to be holding back smiles now. How could they find this funny? Patrick didn't have a grin, but his eyebrows were raised as if he were waiting for her next move. "Let me go," she shrugged free, and pushed her hair back behind her ears.

"Are you done?"

"Shut up," she replied to Patrick. "I'll leave another time when you least expect it."

"That's probably the meanest thing I've ever heard you say," Kate said sadly.

Lily felt a guilty tug on her heart. "You're all being mean. I'm freaking out, trying to do what's right, and you're practically laughing at me."

"Everyone enjoys a good freaking out, dear," Linda said softly. "You've had more stress than the average person, and you're entitled to feel the way you do." She too understood exactly what Lily was feeling.

There was concern in Linda's voice, but in her eyes, there was love. Lily took a deep breath. "I really can't keep going on like this. I love you all so much, I don't want your lives to be like this… stuck with a damn alien with ugly black hair." No one was looking at her with disgust. Jack's face held the same grin his son's did. "I'm sorry," she told them softly.

Everyone moved at once, but Kate spoke up, "I get to hug her first." It happened so fast, she hadn't had time to move. Kate hugged her front, Alex hugged her back, and kissed the side of her face. Patrick circled all three of them in his long, strong arms, and Linda, Jack, Paul, and Sarah formed another tight ring. They all laughed.

"We love you sis," Alex muttered in her ear.

Jack added, "All of us."

Chapter 31

That night, Lily lay in bed listening to the willow branches scape along the side of the house and roof. She could hear the faint sound of the window rattle from the wind, and she felt wide awake. Kate slept quietly beside her in the queen size bed, and Sarah was asleep on the cot by the adjacent wall. Linda and Jack had turned in early, in the room next to hers. The third bedroom on the other side of the family room had two twin beds. Alex and Paul were both probably sound asleep. She wondered if Patrick was still awake. He'd insisted on taking the couch, because he liked being on lookout.

So many thoughts clouded her mind, and Lily couldn't stand the restlessness. She quietly slipped out of bed, and walked over to the fireplace. The orange embers still glowed from the dying fire. She'd glanced at Patrick lying on his back, one arm stretched up behind his head. He wore a green t-shirt and jeans, which she felt couldn't be comfortable to sleep in. Again, her conscience weighed heavily on her shoulders. Patrick deserved a better life. He shouldn't have to sleep in jeans, constantly on watch.

"Can't sleep?" Patrick asked, quietly.

She walked over to the sofa and sat beside him. "Are you always going to sleep with your clothes on and one eye open?" She offered him a small smile.

"Sweetheart, the day is going to come when you and I are going to sleep together in a bed, and believe me… we won't be wearing clothes."

When he pulled her toward him, she fell easily on his chest, her legs curled around his. "I'm sorry about today."

"Quit apologizing, Lil." He kissed the top of her head. "I liked seeing another side of you today. You've seen me at my worst a few times."

She picked her head up, needing to look into his eyes. "No, I haven't. When have you been at your worst?"

"Shooting you with a tranquilizer dart wasn't one of my finest moments. I've done things I'm not proud of." He glided his fingers gently across her arm.

"Well, I can count a few of your really great moments that might cancel out shooting me," her eyes sparkled with humor. "I think protecting me from those men who were trying to take me at the cabin was pretty great. Of course, rescuing me from Hope was even better. Protecting me at Connie's house when you pushed me in a bush…"

"I hid you in a bush." He corrected her.

She traced the bottom of his lip with her finger. "Oh, and rescuing me from Allen and Leo. Let's see… what else am I forgetting?"

"How about when I kissed you on the side of the Webster's house? That was a pretty great moment."

"Oh yeah, and then you did it again on the side of this house. You seem to like the sides of houses."

"Wait till you see what I can do in—"

She cut him off, placing her hand over his mouth, as Paul stumbled sleepily to the bathroom and shut the door.

After a few moments, Lily sighed and moved her hand to his hair. "You've been very patient with me."

He loved her soft voice, her subtle clean scent that he couldn't quite put his finger on, and the way her body molded perfectly with his. "I do really like your black hair, Lil," he said out loud, adding up all the things he loved about her. He ran his thumb down the side of her cheek, his eyes directly on hers. "I'm not going to tell you it hasn't been a struggle taking things slow. But I have an idea of how

I'd like your first time to be. Its' not going to be in a small house with six other people nearby, and it's not going to be when you're scared and vulnerable. It's not going to be quick and rushed." He tucked a piece of her hair behind her ear. "I want it to be perfect."

Joy was not something she was used to feeling very often, but the feeling Patrick gave her, the sweet words he spoke and the tenderness he gave, made her happy. Knowing what a good man he was, she wanted him to be happy too. Not just in the moment, but forever. What kind of life could she offer him? "Patrick, it's probably time we talk about Australia." He had to know by now she was going, and he hadn't said anything about it.

"Yeah, I've been waiting for you to bring that up."

"I'm leaving the country with them, because I don't think we'll ever have a moment's peace in the United States."

"I agree."

She was waiting to see if he'd volunteer to go with her.

He was waiting to see if she'd ask him to go with her.

They both spoke at the same time. "I don't want you to come with me."

"I'm going with you."

"Wait, what?" he asked.

Her heart was racing, and she shifted uncomfortably to the side of the couch. "I don't want you to come with me."

Patrick studied her eyes a moment before a smile stretched across his face. "You're lying, sweetheart."

Lily's eyes flew up to his. She decided to try again. "I'm serious, Patrick. You can't come with me."

He sat up now, pulling her up with him so they sat facing each other, her legs crossed Indian style, and his one knee brought up, touching hers. "I know you now, Lily. I know when you're lying and when you're telling the truth. Right now, you just told a lie."

"You don't know. You can't know."

"Do you remember the first time you looked me in the eyes and told me I had cancer?" He didn't wait for a reply. "You looked

204

me in the eyes and held your breath. Then at the hotel when you were trying to get away from me, you made up that little lie about it being that time of the month and needing…" he put his finger over her lips to stop her from interrupting him. "You looked me straight in the eye and held your breath. Then that day you held a gun on me in the woods, you were really sorry. You glanced down at the ground when you told me how sorry you were for not believing me. You didn't look me in the eyes and you didn't hold your breath. You were telling me the truth. When you told me you loved me, you closed your eyes and you never once held your breath. Just now, you looked at me in the eyes and you held your breath. So I know you're lying to me."

"No I…" She didn't really understand his reasoning, but she was prepared to argue it.

He smiled. "When you lie you look me in the eyes and hold your breath. When you tell the truth you look away. You want me to go with you to Australia, and I am. Your problem is that you haven't yet changed your mind from how you were feeling this afternoon. You want us all to live normal lives without you." He picked up her hand, bringing her fingers to his lips. "The problem is I can't live without you. I don't have a choice anymore. Sweetheart, wherever you go, I'll follow."

"But I…"

"Stop." He reached his hand around her neck. "You'll have to find a way to move past your feelings and get over the idea of freeing me from you. It's never going to happen."

Chapter 32

Alex closed his laptop and leaned back in the kitchen chair. He couldn't say he was sad to leave the little house in the woods, having never felt more restless and confined in his life. He was ready for the Outback, and hoped everything would work out according to plan. It'd taken almost two weeks to coordinate and set things up, and he still wasn't completely finished. But the surprise visit from the police yesterday sped things up. They didn't want to stay another day to find out why the officers had knocked on the door.

He figured leaving earlier than planned might throw a few more complications their way, but hell, he was used to it. The airports had way too tight of security, so they'd have to drive to the Florida Keys, where if all went well, a charter boat would be waiting to take them to Mexico. There, they would board a private aircraft and fly to Australia. All the people willing to help along the way were connections that Danny had secured for them.

Lily was going to have to heal a lot of people along the way, but she had more strength. She'd healed Sarah completely and hadn't passed out from it. Funny how they didn't need money, because the sick and dying weren't interested in gold or green. The pilot who was willing to fly them to Australia would give up all his wealth for his daughter to be cured. Lily would meet the twenty one year old woman on board the aircraft her father would steal from his billionaire boss. He'd risk whatever he could for the chance to see his daughter live. The pilot had seen his daughter suffer enough, so he'd fly Lily wherever she needed to go.

Alex glanced at his sisters and Sarah all sitting together on the sectional. Each of them had a book in their hands, and Kate appeared to be dozing off. Lily had a big smile on her face, and Sarah had a look of concentration. What a trio, he thought. Look at all they'd been through... the year of grieving over Kate, the rescues and worry over Lily. In the end what mattered most was the love they all had for each other. It was this moment right now, right here, which made everything he'd done in life worthwhile.

Sarah's skin glowed with her new radiant health. Her hair was already growing back. She'd had a pampered, rich upbringing, but she was strong and sensible. Alex liked her sense of adventure, and her extremely easy going personality. Perhaps it was having cancer that made her appreciate all the little things in life. He sure as hell did, especially after what his life had thrown at him. He felt simple pleasure watching the three of them reading books.

"It's finally all set," he announced, looking down at his laptop.

All three ladies glanced over. Patrick and his brother had been outside chopping more firewood, and Linda and Jack had gone to the grocery store. When they returned, Alex hoped to have one final dinner together before saying their goodbyes. They would do all their traveling at night.

"I'm ready." Kate had grown bored with the little house. She loved being with her family, but she was ready to move on. Lily had healed her leg, so she had no obstacles to slow her down. The only thing she wished she could do was call Danny's parents. She didn't even know if they knew Danny was dead. She'd love to enter their old house in Virginia and sit in Danny's childhood bedroom. Closing her eyes, she could picture the bay window that she'd crawled through many nights. Alex would be off on some hike with his friends and usually a hot date and she'd be running off to Danny's house. Sometimes she'd bring Lily with her, and the three of them would sit on his bed talking for hours.

"Are you okay?" Lily recognized that deep forlorn look. "What's wrong?"

Kate forced a small smile. "Just having a moment. I miss him so much."

Lily squeezed Kate's arm. "I know." She didn't need further explanation. Danny should be with them. He was the only one missing.

"Once we're safe in Australia, I'll try to reach out to his parents." Alex tried to reassure her. "We just have to be extremely careful right now not to contact anyone we know."

Sarah closed her book and stretched up tall, reaching for the ceiling. Her t-shirt rose up, giving Alex a view of her flat abs.

"Can you do that again?" He smiled and walked toward her.

Kate rolled her eyes, and headed to the bedroom to make the bed. Lily glanced out the window. "Oh no!" she said with alarm, while quickly heading out the door with Alex right behind her.

Patrick had taken a hard right swing at his brother's face. Paul stumbled back, and Patrick punched him again in the gut. "You son of a…" He only paused a second as Alex stepped beside him. "I trusted you!"

Paul's hands went up in self-defense, but he wouldn't fight his brother. If Patrick wanted to pummel him to death, he deserved it. His lip was split open and blood dripped from his chin.

"Stop!" Lily reached for Patrick's arm. "What are you doing?" She was shocked at the look of rage on his face.

"Alex, get the gear and get the girls in the car. We have to get out of here immediately!" He turned back to his brother. "How much time do we have, Paul?"

Paul stumbled, putting his hands out as if for balance. "I'm sorry, Patrick. I told you I didn't follow through with it, I changed my mind."

"What are you talking about?" Alex hesitated, before going inside, and shouted at Sarah, "Get the bags in the car quick! We're leaving now!"

"Do you want to tell them, or should I?" Patrick asked his brother.

"Lily, I'm sorry. I didn't know what kind of person you are." Paul shook his head, the pain evident on his face. "It was before I had the chance to get to know you and your family. It was a mistake."

"It's more than a mistake."

It scared Lily to hear the ice in Patrick's voice toward his brother. If it was over her, she had to make it right. She didn't want Patrick to leave the country hating his brother, and whatever mistake Paul made, he was clearly remorseful.

Everyone turned at the sound of tires crunching gravel. "Jesus, we have to hurry. Get in the car!" Patrick grabbed Lily's hand and was relieved to see Alex moved faster than anyone. He wasn't the type to stand around asking questions. When he sensed danger, he moved.

Kate was shoved in the back seat between Lily and Sarah. Patrick hit the gas pedal, jolting everyone forward. He was taking a back trail behind the house, and ignored everyone's questions.

"He turned us in for the bounty on Lily!" Patrick tried to keep control of the car, while his gut churned. "He's the one that Lily spoke to on the phone back in Canada. When my old boss Jeffrey found the phone I'd dropped in the hotel, he had Paul pretend to be me. Paul was helping to set the trap for delivering Lily."

"Oh, God," Kate whispered, her heart sinking.

"We were there for over a week, why didn't they come for us sooner?" Alex glanced out the window. "Hang on you guys!" The car was dipping and rocking over the rough forest branches and potholes. "Patrick, slow down before you blow the tires!"

Patrick eased off the gas, trying to get a grip on his anger. He knew something had been wrong with Paul from the moment they'd first arrived. He never would have imagined it was because his brother had betrayed him. "I guess he changed his mind once he saw us all together. He claims he sent Jeffrey on a wild goose chase, giving him the name of some fake location." But that didn't matter to Patrick. His brother had lied. He'd used the information he'd given him, and even pretended to be him.

209

Suddenly gunshots echoed through the forest. The back window shattered and glass blew through the car. Kate screamed. Not quite the same blood curdling scream from when she was ten years old and set on fire, but close enough to make Lily's heart skip a beat.

"Get down!" Patrick yelled.

"Is she shot?" Alex reached for Sarah, the fear evident on his face.

Lily lowered herself to the floor behind Patrick's seat and examined Sarah. The side of her face was bloody, but it looked like it was from glass. Lily took her hand as Kate tried to nudge her awake.

"Oh God, I think they shot her!" Kate yelled.

Lily quickly sent her healing energy into Sarah's unconscious body, and glanced at Kate, who was lying low over Sarah's back, trying not to bounce with the car. Her eyes were wide and terrified as more bullets ricocheted off the sides of the car.

"I've got five on my side!" Alex shouted to Patrick.

"Four on my side, and two in the back. Start shooting, they have us surrounded."

Touching Kate's hand, Lily looked in her sister's eyes. "I love you. I love you all." She opened her car door and jumped out. Patrick slammed on the breaks, but the tires were already blown. Smoke blew up in a thick black cloud in front of the car.

Lily quickly got to her feet and threw her hands up. "Don't shoot!" She quickly scanned the forest, and found who she was looking for. Jeffrey came walking toward her, wearing the same solid, dark hunter-green clothes that he'd had on at the cabin. His grin was cold and calculating.

"Wise choice, Lily," Jeffrey sneered as he approached her. She glanced away to see everyone she loved being dragged from the car and shoved to the ground.

"Don't hurt them! I'll do whatever you want. I'll go willingly, but please don't hurt them." She couldn't bring herself to look at Patrick, for fear she'd see panic and disappointment in his eyes, or the devastation she knew her brother would show.

Jeffrey wore a smug smile. The shadows below his eyes and the yellow of his teeth made him appear sinister. "I've got my orders, Lily."

She turned as two government agents pulled Patrick and Alex to their feet, holding guns to their heads. Now she looked from face to face, and saw only steel expressions. They were so alike… both commanding figures, identical in their strength, their skill and competency. They would never beg for their lives, and never back down. They were the type of men who faced anything with pure iron coursing through their veins. Oh how she loved them.

"I have orders to bring back you and Kate. However, Alex and Patrick will die." Jeffrey moved over to Sarah and bent down to her level. She was on her knees next to Kate, who was still holding her hand. "And you, Sarah Walker, have made the unfortunate mistake of hanging with the wrong people." He glanced at his agent beside her. "She gets a bullet too."

"Jeffrey, you evil bastard, I'm going to—"

"No!" Lily jumped in front of Patrick when Jeffrey aimed his gun at him. She then turned and wrapped her arms around his waist, her face pressed against his chest. She let loose her tears, when his arms came around her.

Kate stood, helping Sarah to her feet, and both of them went into Alex's arms.

"That's enough," Jeffrey said, and raised his gun to Alex's head.

Lily turned to take her brother's and sister's hands, but from the corner of her eye she saw that Jeffrey was going to shoot Alex.

One gunshot suddenly followed another, and before she could understand what was happening, she was on the ground, Patrick's heavy body lying on top of her. Everything happened in a blur. In the span of just a few seconds, she saw bodies fall to the ground, out of the corner of her eye. The scene unfolded as though it were happening in slow motion. Gunshots continued popping as she squeezed her eyes shut.

Chapter 33

For a moment she was back in the blue room at Hope Hospital. She was lying on that same mattress, the blue walls closing in on her. The pain in her stomach from hunger was nothing compared to the burning, unbearable ache of knowing Patrick was lying dead on top of her, and Alex was dead beside her. She'd gotten them killed.

Jumping from the car had been her way of trying to save them, but it hadn't worked.

Her body shook, and her sobbing was so intense she couldn't find air to breathe.

"Lily, it's okay. Sweetheart… we're okay. Open your eyes." Patrick's hands were rubbing the sides of her face. He was putting his body weight on his arms, so he wouldn't crush her. "Open your eyes, Lily."

Lily had a vague sense of Patrick's lips trailing along her face, but she knew she was dreaming it. She was back in that blue room. They were dead, and she couldn't breathe. She gasped for air, but the weight on her chest was crushing.

"Lily, we're all alive," Kate's voice sounded strained and hoarse. "Please, Lil, open your eyes."

"She's hyperventilating. She's having a major panic attack." Alex set his hand on Patrick's shoulder. "Maybe you should get off her." He stroked the side of Lily's cheek. "Lily, Jeffrey is dead. It was him and his men who were shot, not us."

With the words that finally penetrated her mind, Lily opened her eyes. When she saw Kate, Alex and Patrick all mere inches from her face, she heaved again, the words choking in her tight throat. "Oh God… please let this be real!" The words were almost incoherent, as she gulped deep breaths of air.

"That's it, take deep breaths, baby. We're all okay." Patrick soothed her, rubbing his thumbs along her tear streaked face. He'd seen Jeffrey's face blown apart from a bullet, right before he'd been able to pull the trigger.

As other shots were fired, he'd fallen on top of Lily to protect her. But he understood what she thought had happened. She thought they were all dead.

Lily's eyes blurred, but she could see Alex's face. She felt Kate's hand on hers, and Patrick's breath was warm whispers across her damp cheeks. When she tried to move, Patrick got to his knees and helped her up. Lily's eyes quickly swept the ground. Blood, mangled faces, and bodies lay all around.

"Don't look." Kate tried to block her view. "It's awful." She'd seen Jeffrey's gunshot to the head, and was still in shock. Her tears would come later, but right now she was focused on Lily, who was still shaking and finding it difficult to breathe.

Patrick held Lily tight to his side. The forest was spinning, and she still couldn't catch her breath, so she clutched Patrick's shirt, her fingers squeezing tight to the flannel fabric.

"I've got her." Patrick swept her up in his arms when he felt her knees give way, knowing she hadn't the strength to stand. "Just take it easy, baby, I've got you." He glanced around at the dead bodies that had fallen, some face down, and others sideways with blood covering their face. And while other men with guns had a made a circle around them, they weren't aiming their guns at Patrick, Alex or the women. They were patiently waiting, allowing Patrick to comfort Lily.

Lily drew in another deep breath, and wiped her tears. "What happened?" She glanced at Kate and Sarah standing on each side of Alex, their arms through his. Their faces were red and wet too, and Kate still had tears dripping down her chin.

213

"We're surrounded by men with guns, but I don't think they're government." Alex moved closer to form a tight-knit circle around Lily. "But whoever they are, they just saved our lives." He'd seen Jeffrey getting ready to pull the trigger, when suddenly the men shot Jeffrey and all his men at once. It had happened in seconds, and was a very close call.

"I can stand now, I think." Patrick set her on her feet, but kept his arm tightly around her waist, anchoring her to his side.

A man walked up, and cleared his throat. Patrick instantly recognized him. He was the man who'd taken out the agents at the cabin, when Jeffrey had tried to take Lily. The man was still wearing the same red baseball cap.

"Who are you?" Patrick asked him.

"That's the man I saw outside of Ian's house, just before I hid and they tied up the Webster family," Lily told Patrick.

"I'm the good guy," the man replied, with a wide grin. He turned toward his left as another man walked toward them.

Patrick glanced at Alex. They'd already counted how many men were standing around them. Five to their right, eight to their left, and Patrick had seen a few sharp shooters up in the trees. All the men wore casual clothes, jeans and flannel shirts with thick jackets. Some were hunting jackets, and others wore nicer leather coats.

"I'm the man in charge." An elderly gentleman with stark white hair, short and balding on the side, held his hand out to shake hands with Alex. "My name is Doctor Gary Price. You may call me Dr. Price."

"What do you want?" Alex refused the man's hand, hoping he'd make his demands fast. He'd probably want Lily to heal someone.

"I don't need healing, if that's what you're wondering," Dr. Price replied. He held his hand out to Lily. "I've been watching you for 23 years, Lily. It's truly a pleasure to finally meet you in person." He lowered his hand when no one was willing to shake it, and set it on his cane. Turning, he smiled at Kate. "You too, sweetheart.

You're both much more beautiful in person. I don't care for the new hair, but it was wise to change your appearance."

Kate stared at the older man in his gray suit and black tie. He looked so out of place standing in the forest surrounded by bloody bodies, smiling as if they were friends. She moved closer to Alex's side and waited for the old man to expound.

"You're going to want to come with me and hear what I have to tell you. It's a long story, and I'm not a fan of this chilly weather." With a twinkle in his eyes, he stared at Kate. "And you... I have a wonderful surprise for you."

Kate and Lily shared a look of apprehension with each other. They didn't know what to think of this elderly gentleman.

"She's not going with you alone. You'll have to finish what Jeffrey started if you think you're taking her."

"Mr. Reeves, I'm happy to hear you say that," Dr. Price replied. "I'm thrilled with how well you and Alex have protected the twins. You certainly turned out to be a pleasant surprise."

Doctor Price nodded his head to Alex, knowing he was about to demand answers. "Soon you'll find out why. I think you'll agree that the women are extremely upset, and have been through enough. It's hard for me to stand on these old legs for too long, and there's much I need to share with you. I'd like to invite you all as my guests back to my house. It's not far, and I have transportation just up ahead." He tipped his head in the direction he'd come from. "Should you choose not to come as my guests, Kate will miss out on her wonderful surprise, as will the rest of you."

"We'll go," Kate replied almost immediately. She wanted out of the forest, away from the dead bodies, and she was curious what the surprise would be. No matter what his intentions, the doctor had saved Alex and Patrick from being killed. He had enough men with guns that could easily force them to comply, yet he was offering.

As they walked through the woods, Patrick wished a giant sinkhole would open up and swallow all the men with guns, along with the doctor who walked slowly behind them with his cane. He needed to be alone with Lily. Just to hold her, and kiss her the way he had every night at his house. She was still upset, but her breathing was steadier. He knew that the human body didn't just bounce back easily from severe shock.

Chapter 34

Lily held Patrick's hand as they walked through the woods. She smiled softly when he tried to help her over tree trunks or push branches out of her way. She felt his need to touch her, which was probably as intense as her need to touch him. Now, glancing back at the thick forest, she almost wished they could disappear in it. She loved the way the trees had swallowed them up. The ground was thick with brown leaves that crunched under their feet. Twigs snapped, and birds still fluttered their wings from tree to tree. The forest, and walking, both helped soothe Lily's frayed nerves. The cold temperatures had not bothered her, the way it had Sarah and Kate.

"I've spent a lot of time walking in the woods with you. I'm pretty sure I could walk forever with you."

Lily glanced up at Patrick, feeling her heart squeeze. How she loved that man and couldn't wait to be alone with him. Her mind praised God again for his life and Alex's. Lily turned to see her brother arm in arm with Sarah and Kate on each side of him.

When they finally reached the gravel road, they saw the parked black stretch limousine. Dr. Price had a slower, more bent gait, and hadn't been able to walk as fast, so they stood waiting for him to catch up. They were still surrounded by men with guns, but one of them, the man Lily recognized from both the cabin and Ian's house, unlocked the limo and opened the door.

"What's your name?" Lily asked him, as he smiled at her.

"Chip."

Lily remembered the way he'd tried attacking Patrick in the

backyard at the cabin, after he'd killed some of Jeffrey's men. Patrick had blocked his swing and knocked him out cold.

He'd helped them escape Jeffrey at the time. Then she'd seen him again standing outside the Webster's house. He'd been with the men who had locked up the Webster family, while she hid in Ian's desk. At least he hadn't killed the innocent family that was helping her. "You've been following me a long time." She examined his face. He had a short beard and mustache, and brown eyes. He reminded her a little of Fred Brown, the man she'd cured on the way up the mountain. He had that similar outdoor sportsman look.

Chip nodded his head, and moved aside as Patrick followed Lily into the limo. The seats were dark gray leather, and a bottle of wine was chilling over ice in an elegant bucket. There were track lights above and soft throw pillows in the corner. Limousines were almost a thing of the past. No one used them anymore, since gas was expensive. Even the rich settled for fancy hybrids. She'd never seen the inside of a limo before, and when Sarah gasped, she assumed neither had she.

"Who the heck is this guy?" Alex slid across the seat beside Sarah.

Doctor Price entered the limo last. "Make yourselves comfortable. I think the ladies could use something a bit stronger than wine." He opened an overhead cupboard above Patrick and pulled out a bottle of brandy. Everyone sat quietly watching him, as he found five rock glasses and filled each one.

Patrick sniffed the golden brown liquid before tipping his head back to empty the contents. The soothing liquor was just what his tense body needed.

Alex took a sip, but then set his glass on his knee. "I'd like you to get to the point. Who the hell are you, and what do you want with us?"

The doctor gave a dramatic sigh. "Okay." He tapped on the glass indicating to the driver to start moving. Lily scooted closer to Patrick's side as the limousine crunched the gravel on the road. The brandy burned her throat, but added warmth to her stomach, which was still very much in knots.

"Your mother wasn't raped." Doctor Price paused seeing that his opening line immediately drew everyone's attention. "And you're not an alien. I happen to know exactly what you are, and why your DNA is different, and I'll explain more when we arrive at my house."

"No, explain now." Alex knocked back his drink, and adjusted his hat.

Dr. Price set his eyes on Lily. "Did you know there are many animals that can regenerate? Certain species can grow or regrow new parts of their bodies to replace those that have been lost or damaged." He lifted his arm in the air, his long-sleeve black shirt raised over wrinkled skin, showing his age to be easily around eighty. "There is a clam known as Dynastic Clam, which can live for five hundred and seven years, and bowhead whales have the capacity to live about two hundred years."

"What does this have to do with us?" Alex was losing his patience. "Get to the point."

"Alex," Kate whispered softly. With her eyes, she asked him to calm down.

"Lizards are fascinating creatures. A Salamander can grow a new tail," the doctor continued, ignoring Alex's scowl. "Flat worms can be cut into pieces, and each piece can grow a new worm. The stem cell processes of many unique species resemble a super power that we can't quite understand. And yet it's real. And for many years scientists have studied these remarkable creatures, with the idea that perhaps humans could one day have these qualities through stem cells and genetically altered DNA."

"I'm listening." Lily felt there had to be a point eventually, and since his eyes were so intently on hers, she tried to mask her uneasy impatience.

The doctor leaned forward. "Before you were born, your mother was in debt and about to lose her house. She'd been denied a loan, and was desperate. Your mother had heard from a friend that

219

a group of doctors were giving thousands of dollars to people who were willing to be live test subjects in an experiment."

"Oh God," Kate whispered, shifting nervously in the seat.

"The test subjects were all female, and they didn't know they were being given live embryos. Embryo's that were man made." The doctor's eyes lit up. "Different strands of DNA, some from lizards and worms, and stem cells from these unique creatures that do in fact have super powers to heal, regenerate, and live for hundreds of years, were successfully coded and transplanted into embryos. The technology to replicate DNA and clone these stem cells was created by one man... one man who had a vision and desire to create human beings who could restore their own bodies."

"You?" Lily guessed, from the satisfied grin on his face.

"I feel sick," Kate whispered.

Sarah glanced at Alex. "Your mom offered to be a test subject, and was given..." Her eyes widened as she mentally put the pieces together. "Oh my... gosh."

The doctor leaned back in his seat. "We impregnated sixty two women, and then brainwashed them. That was another experiment, but that's also a different story. The single women were made to believe they'd been raped. We chose women from different parts of the country, and all of them were single, struggling to survive, and had healthy young bodies. The rape was the explanation for their pregnancy, and we needed them to believe it."

"You sick bastard." Patrick held Lily close when he felt her tremble. "What you did was illegal."

"Yes, and I'm not proud of it. But none of the women died, and all the babies were either miscarried by the third trimester or stillborn. Except for one mother who miraculously carried twins."

Alex tipped his head back, and closed his eyes. "Jesus."

"You're my miracle, Lily." Doctor Price leaned forward again, his eyes dancing. "You're a fluke enigma... an accident in the experimental game of science."

Alex remembered the day his mom was escorted home in a

220

police car. She looked distraught, and that's when her eyes had taken on the haunted look that had somehow changed her. "My mother was brought home by a policewoman. She told me my mother was attacked and sexually assaulted." Alex remembered the woman's words, as if it had happened yesterday. "She said, 'your mom may be pregnant as a result, but you can help her raise the baby'." Alex had thought the comment was a strange thing to say to a young boy. "By the time mom discovered she was pregnant, she was coping, but she wasn't the same person. It was like she was living in an imaginary world, and she was telling people that the father of her child was away in the military." Now Alex knew it was all part of a scientific brainwashing, and her reality had been purposely altered. What a cruel and sick thing to do. His stomach lurched with a desire to beat the doctor.

Lily met Patrick's eyes to see how he was processing the information. He wasn't pale like Kate was. She turned an angry glare toward the doctor. "You ruined my mother. Whatever you did to her mind ruined her." She thought about the empty shell of a woman who sat in a mental hospital with intravenous tubes and mumbled nonsense. "I can't forgive you for that."

"No, I suppose I don't deserve your forgiveness. But I won't apologize for conducting the tests, because you were created. The accidental miracle of science, and now as a result, we have a genetically modified human being who can ensure the human race will live on."

The limo slowed to a stop. Everyone peered out the tinted black windows. They were still surrounded by forest, but in the middle stood what almost looked like a castle. The front of the house was rounded white brick and stretched too far up for them to see from the car. The lawn was beautifully manicured and still very green for the time of year.

As everyone exited the car, each person stretched their arms and rolled their heads over tense neck muscles. Two more black pickup trucks pulled up behind the limo, and a few men jumped down from the bed of the truck. They awaited further instruction from the doctor.

Lily felt sick. Human beings were capable of such horrific crimes. It was something she always suspected, but the truth was even more abhorrent than she could have guessed. She imagined her mother's face, the familiar image that so often popped into her mind, of her mother singing "You're not human," and holding a lit match over her and Kate. A group of scientists had messed with her poor mind, from an experiment her mother had volunteered for. Lily reached for Alex's hand. "I'm trying to comprehend all of this."

When Alex pulled her into a tight hug, she sagged against his chest. He softly spoke in her ear, "Mom was trying to get money to keep the home I loved. She did what she did to protect *me*."

"Don't start blaming yourself, Alex," Kate said standing close. "The only one who gets blame is Dr. Price." She hated doctors, and their superior attitude, their god complexes, and their ability to harm humans in the name of science. She felt a strong desire to take the old man's cane and beat him with it. She loved her mother, and losing her had been a pain she still struggled with.

"If you'll follow me inside, I'd like to give Kate her surprise. I'm thinking with the way you're all looking at me, I need to earn a few points."

Kate moved away when the doctor tried to offer her his arm.

The house was stark white, with tall windows that let in tons of light. It was late afternoon and the sun was already lower in the sky. Giant colorful art canvases adorned the walls to offset the white paint. The neutral-colored furniture was modern with a sense of simplicity. Angled walls curved and squared off the sections of the house.

They kept walking until they reached the kitchen. A huge, wide open room appeared so white and clean the marble floor glistened and the white counter tops held reflection. An enormous crystal chandelier hung over the S-shaped center island and the cupboards were white with large steel handles that matched the stainless steel appliances. It was crisp and cheerful and yet felt eerie at the same time.

Kate whirled around to face the doctor. "What surprise do you have for me?" She wanted out of the house.

"Bring him in," the doctor ordered Chip.

As if having sensed Kate's feelings, Lily moved to take her sister's arm. They all stood close, keeping their eyes on the door that Chip had walked through.

Then there he was, and the room suddenly exploded with voices.

"Danny!" Kate was the first to run into his arms. He'd moved to her, picking her up off the ground, and barely waited for her to land on her feet before his mouth crashed down on hers.

Lily waited with tears in her eyes, and her heart aching with joy.

"We thought you were dead." Alex moved in and hugged his best friend, reminding them that they weren't the only ones in the room waiting to say hi. "Damn good to see you, buddy."

"You look good." Danny glanced around, "You all look great."

"I told you I would deliver them all to you in one piece," Dr. Price said from the other side of the room. He too was smiling, and enjoying the reunion. "I kept my end of the bargain." The deal had been that Danny would help him find Lily and Kate, and in return the doctor would use his money and manpower to keep Lily from falling into the hands of the government again. It allowed Danny to offer more help in secret. "It was safer and best for the government to believe Danny was dead." And Danny almost had died, but Dr. Price's men found him in time and saved his life.

Danny turned from Dr. Price to Alex, still holding Kate tightly. "My base was flooded by a group of men we think belong to a new organization that believes Lily is an alien. When they found me at my base, they stole my information and used it to go after Lily. I was afraid they would find Sage, and capture Lil. Chip found their dead bodies at the cabin, so it gave me hope that you and Lily were okay."

Lily remembered the first group of men Patrick had been

223

forced to kill at the cabin. The one man had practically broken her arm, twisting it behind her back. They were men who claimed they knew Danny. Now the pieces were coming together. "Those men tried to take me, but I had help." She offered Patrick an appreciative smile. "They told me you sent them, but I knew it was a lie." It concerned her that new organizations were being formed by ordinary civilians. It was bad enough the government was after her, but now she'd face threats from other groups of people who were on a mission to find her.

Danny's tender smile faded as he responded to Lily. "Those men were ruthless and smart, and had a lot of manpower. You're lucky you escaped them. They shot me, and I probably would have bled to death, but Chip saved me." Danny regarded Chip as he moved into the kitchen holding a tray of champagne glasses. "I was also hit on the head and spent a couple days in bed with a concussion." Kate reached her hand up to touch his head, and he took her hand, kissing the inside of her palm. "I'm fine, babe." He kissed her again. "I missed you so damn much."

Alex rolled his eyes, "Okay, reunion time is over. Let's move out." He took Sarah's hand, and glanced back at Danny. "By the way, this is Sarah," he tipped his head, "and that's Patrick."

"I know." Danny smiled. "I'm happy to meet you both." He offered a nod to Patrick.

Patrick nodded back. "I've heard a lot about you, and I'm glad you're still alive."

Lily embraced both Kate and Danny. "We've had a terrible day, but you just made it all better." She liked that he looked healthy and unharmed. He was wearing blue jeans and a white button-down shirt. He smelled clean and his short sandy blond hair was combed back, giving him the distinguished look that Kate found so appealing. Lily reached for his hand to feel his body.

"I'm okay, Lily. Honestly, I don't need healing." He kissed her cheek.

"We have so much to tell you," Kate said, smiling through her

224

tears. "So much has happened."

"I already know everything," Danny told her, gently kissing her cheek. "I was being kept updated on everything that was happening to you guys." Danny tipped his head toward the doctor. "I was treated well here. Doctor Price has been watching out for you a long time. Chip was following you to try and bring you all here sooner, but you kept getting away from him, and in the end it looks like you didn't need our help."

"Actually, an hour ago they did need my help, and I was there." Chip winked at Lily.

"Yup, and now it's time for all of us to leave." Alex turned a knowing expression to Patrick. They'd discovered the secret to Lily's healing power, and they'd gotten Danny back. The perfect end to what started off as a terrible day.

"Not so fast." Dr. Price limped into the center of the room without his cane. "I've got one more pleasant surprise for all of you." He signaled to Chip, who obviously understood the cue and left the room again. "I wasn't responsible for the horrific tests that were done on you, Lily. That was a government agency with which I'm not affiliated. And I was working on your release, but Danny and Alex beat me to it. However, I did manage to obtain all their research on both you and Kate."

"Here we go," Alex muttered under his breath. He'd been waiting for the catch.

The doctor turned to Kate. "Kate, we find it interesting that most of the genetically modified DNA and stem cells died inside your body, leaving only the human cells. However, according to your tests, it appears as though some of the manufactured cells may be dormant inside of you."

"I don't know what you mean," Kate replied, holding tightly to Danny.

"It means that perhaps your children will one day have a unique ability. Perhaps they will have the potential to grow a new body part, or live longer than the human race does now." He watched the look

225

of skepticism and concern on Kate's face as she processed what he was saying. "Or perhaps one day you'll discover an ability you didn't have before. We don't really know what will happen, but it's fascinating you're alive with manufactured cells, which makes you as important as Lily." He patted Kate fondly on the arm, before addressing the others. "Lily, you're a phenomenon we can't duplicate, nor figure out." The doctor pulled a white bar stool from under the island, and hunched himself on it. "My hope is that you'll both have many children. Perhaps you'll be the beginning to the next step in evolution." He shook his head sadly. "We've destroyed our planet. Nuclear radiation, wars, famine…" He set his weary blue eyes on Lily. "Humans will eventually become extinct, by our own doing. But you Lily… you alone could keep the human race going with a new body… a body that can't be destroyed by cancer, disease, and wounds." He held his hand out as Chip entered the room carrying a blue folder.

"I consider you my creation," he continued. "Without sounding condescending, I'm extremely proud of you. And it's important to me that you survive." He glanced around the room at each person. "All of you." He opened the folder. "I want you to find love, marry, and have lots of children. If we're lucky, one of them will have your healing ability." He looked directly at Kate. "Perhaps the dormant cells inside you could be passed to your offspring as well. If there's even a small chance one of your children will have healing genes, they could henceforth start the beginning of a new evolution of mankind." The doctor's smile faltered. "Lily, if you die, the hope dies. There isn't anything we can do to recreate you. I've spent my life trying."

Lily's heart clenched at his words. "I'll never be safe. I'll never have a life with a family and children, because as long as I can heal people, someone will always want to use me. The government isn't going to let me go." Lily's eyes swept past Kate and Sarah and landed on Patrick. "They will never be safe, and I won't bring a child into this."

The old man held out a few photographs to her. "These will be on the cover of every newspaper and magazine. They are already circling the Internet and every social media site, and will be on all the news stations."

"Oh my gosh." Lily flipped through the pictures, handing them to Patrick and Alex so they could see.

"How did you do that?" And so fast, Alex wondered.

"My men were up in the trees taking pictures when Jeffrey had you surrounded. We captured photos of you lying on the ground, and when Jeffrey aimed the gun at you. The rest was easy to Photo Shop. No one will know exactly where the photos came from, but there will be a real crime scene in the forest. Bodies will be found, and the world will think that all four of you are dead." They'd left Sarah out of the photos altogether. The pictures looked extremely real, showing all their bodies covered in blood. They'd gotten a close-up picture of Lily when she'd been hyperventilating in shock, and the picture would appear to others that she'd been shot, and was struggling.

The doctor held up his phone. "We've got video of the government agents aiming their guns at you. We've got enough on tape to convince people what we need them to believe."

Chip folded his arms across his chest and added, "There are always conspiracy theories, and those who won't believe. But once you've disappeared from the planet for a long time, people will begin to accept that you're gone."

The doctor stood up from the stool and slowly walked over to stand in front of Lily. "Everything you need to start a new life is in this folder." He placed it in her hand. "I'll continue to watch out for you. We're working on eliminating the threats."

Lily glanced down at the folder. Somehow the passports that Alex had gotten were already in there along with new birth certificates and social security cards. It meant that perhaps one day she'd be able to have a life under this new name and identity.

"You did a nice job changing your appearance. You're no longer easily recognizable."

"I don't believe this." Lily handed the folder to Alex. "Is it possible we could actually have a life in Australia?" It's where she knew Alex wanted to live, and until this point, she hadn't really believed it was possible. She glanced at Danny knowing he was behind some of it.

"You'll be living in a very secluded area. Your home, transportation, money, everything you need is provided. There are safety guidelines, should you require them." Dr. Price handed Lily a glass of champagne. "You are a miracle Lily… the hope for mankind. You have a good heart and human blood coursing through your veins. For whatever reason, God allowed our experiment to work on you. I believe he allowed it so mankind will evolve from the destruction we've created. Humans will become stronger and more resilient."

Kate's voice trembled. "What about our mother?"

"I'll make sure she continues to get proper care. I'll have someone send you photos and updates on her, but you won't be able to have contact. People need to believe that she has gone under the care of the State since you're all dead. The government will be watching her."

Danny saw the pain in Kate's eyes, and gently rubbed the back of her neck. "You'll see her again someday, sweetie."

Lily felt the heavy ache in her chest. The doctor had thought of everything. He'd saved Danny, when he could've been killed, and she knew now that Chip wasn't trying to harm her. Instead, he'd been following her to protect her. And an hour ago he'd kept everyone she loved alive. She swallowed hard, and searched the old man's face. This old man who had given her all the facts she never knew, a scientist who had implanted her and Kate into her mother's womb… the old man who had played with DNA and stem cells, altered her life, and had somehow created her. She stared at his deep wrinkled eyes, and realized this same old man who started everything was now going to finish it. He was going to save her.

www.ingramcontent.com/pod-product-compliance
Lightning Source LLC
Chambersburg PA
CBHW030305200626
46816CB00002BA/768